ALL I HAVE TO GIVE
THE SUCCOURI SAGA

MERIDITH GIBBENS

2023 Meridith Gibbens

Published by Meridith Gibbens

http://meridithgibbens.com

All rights reserved

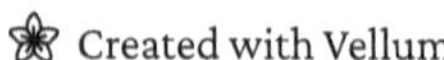 Created with Vellum

STAY INFORMED

Be the first to hear about new releases, including the next book in this series.

Go to: http://meridithgibbens.com

Click "Subscribe to stay informed".

Thank you for your kind support.

CONTENTS

Dedication   vii

1. The Dream   1
2. The Ride   7
3. The Memory   14
4. The Hospital   21
5. The ICU   37
6. The Prediction   51
7. The Learning   62
8. The Concern   73
9. The Park   87
10. The Dinner   104
11. The Mistake   117
12. The Choice   127
13. The Anticipation   140
14. The Date   155
15. The Kiss   174
16. The Rescue   189
17. The Revelation   199
18. The Recovery   215
19. The Answers   226
20. The Goodbye   242
21. The Warning   256

Acknowledgments   267
About the Author   269

DEDICATION

In love and gratitude to my husband, who has always seen just me and whose love and care for me makes me feel whole in his presence,
and to my parents, who have taught me how to accept and love myself despite the difficulties and challenges I face.

CHAPTER 1

THE DREAM

Callie squinted in the bright sun, which stung her eyes. After a moment of rapid blinking, they adjusted to the light, and she eagerly gazed at the world around her. Though her view was limited, she nevertheless smiled in delight at what she saw.

Stretching out before her was a meadow teeming with vibrant, fragrant flowers. A light breeze played with her curls and flooded her senses with some of nature's most pleasing perfumes: lavender, honeysuckle, and sweet alyssum. Though she enjoyed the fragrances, Callie couldn't see the flowers individually. They appeared to her as overlapping swirls of muted color, blending together in a never-ending, depthless expanse.

As she closed her eyes to enjoy another pleasurable scented breath, the sunlight, which had bathed her in warmth, blinked out of existence.

Fear ripped through her as she opened her eyes but saw nothing except for a few fading, ghostly images, dancing like ominous shadows around her. Even these soon vanished into the cold darkness. Silent stillness smothered her, cutting her off from every available sense she had to relate to her surroundings.

When she inhaled, she coughed, as the air now reeked of ash and burning rubber. Whatever was under her feet crunched like broken glass, and the sound echoed sharply in the eerie emptiness. Just as she was about to scream, to call out desperately for help, her surroundings shifted once more.

The sunshine and flowers returned. As her eyes refocused, she gasped, and her heart pounded violently with excitement. Though she didn't understand how this was possible, she could see the world around her as she'd never seen it before, and it was spectacular! The flowers in the meadow weren't blurred masses anymore. Each one now possessed a distinctive shape and vivid color. She delighted in the beauty of a large black-eyed Susan with a dark lumpy center and sprays of golden petals, a deep red wild rose with layers of overlapping circles, and stalks of lavender lifting their spikes of flower heads, swaying in the breeze. Overwhelmed, she let out a laugh that sounded childlike in its pure joy.

All at once, she had the urge to run, to see everything there was to see in this new and brilliant world, but as she took her first excited step and her foot hit the ground, she heard the sound of crunching glass again, and everything vanished.

Darkness enveloped her like she'd been wrapped in a black shroud, and her heart constricted in terror and despair.

"No! No! Don't go away!" she begged, reaching out in vain to grasp something that was no longer there. "I want to see it. It's beautiful! Oh please!"

. . .

"CALLIE! CALLIE! WAKE UP!"

For a moment, she was disoriented, and she kept her eyes shut tight. Then she felt a hand on her shoulder, shaking her.

"Hon, you okay?"

Recognizing her dad's soothing voice, Callie sat up slowly, though she couldn't yet focus her eyes.

"You were screaming, Cal. Nightmare?" Her dad reached out, and she leaned into his warm embrace.

"I guess so," she mumbled, still confused by the contrasting images. "But the weirdest one I've ever had. It felt real. Totally real!"

Holding her, he tenderly stroked her untidy curls. After a moment she sat back, so she could look at him. "In my dream, I could see, Dad. I saw flowers like you can. Well, at least how I think you can." Her voice was wistful, as her heart pulsed with the desire to return to that place.

Her dad placed his hand affectionately on her cheek. "Wow! That sounds like a gift, not a nightmare."

Callie shook her head. "It kept coming and going, like it was being given and then ripped away. And then it was dark. Total, frightening darkness."

When she shivered at the memory, he pulled her close again. "I'm sorry," he whispered. "That's awesome and awful at the same time. You know, if I could give you my eyes, I would, Callie Flower, no question."

She smiled at his generous heart. "You tell me that all the time. But, you know what? I'd never let you do that because I love you too much, and you're too important to the city, to the family, and to me just the way you are."

Abruptly, he pulled away from her but kept his face close enough for her to see his sincere expression.

"You don't need perfect sight to be important. You see

plenty, and there's no one more important to me, your brother, and many more whose lives you have and will touch. You see from the heart, and that's the real twenty-twenty. Do you hear me?"

As she nodded, Callie marveled at how he always knew what to say to make the pieces of her world fall into place again, to help her find the right perspective, or just to cheer her heart.

"I'm alright now." She teasingly pushed him away. "Get out of here."

Usually, her dad had left for work before she got up, so she knew he was probably running late.

"Yes, ma'am." Performing a mock salute, he kissed her forehead and then stood up to go. Just before he left her room, he stopped and turned back. "Remember, just do today, Callie Flower, just today."

Callie smiled at the familiar reminder. "Love you, Dad."

"Love you too," he replied as he disappeared into the hallway.

Callie's dad, Ronald LeVray, was a well-respected prosecutor in their suburban Midwest town. He'd been unusually busy lately, working on some difficult but consequential cases that had kept him away from home more than he liked. Only about a year from retirement now, he'd seemed uncharacteristically tired recently, which made Callie glad for the upcoming change.

Callie's dream had put her behind schedule and, by the time she headed downstairs, she realized her younger brother Lee, a senior at the local high school, had also left. With only a few months to go, he had recently contracted a bad case of "senioritis," which Callie was trying to cure, so he would finish strong and be ready for college in the fall.

"Don't give up when the finish line is in sight," she had

teased him a few days prior, standing on her tiptoes and tousling his short curly red hair.

Tilting his head and crossing his arms, he'd looked at her with a teasing grin. "If I wait for it to be in your sight, Sis, it'll be a long wait." He lifted her off the ground and kissed the top of her head. Only Lee could tease her like that and be more endearing to her for it.

After he set her down, she put one hand on her hip and returned his teasing grin. "Hmm… Well, if you don't graduate and go to college, you'll live forever with the knowledge that I'm smarter than you!"

Lee shook his head and chuckled. "I'll never doubt that no matter how many years of college I complete," he responded in his irresistibly charming tone.

Currently, Callie worked from home, a convenient arrangement since she couldn't drive due to her impaired vision. She'd graduated from college a year earlier with dual degrees in English and journalism. Though she loved writing, since she was just starting out in her career, she was paying her dues primarily by editing others' work.

Callie carried her mug of chai tea into her home office and set it on the desk. Though she was still feeling somewhat shaken by her odd dream, as she booted up her computer and started her workday, she fell into a familiar routine, and the images, both good and bad, began to fade as dreams often do.

As she was putting the final touches on her third file, her phone buzzed, startling her from her deep concentration. She snatched it from the edge of her desk.

"Hello?"

"Miss LeVray?" an unfamiliar voice asked hesitantly.

"Yes, this is her," Callie replied as she leaned back from

the keyboard and tapped her index finger nervously on the desk.

"Miss LeVray, I'm a nurse at Saint Luke's Hospital, and I'm calling to let you know that your father has been admitted after collapsing at his office this morning. The doctors are working on him right now, but it would be good if you could come as soon as possible."

As she tried to process the woman's words, her heart raced. "What... What's wrong with him? I just saw him. I mean, he was fine this morning."

"The doctors will be able to tell you more when you get here. Please hurry, Miss LeVray!"

Callie struggled to accept what she was hearing. Surely, they'd made a mistake!

"Um, alright, thank you," she finally managed, her voice weak and shaky.

After hanging up, she sat back in her chair, trying to make sense of the news. Her dad was healthy. He had to be alright. But then she remembered his recent weariness. His job was stressful, and she had worried about the toll that stress took on his health.

He was her rock, the center of her universe, and the person who made her struggles and obstacles seem less scary and immovable. He'd taught her to be strong, to find a way, to keep fighting. And he believed in her, as did Lee, and that was why, most days, she believed in herself too.

Shaking her head, she tried to clear her thoughts. She had to get to the hospital as soon as possible. Though she lifted her chin in a bold stand against the panic that was threatening to overtake her, a betraying tear still managed to trace its way down her cheek.

CHAPTER 2
THE RIDE

Ben had just finished filling the gas tank of his dark gray Range Rover when he heard his phone buzz. Leaning across the driver's seat and pulling off his gloves, he retrieved it from the center console and stared at the screen. A new ride request was displayed there, and the address was only a few blocks from where he was, so he tapped "accept" to claim the job.

"Busy day," he mumbled to himself as he started his engine and connected his GPS to the address. It was only mid-morning, but he had already completed three rides, taking two people to work and one to the airport. Though he was new to this type of work, and it certainly wasn't what he had planned to be doing with his life, he liked being out and about, and he found the job satisfying and, so far, safe.

His passengers sat in the backseat, usually on the opposite side of the car, so the distance and barriers gave him a sense of security.

And these were strangers, most of whom were quiet and didn't want much in the way of conversation, though a few made small talk. He liked being with people, having had his fill of isolation, but he couldn't allow himself to get close to anyone. Experience had taught him that hard lesson.

Proceed with caution, he reminded himself, not wanting to get complacent even though this appeared to be a workable situation.

He didn't want to move again, run away, and change his whole life around, at least not yet. This town had only been home to him for a few weeks, but he liked it. The people were friendly, and the pace of life was more laid back than in some of his previous residences.

A kind woman he'd met at a restaurant when he'd been passing through had engaged him in conversation and convinced him to stay. She worked part time at a nearby high-rise apartment building, and she had helped him get a place there.

Don't get attached, he reminded himself. *You never get to stay long.*

As he approached his destination, anxiety gripped him as memories of so many escapes and close calls overtook him.

Get a grip, Ben! You're fine. This is working.

Lantern Street was in a quiet, pleasant upper-middle-class neighborhood. The houses were all about the same size, but they were custom designed, each with its own unique architecture.

As he looked for the address, the mid-morning sun reflected off windows and mailboxes, sending streaks of blinding light across his vision. He mumbled the house number as he searched.

Ben pulled into the driveway of an elegant yet unassuming house midway up the street. Bright white paint gave the traditional two-story home a clean, fresh look. The yard was well maintained with manicured bushes lining a walkway that led to a spacious front porch. It was January, so everything was colored by the winter-brown characteristic of the season.

Putting his vehicle in park, Ben waited, knowing that the ride service app would alert his passenger to his arrival. As he waited, he glanced at the destination for this job: Saint Luke's Hospital.

Why the hospital? he wondered. The passenger's name indicated that she was a woman. He wondered if she was sick or visiting someone who was sick, or maybe she just worked there.

Defensively, he pushed down his familiar, almost instinctual feelings of empathy. Many might find this trait to be a blessing, but for him, it was not. Once more, unpleasant memories pulled him down into a dark yet familiar pit of emptiness.

Ben was startled and relieved when he heard the back door open, pulling him back to the present.

As his passenger, a young woman, settled herself noiselessly in the backseat, Ben glanced at her in his rearview mirror. Her face held an expression of distress, but Ben couldn't help noticing that she was quite attractive. Her shoulder-length light brown hair hung in loose curls around her face. There was a hint of red in it that tinted it auburn in the sunlight. Her coral-colored blouse, though partially obscured by her coat, looked dark against her fair skin. She wore dark sunglasses, so Ben couldn't see her eyes, but there was a soft strength in her features that left him with the impression that she was vulnerable but not fragile. Still, the sadness he saw in her instantly grabbed his heart.

Watch the empathy! he scolded himself. He couldn't stop what his heart felt for people, but he had learned to control it, push it down, and cage it, which kept things safe for him and, more importantly, for others.

"Good morning," Ben offered casually. "You're headed to the hospital today, right?"

"Um, yes, thank you," she replied distractedly as she pulled her phone out of a small purse, which she held on her lap.

Ben switched the GPS to his new destination. Though he was getting good at finding his way around town, he still didn't trust himself to navigate without it.

As he pulled away from the curb and picked up speed, he unavoidably heard her side of the phone call.

"Lee, oh good. I'm glad you got my message... I got a call that Dad is in the hospital... No, I don't know. I mean, they wouldn't tell me over the phone... No, I'm using a ride service... Yes, meet me there when you can... I know, me too."

When the call ended, she let out a sigh, and in the rearview mirror, Ben saw her purposefully lift her chin. He chuckled under his breath, knowing that gesture well. Conjuring up courage was one of his own constant acts of necessity. Despite her effort to project strength, Ben saw a tear escape past her sunglasses and streak down her cheek.

His instinctive sense of empathy rose again, but he pushed at it with all his might, like bracing a fortress door against the onslaught of an attacking army.

She's a stranger, he reminded himself. *It's not your problem.*

They rode in silence for a few minutes as the woman fought to control her emotions and Ben struggled to stay aloof and uninvolved. The fact that she was attractive and had something very vulnerable about her that he couldn't quite put his finger on, tapped directly into the deep stores of empathy within him, making the battle harder.

Ben got on the freeway, but after a moment of acceleration, he saw brake lights ahead, and traffic began to slow. He glanced at his GPS, which was flashing with an alert of an accident ahead and slow-moving traffic.

Now it tells me, Ben complained inwardly as he tapped the brakes and came to a stop behind a semi pulling two trailers.

The truck blocked his view, but the traffic in the adjacent lanes wasn't moving either, so it didn't matter. They were stuck.

"I'm sorry," Ben offered his passenger. "It looks like we're stuck for the moment."

"Can we get off and take another route?" she asked, her voice tinged with panic.

Ben was confused and a little annoyed at the question. Surely, she could see their predicament and that there weren't any alternatives at the moment.

"If we get to an exit, I can try, but for now there's not much I can do."

She fidgeted with the strap on her purse, running it between her thumb and index finger.

Several minutes went by, but the traffic remained gridlocked. The silence in the car was broken when her phone buzzed, and she lifted it to her ear.

"Yes? Lee? No, you've got to be kidding me! Well, I'm stuck too. Traffic jam, I guess. I don't know... Okay, I'll call them."

When she ended her call, she asked her phone for the hospital's number. Ben heard her inquire about her father's condition, but she didn't seem to receive any direct answers. When the call ended, she took several deep, shaky breaths. Whatever they told her, it was enough to scare her. The battle to keep his walls up raged on.

As there was currently nothing else to look at, he couldn't keep himself from occasionally glancing in the rearview mirror. She seemed completely unaware of his attention toward her, which Ben found curious. She dropped her head into her hands and massaged her forehead, looking lost, like she didn't know what to do next.

And, here she is, Ben thought, *all alone in this car with a stranger.*

Despite his mind screaming at him to stay detached, he couldn't avoid the ache in his heart in response to her circumstances. He knew what it was like to worry about someone he loved and not know what had happened to them. His special skills in empathy weren't needed for that, as his personal experience informed him all too well.

"Miss, I don't mean to invade your privacy but...Are you alright?" Ben asked, trying to communicate a sense of calm and assurance.

To his surprise, she responded immediately. "My dad was taken to the hospital after collapsing at work today. I don't know what happened. They won't tell me anything except to get there fast. My brother's car won't start, and he's at the high school, and now we're stuck, and what if...?"

Her words flowed out in a rush, and Ben was sure she hadn't meant to say all of that, but it was like a pressure valve had opened, releasing all of her built-up tension.

Fresh tears slipped past her sunglasses, and she removed them to wipe her eyes. Ben caught a glimpse of green before she put them back on, apologizing for her outburst of emotion. He wondered why she kept the sunglasses on at all. Without thinking, he glanced at his gloves, not knowing why he connected the two objects in his mind.

The cursed traffic made him angry now. He didn't want to keep this woman from her dad, and he knew it was uncomfortable for her to be in such a situation with a stranger.

Well, at least maybe I can help with the "stranger" part, he decided, though the wall defenders in his head screamed all the louder in protest.

"I'm Ben," he said. "I'm going to do my best to get you there as soon as possible. Don't let yourself think the worst. Just keep taking deep breaths and hang in there. We'll get there."

The words came out soft and gentle. A calming presence was part of his curse. He knew it made people trust him. Usually, he kept it locked away, but he couldn't resist offering it to this hurting woman in a moment when she didn't have anything or anyone else to comfort her.

And it seemed to work. She took a deep breath and leaned her head back against the seat. She put her hands in her lap, and this time there was no fidgeting.

"I'm Callie. Thank you, Ben."

She conveyed such genuine gratitude and relief that the protective wall around Ben's heart weakened, but only for a moment.

CHAPTER 3

THE MEMORY

They spent several more minutes at a standstill before the brake lights in front of them went dark, and the whole group of vehicles began to inch forward, like a swarm of sluggish insects. Ben kept his distance in case of a sudden return to gridlock, but soon they were moving at a slow but constant speed.

Callie's posture relaxed as they made progress toward the hospital and answers to her questions about her father's condition.

"Well, it looks like we won't have quite as much time to get acquainted after all," he said lightly, hoping to raise her spirits and perhaps coax a smile from her. She offered a weak one, but it faded quickly.

As they rounded a curve in the highway, the accident that had caused the traffic backup came into view, and Ben felt his stomach tighten. A small white car and a semi-truck had collided and now stood at odd angles on the shoulder. The white car had taken the brunt of the accident, and the entire right side was caved in. Ambulances were parked nearby, and a stretcher was next to the driver's side door.

Ben's eyes fixed on the white car as they slowly passed by and he remembered another one like it, which had taken an even worse beating. The memory was over four years old now, but it still sent fresh pain and sadness through him.

HE HAD BEEN DRIVING WEST, about sixty miles from the Denver Metro area, far enough to be well clear of any heavy traffic. It was dark and raining, one of those rains where individual droplets disappear into great heavy sheets that make one feel like they are being smothered beneath them. The terrain wasn't mountainous yet, but it was etched with hills and shallow ravines. Ben was driving cautiously, as he wasn't familiar with that stretch of road, and visibility was poor.

A small white car passed on his left in a blur of vapor and spray and then pulled into his lane. It wasn't speeding, but its driver was obviously more comfortable navigating in this weather than Ben was. He watched the taillights, using them as a guide in the torrent.

From the corner of his eye, Ben saw the silhouetted shape of a deer run out onto the road, followed by the squeal of tires. Slamming on his brakes, he watched in horror as the white car hydroplaned off the side of the roadway and rolled over before disappearing into a dark ravine.

Pulling over to the shoulder, Ben grabbed his phone. He turned on its flashlight and then called 911, knowing that a signal and rescue might be hard to come by out here in this remote area. The first two tries were futile, but on the third desperate attempt, he reached a dispatcher and did his best to describe what had happened and where he was.

When he hung up, he shone his cell phone flashlight

down into the ravine. Thankfully, it wasn't too deep, and Ben spotted the white car. It had landed driver's side down at the bottom and had taken a battering on the way. Rain poured through its shattered windows, and the car's body was dented and buckled in multiple places.

Heart pounding, Ben thought about the driver, trapped inside with his or her door facing the ground and likely in bad shape, if the driver was still alive at all. Gripped by a sense of urgency, he scanned for a way to get down to the car. The sides of the ravine weren't steep, and in normal conditions, it wouldn't have been too tough to traverse, but the rain and the dark were not going to make this a normal descent.

As he started down toward the car, Ben slipped with every step and rain quickly soaked him through. It was a spring storm, so thankfully it wasn't overly cold, but the water dripping off his hair and into his eyes added to the struggle. His right leg caught on something that sliced into him, but he ignored it and kept going.

Turning to face the sloping wall, he grabbed onto whatever he could. Everything was covered in slimy mud, which also caked his clothes and his hair as his descent became little more than a controlled slide. He landed hard at the bottom, falling onto his back before scrambling to his feet and bolting for the car.

One headlight still cast its eerie light across the scene, and Ben was grateful for the illumination. As he approached, he heard the driver moaning. Though relieved he was alive, the feeling was mingled with heartbreak at the sound of desperation.

When he pointed his flashlight into the car, he gasped at what he saw. The man was slumped against the door, glass shards glinting all around and in him. Blood gushed from a large gash across his head, and it ran down both of his arms. Ben couldn't see his legs but judging by the position of the steering console and the man's body, he knew he was trapped. There was no way Ben could pull him out on his own.

The man cried out in acute agony. Desperate to help, Ben searched for a way to get to him. He went around to the roof of the car, but he couldn't maneuver around the steering console and a large section of the hood, which had folded like an accordion. So, he shifted to the front of the car and climbed up on the upturned side. The windshield was gone, shattered into thousands of tiny pieces that shimmered in the mud around the car. Grabbing the windshield's frame on the passenger's side with his left hand, he stretched his right arm as far as he could toward the injured driver.

"It's going to be alright!" he shouted through the pouring rain. "Can you move your arm at all? Can you reach me?"

The driver opened his eyes. Now that Ben was closer and could see him more clearly, he realized he was very young, almost a boy, maybe seventeen or eighteen. His bloody black hair stuck out in every direction, and his dark, terror-filled eyes struggled to focus through the pain and darkness. From the dazed look in his eyes, Ben could see that he was about to lose consciousness.

"Stay with me!" Ben pleaded. "Can you reach me? Can you lift your arm?"

"No," came the weak reply, which Ben had to strain to hear over the sound of the pounding rain. "I can't move." His face contorted in pain as he cried out once more.

Swinging himself over the side of the car, Ben kept his grip on the frame of the windshield and let his foot slide until it caught the edge of the dashboard. He slid his left hand up and around the top of the windshield, slicing his skin on jagged metal and shards of glass. This positioned him higher and closer, but with the rain making every surface slick and the near complete dependence on his left hand alone to hold his body weight, Ben wasn't sure how long he could maintain the stance.

He stretched his right arm toward the driver again. As he did, it scraped against some protruding plastic or glass he couldn't see in the near darkness, carving a deep gouge into his flesh. The boy saw it and gasped just as Ben's hand came into contact with his upper arm.

"You'll be okay." Ben tried his best at a soothing tone despite his own pulsating strain. "Just don't move, and take deep breaths. I called for help, and they'll be here soon. Hang on, and I'll hang on to you."

Despite his words, Ben knew this boy was in trouble. The left side of his face was covered in gashes. His right leg was pinned and his left leg was twisted and crushed.

Ben talked to him as best as he could. He asked his name and told him his. Soon, Ben's left hand began to shake, but the boy grew calm. The bleeding on his forehead gradually slowed, and his breathing took on a more even rhythm.

Twice, Ben slipped and fell into the pool of muddy water around the car, but he pulled himself back up, driven by the return of the young man's desperate cries, until he could reach for him once again.

When he returned to the boy after the second fall, Ben barely had the strength to grip the frame and hold on. When he caught hold of the young man again, fresh blood soaked his hand.

Seconds ticked by like hours, and Ben's whole body

began shaking violently, but eventually, he heard sirens approaching, and he willed himself to stay in place until they arrived. The boy stared at Ben with questioning eyes as his cries subsided, but Ben couldn't speak anymore.

Voices shouted from the top of the ravine, and flashlight beams floated around them. Ben clung to the vehicle with everything he had, determined to stay in position for a few more moments.

The next thing Ben remembered was a hand shaking him awake and chaos all around him.

"Are you alright, sir? Are you hurt?"

A paramedic stood over him, but Ben looked beyond him. All he could do was sit and watch, weak, exhausted, drenched, and muddy as they cut the driver loose. When they lifted his limp, silent, bloody body onto a stretcher, Ben knew he was gone. He had done all he could to help, but in the end, it hadn't been enough.

"Ben?"

Callie's voice startled him back into the present, but his heart still pounded from the bleak memory.

"I'm sorry, what?"

She'd obviously been talking to him, but he'd missed it completely.

"Are you alright?"

Ben nodded, but she didn't seem to notice. After a moment of awkward silence, she spoke hesitantly again, seeming to feel uncomfortable asking her question as she sensed something was upsetting him.

"I was asking how long it would be until we reach the hospital."

Shaking off the past, Ben struggled to refocus. "We're

about eight minutes away," he reassured, trying for a clear, steady voice.

As the accident scene faded in his rearview mirror, the traffic picked up speed. Ben wished his lingering doubts, regrets, and failures could fade away and be forgotten just as easily.

CHAPTER 4

THE HOSPITAL

Seven minutes later, Ben pulled up to the front entrance of the hospital.

"Sorry it took us longer than usual to get here, but I really hope your father's condition isn't serious," Ben said as he twisted around for the first time to look directly at Callie.

To his surprise, she hesitated. "Ben, I hate to bother you, but, well, I don't see well, and I've never been here before. Would you mind walking me to the front desk? I can find someone else to help me from there."

For a moment, Ben was confused, trying to process her words. She couldn't see well. What did that mean? How much could she see? How did he not notice? The sunglasses, of course. He should've known. But he couldn't help her. She was exactly the kind of person he needed to keep his distance from. He'd end up having to run again. Panic paralyzed him, and there was an awkward moment of silence while he wrestled with it.

"I'm sorry to bother you with this," she continued,

reacting to his silence, "but it shouldn't take more than a minute."

Ben struggled frantically to find words to reject her request, but even if he could find them, he couldn't speak them. What was he going to do, leave her here by herself when she couldn't see where she was going? He couldn't do that, but he couldn't help her either. Feeling trapped, he began to sweat. He was sure his panic was evident in his face and stiff posture, but then she probably couldn't see that.

His eyes fixed on his gloves, lying in the passenger's seat. Maybe he could make this work. He was wearing a coat, and he could slip the gloves on and be careful. Taking a deep breath, he tried to rid himself of the panic before he spoke.

"Um, alright, just a minute," he forced out a little too briskly.

She must think I'm a terrible, heartless person, he thought as he pulled into the nearest parking spot and turned off the engine.

After pulling on his gloves, he tugged at his coat sleeves, coaxing them as far down as possible.

This will be alright, he tried to reassure himself.

By the time he circled the car to Callie's door, she was already standing nervously, her purse gripped in her left hand. Ben halted a few feet from her. Fully visible to him now, Ben's earlier impression of her attractiveness seemed an underrated assessment. About five inches shorter than him, she was slim and feminine, and she possessed a graceful quality that was rare among her generation of women.

The part of him that was just Ben, the man, wanted to move easily toward her, but he was practiced at subjugating any part of him that threatened to expose *that part*, so he approached cautiously. Typically, women interpreted his hesitation as a lack of interest, so they moved on, but as he stood there, unsure what to do, he realized Callie likely wouldn't notice and, therefore, wouldn't respond that way. This thought both relieved and frightened him.

"Do you... Do you want to take my arm?"

"Yes, please," she replied timidly.

When she lifted her right hand, Ben carefully inserted his forearm beneath it. As her small hand gently circled his arm, Ben's breath caught in his throat.

Because of who he was, he rarely allowed anyone to touch him; he couldn't. The sensation was unfamiliar and foreign. Presently, as he guided Callie toward the front of the hospital, he became acutely aware of the existence of a gaping hole within him, one that human contact and affection were meant to fill.

Turning to him, she smiled despite her current circumstances and his rude hesitation to help her. "Thank you," she said as she squeezed his arm.

"Sure, no problem." Ben tried to make his voice sound genuine and kind despite his overwhelming anxiety.

Her smile was radiant and undeservedly trusting, and it filled his heart with something he found difficult to describe. It was like tasting something he'd never tasted before and discovering later that he craved it despite being oblivious to its existence until that moment.

As they approached the hospital doors, Callie's phone buzzed, and she stopped to reach inside her purse. When she let go of his arm, a strange mixture of relief and disappointment came over him, and he ran his gloved hand through his hair several times, trying to unwind the tangle of unexpected emotions.

Callie spoke to her brother once more as Ben listened, trying not to notice the beautiful way Callie moved her hands when she talked or how the sound of her voice was so musical that he imagined he could close his eyes and enjoy the tone of it for hours.

Ben had never known anyone with significant sight loss before. Callie was so lovely in the way she moved that if not for her telling him, or needing his help, he wouldn't have guessed she couldn't see well.

"My brother will be here soon, I think," she informed him as she tossed her phone back in her purse. "A friend is giving him a ride."

Ben slid his arm back under Callie's hand, feeling her warmth as she pulled close to him again, and they continued toward the hospital's front doors.

The lobby was crowded and loud. Padded blue chairs dotted a waiting area to their left, and nearly every seat was taken. Nurses, doctors, and staff darted to and fro behind the waiting room, disappearing into winding hallways that crisscrossed in different directions. A reception desk with a sizable crowd in front of it lay to their right. The smell of bleach and antiseptic lingered in the air.

"I can probably figure it out from here," Callie said unsteadily as she dropped her hand and seemed to look around, taking in whatever she could of the busy scene. Though Ben had no idea what she could see or do here on her own, he felt it would be cruel to leave her in this chaos.

"It's okay. I'm not in a hurry. I'll just make sure you find someone to get you to your father."

Removing her sunglasses, Callie turned her emerald-green eyes to him. They were as lovely as the rest of her, but there was something exotic about the look of them. That was the only way Ben could describe them as he stood there wondering what she could see of him. The shape of her pupils and the way her eyes tracked were distinctive, but her eyes still reflected her warm and generous nature, and Ben was intrigued and lost in their revelations. Though he didn't intend to stare, he felt frozen in place as she focused on his face.

The line in front of the reception desk moved, and Ben guided Callie forward, forcing himself to look away from her, so his heart wouldn't keep drawing him closer to the edge of disaster.

Just help and then get out, Ben, he chided himself. Of all the people to meet, why her? There would be no hiding who he was if...

The line inched forward as each person's questions were answered or their needs addressed. Many were given clipboards and sent to the island of blue chairs to complete paperwork. Finally, it was Callie's turn.

The woman behind the desk had a rushed look on her face, and she nodded to Ben and Callie as they approached, her gray bun bobbing as she moved. Ben had never thought about how rude it was for people not to speak in greeting. Knowing that Callie likely couldn't see the silent acknowledgment filled him with sudden indignation toward the woman, which he knew was probably unfair.

Ben cleared his throat and Callie seemed to understand what he was indicating.

"I'm Callie LeVray. My dad was brought here. I guess he collapsed at work. They told me to come soon. I..." Her voice trailed off as tears formed in her eyes.

"What's your dad's name?" the woman asked as she looked from Callie to Ben.

Ben glared back at her. He didn't like this woman. Why was she looking at Callie that way?

"Ronald LeVray," Callie replied, trying to keep the tears from overflowing.

Letting go of Ben, she crossed her arms, trying to calm her nerves.

The woman tapped at her keyboard and puffed air through her teeth as she scanned her screen. "He's in the ICU," she said softly, finally showing a measure of compassion that Ben judged to be long overdue.

"Go to the third floor and check in at the desk. Tell them who you are, and a doctor will come and speak to you about your father's condition."

When she opened her mouth to speak, Ben interrupted. "Thank you. We will."

Without thinking, Ben clasped Callie's hand with his gloved one and circled it back around his arm. He didn't wait for her to protest before moving away from the desk and toward a set of elevators on the back wall.

"Ben!" Callie exclaimed after they'd moved away from the crowd. "You don't need to go. I can get help. I can—"

"I'm not leaving you in this crowd. It's too crazy here. You'll be waiting a long time for someone to help you, and you need to see what's going on with your father. I'll just wait until your brother gets here. It's not an inconvenience. Really, it's fine." It all came out so quickly that Ben didn't have time to consider what he was doing.

Stopping, Callie pulled her hand away from him so abruptly that Ben worried she may have lifted his sleeve in the process. She spoke softly but insistently. "That's so kind, but this isn't part of your job. I, well, I'll have to pay you something for this if you insist. I really don't want you to trouble yourself. It's not fair to you."

Ben had the urge to put his finger over her soft pink lips

to silence her considerate objections, but he still had enough self-control to squelch the desire.

"Don't worry. I'm done driving today, and I'm, well, I can spare a few minutes to get you to the right place." Ben hoped his statement came across as caring, as he wanted to be a comforting presence, even though he and Callie were near strangers. It occurred to him that she might feel confused by his insistence, given his initial hesitation to even help her to the front desk.

However, Callie hesitantly took his arm again, dropping her head in surrender to his kind offer. "Thank you," she breathed in a relieved-sounding whisper as they got into the elevator.

CALLIE STARED into the emerging light, as the elevator doors opened onto the hospital's third floor. Ben guided her through what felt like an endless maze of hallways in search of the ICU. Once her eyes adjusted to the light again, she was able to make out doorways, carts, and the few people who passed them on their way to the check-in desk.

Callie's mind returned over and over again to unanswered questions about what had happened to her dad. She could hardly stand any more delays. But at the same time, the fear of what she might learn made her knees shake. Learning that he was in the ICU had heightened that fear. Whatever was wrong with him was obviously serious. A part of her knew that someday she would have to learn to live without him, but that reality had always seemed so far off in the future, far enough that she could pretend it didn't exist at all. Now, that possibility loomed over her and threatened to turn her whole world upside down.

All she wanted to do was sit and weep, but she wasn't

sure yet if that was necessary, and even if it was, it felt awkward and improper to react like that in such an unfamiliar public place and with a stranger by her side.

Thinking of Ben as a total stranger certainly should have been the way she perceived him. Besides his name, she knew nothing about him, and a little over an hour ago, she hadn't even known that much. It was curious to Callie that he didn't feel as much like a stranger as he should have. There was something oddly familiar about him, and when he offered her comfort in her distress, her heart had responded right away. Typically, only her father or brother could put her at ease like that.

When they entered the hospital and she removed her sunglasses, she'd been close enough to catch some details of his face. He had thick dark brown hair that hung in a loose yet styled way, strands of it falling attractively over his forehead. She couldn't make out his eye color, but his face was handsome, with a hint of boyish charm. He was several inches taller than her five-foot-six-inch frame, and from holding his arm, she assessed him to be strong and well-muscled.

He had a kind and gentle way about him, but he was hesitant and guarded too. It was as if being himself was new to him, like he'd been asleep or unconscious. He seemed unsure about how to express a part of him that was natural but forgotten. Though she recognized that these were strange impressions, and she had no idea where they came from, it was uncanny how often her inability to see well seemed to be compensated by a kind of intuition about people that helped fill in the gaps.

After winding through more hallways, they finally reached a reception area. Thankfully, there was no line this time, so Ben led her straight up to the desk.

"Good morning. Can I help you?" came a friendly voice as they approached.

When Callie tried to answer, her voice stuck in her throat. She wasn't sure she wanted to ask or know. Standing here, finally so close to answers, she didn't think she could face them.

"This is Callie LeVray," Ben spoke up next to her. "She's here because someone called and said her father, Ronald LeVray, was brought here this morning."

Relief and gratitude filled her as she leaned into Ben's arm to communicate her appreciation. *How did he know I needed help because I couldn't speak through my emotions?*

Here was yet another way that Ben didn't seem like much of a stranger at all.

"Thank you," she whispered, glancing at him as she pushed a loose curl behind her ear.

"Oh, yes," the woman behind the desk said. "Have a seat, and I'll find the doctor to talk with you."

Callie tried to read her voice. It sounded serious but steady, not despairing or distressed. Whether or not that was accurate, she didn't know. Without being able to see her face clearly and with her own raging emotions clouding her judgment, she couldn't be sure.

Ben guided her to a small cluster of chairs situated against a bright window. The early afternoon sun streamed in and warmed Callie's shoulders as she sat down, releasing Ben's arm. She took off her coat and folded it in her lap, but she noticed Ben didn't do the same. As the minutes ticked by and her anxiety built, she covered her face with her hands, attempting to take control of her racing heart.

"Are you alright?" Ben asked with genuine concern.

"I'm trying," she said with a sigh. "I'm trying not to think or imagine the worst case, but my mind keeps going there. I, well, I can't think of my world without my dad. I don't want to think about that."

"Tell me about him," Ben said, surprising her by asking. "I've never met my father, so I'm unfamiliar with the experience of what having one, much less a good one, is like."

Callie knew he was trying to distract her, take her mind away from the impending news and imagining the worst, and she appreciated the gesture.

"Well, I didn't have a mom for much of my life, so I'm like you, lacking that kind of normal experience. My dad, though, has been everything to my brother and me. By day he's a prosecutor, helps to convict and put away bad guys, like a real-life superhero." She paused to smile at her analogy. "Then he takes care of my brother and me with a level of love and commitment that I'm not sure any two parents could rival. And on top of all of that, he has a daughter with, well, with my unique situation to handle, and he has never made me feel like that ever caused him an ounce of trouble or stress, though I know it surely has."

Leaning back in her chair, she felt the sun's warmth seeping through the cold brought on by the dread and anxiety raging inside her. Ben shifted toward her, but he didn't reach out or invade her space.

"Wow!" he exclaimed, chuckling. "It sounds like kryptonite wouldn't stand a chance."

Smiling, Callie held out her hands, palms up, in an exaggerated shrug. "Not a chance, I'm sure."

"Well, then, we'll have some faith in his ability to beat this, whatever this is," he said, leaning back again against his seat.

Callie sensed his gaze focused on her as he tried to boost her courage. "I'm trying to keep that hope," she whispered.

"Hope is a powerful thing, and sometimes it's the only lifeline we've got."

Ben's voice held a sense of wisdom that only came with experience. Callie found herself wondering why he expressed an understanding of the importance of hope but seemed so drained of it himself. Though she had no idea why, she felt moved by the pain in his voice. She leaned forward, needing to understand it. "Is this, I mean, have you faced this kind of thing before or..."

She let her question fade, suddenly feeling like she was prying into secrets that weren't her place to unearth.

There was silence between them for a moment, and Callie, like so many times before, found herself wishing she could read the face of another human being and see the message in their eyes.

Ben seemed to be about to speak when he straightened, and Callie became aware that someone had taken the empty seat on her left.

"Miss LeVray?" a voice asked.

Turning, she saw a man in a white coat facing her. "Yes!" she replied, jumping to her feet.

The doctor stood and placed a hand on her arm, likely afraid she might lose her balance due to her sudden motion. "I'm Doctor James Karl, and I've been taking care of your dad. Can you and your, um, well, can both of you please follow me, and we'll talk in a private room about your dad's condition?"

"Oh I, well, I..." Callie didn't know what to do. She didn't want to impose upon Ben anymore, but she wasn't sure if she could handle facing the news alone.

"Callie, you go with the doctor," Ben said, solving her dilemma. "I'll watch for your brother and be here to let him know where you are." Ben paused. "She'll need your arm,

Doc," he said. Doctor Karl quickly retraced the few steps he had taken to offer Callie his arm.

She appreciated Ben's thoughtfulness in resolving the awkward situation, but she felt sad, realizing she'd likely never see him again. Then she scolded herself, not understanding why his presence had so quickly become something comforting and even desired.

Offering Ben a smile, she thanked him again before taking Doctor Karl's arm. Though each step felt as if heavy weights had been strapped to her ankles, she allowed him to lead her down the hall and into an unmarked room.

Ben had no idea what Callie's brother looked like, but he figured he would arrive at the desk looking as frantic and lost as Callie had upon their arrival. He positioned himself in a spot where he could see the check-in desk as well as the closed door that Callie and Doctor Karl had disappeared behind.

Looking down, he realized he still wore the black gloves that protected him, but which now caused him to sweat in the warmth of the hospital. Sliding them off as well as his coat, he stashed them next to him, ready to quickly put them back on if needed.

As he glanced down the hallway at the door that Callie had entered, he wondered what news she was hearing and his heart tightened in his chest. He was afraid for her, this strong yet vulnerable woman. Though he had only known her for a short time, he somehow felt connected to her in a way that was impossible to understand. Was she strong enough if the news was truly bad?

Ben was amazed at the courage she displayed. It had to be overwhelming to carry around so much hardship, like a heavy weight on her back, only to have more piled on. But Callie carried it with grace. She didn't complain or feel sorry for herself. She didn't seem jaded by the hand the universe had dealt her either. She was kindhearted and caring, tuned in to the burdens of others.

Perhaps that had something to do with her father, whom she so obviously admired. Ben supposed that if a person felt sufficiently loved, accepted, and treasured by another human being, so many of the worst tragedies and difficulties of life could be endured.

He chuckled humorlessly at that thought. He had had something like that once, until his world collapsed around him, and the acceptance that had been given turned lethal for the giver. Loving Callie likely brought her father joy, but loving and accepting him had brought tragedy and destruction. He couldn't let anyone offer that to him again no matter how much he, like every human alive, needed it.

Ben huffed bitterly. *If I even am human.*

The world might be a difficult place for those like Callie, but for him, the world was intolerant, scared of what it didn't understand.

But maybe someone like Callie... Shaking his head, Ben pressed his fists into his knees. *You've been down that road,* he reminded himself. *It's worse for them because they win, but then they lose, and the second loss is worse than if they had never known what it was to win in the first place.*

He needed to walk away now. It wasn't possible to be, well, to be anything to Callie, not even a friend. It would hurt her, break her. That weight on her back, he would turn it into a crushing burden that she'd never get out from under. He couldn't do that to such a trusting and beautiful soul.

Grabbing his coat and gloves, he stood and started

toward the hall that led to the elevators, just as a worried-looking teenager rushed around the corner and approached the reception desk.

"I'm Lee LeVray," he panted, evidently having sprinted through the halls to get there as quickly as possible.

"My sister, my dad..."

Catching the eye of the nurse behind the desk, Ben came up beside Lee, clearing his throat to get his attention.

"Lee, I'm Ben. Your sister is in with the doctor. I'll show you where."

When Lee looked at Ben, Ben saw Callie's eyes staring back at him, though they lacked the exotic quality. Lee also had Callie's curly hair, though it was short and a striking shade of red. He was only an inch or so shorter than Ben, so they nearly looked eye to eye as Lee hesitated for a moment, trying to figure out who this stranger was.

A resignation birthed from urgency settled into Lee's expression, and he motioned to Ben to lead the way.

Guiding him past the seating area and down the adjoining hallway, Ben stopped at the door that Doctor Karl and Callie had entered.

"Doctor Karl led her in there to talk privately about your father. I'm sure she'll be relieved to have you with her."

Pausing at the door, Lee looked at Ben, a smirk raising the corners of his mouth. "Does my sister have a secret life I don't know about, or are you some kind of hospital helper person or what?" The question wasn't confrontational but instead conveyed simple curiosity, mixed with amusement.

Ben cleared his throat, unsure how to sum up the day in a way that didn't sound outlandish or make him appear like some kind of crazed stalker, or worse. "Well, I'm actually your sister's driver. She needed some help when we got here, and, well, the hospital was so busy I didn't want to leave her here alone, and…" Ben trailed off, not sure where to go from there.

Raising an eyebrow, Lee stared at Ben, as if sizing him up like a protective father might do to his daughter's new boyfriend.

After an awkward moment of silent scrutiny, Lee offered a satisfied grin and held his hands up in surrender. "We'll just go with 'Good Old Uncle Ben' then," he teased, slapping Ben on the arm despite his anxiety about his dad, which still manifested in his tight jaw and anxious shuffling.

Ben instantly liked this kid. He had an open, easy-going way about him, even in such circumstances, that warmed up the space around him and everyone in it. Lee was clearly one of those people who never met a stranger, possessing the ability to connect quickly with others.

Lee started for the doorknob but then paused, turning his eyes back to Ben. "Don't go away, Uncle Ben," Lee ordered. "If Callie trusted you to lead her here, then I want to call you a friend, and if I know my sister, which I definitely do, I'm sure Callie already considers you one." Without giving Ben a chance to respond, he opened the door and stepped inside.

Slowly, Ben turned to head back to the waiting area. He wasn't sure what to do. He should go. He definitely needed to go, but now he couldn't go.

Was it true? Did Callie already consider him a friend? Did she need him in some way? He knew that neither she nor Lee had a ride, so his presence there could still be helpful to them. The kindness in Lee's words thawed the barren wilderness of Ben's heart, like the first warmth of springtime after a long, harsh winter. The resemblance between Callie and her brother went far deeper than eye color and curls. Ben wondered if their father carried the same kind of heart. From what Callie had told him about her father, it seemed likely that he did, and Ben found himself wanting to meet the man and find out.

He'd been ready to walk away, to move on, to leave this family, leave Callie, protect her from him. That was what he should do. But their open, accepting hearts, even in such a terrible moment of worry and potential loss, held him in place. He hadn't known such kindness in a long time, and it was something he desperately needed in his isolated world, but he knew he would likely regret allowing any of his walls to come down.

Sitting down, Ben put his head in his hands, his hair spilling over his fingers. If there was any chance she needed him, even a little, he couldn't leave. He couldn't run. Not for now anyway.

CHAPTER 5
THE ICU

An hour later, Callie was sitting by her father's hospital bed, her hand covering his as the monitors beeped and the life-support devices pushed air in and out in a steady but ominous rhythm. Lee paced behind her, never comfortable with sitting still or being idle, even under normal circumstances. Every few passes, he paused and rested his hand on Callie's shoulder for a few seconds before resuming his pacing.

"Lee! You're going to drive me crazy," Callie scolded gently, though she knew this was his way of coping with their situation.

Ronald LeVray had suffered a severe stroke. He was unconscious and unresponsive. The doctors were doing everything they could to manage his vitals and keep him alive, but there were no guarantees. This was about as much as Callie had understood of her and Lee's conversation with Dr. Karl. The doctor had not sounded optimistic, but he reassured them that he wasn't giving up either. Only time would tell if her father would wake up and recover.

The shock had sent Callie into Lee's arms as they both shed tears over the bad news they had hoped would never come.

"Dad's tough," Lee had comforted. "Really tough, Callie. Don't underestimate him. He knows we need him, and he'll fight like hell."

Normally, Callie would have scolded Lee over his occasionally loose tongue, but she simply didn't care about that now, and she was comforted by the sentiment.

"Kryptonite can't touch him," Callie muttered to herself, as she wiped her eyes and nose with a tissue.

"What?" Lee pushed her shoulders away from him, wrinkling his brow in confusion.

"Nothing." She shrugged. "Just remembering an earlier conversation."

Sitting here now, listening to the machines breathe for her dad and signal his heartbeat and witnessing Lee's nerves working themselves out on the tile floors around her, Callie wasn't so sure. Her dad's job was stressful, with life-and-death consequences. If he failed to put away a criminal, innocent people could be hurt.

His most recent case had been against a drug dealer who was evil enough to trick kids and teens into taking pills laced with lethal doses of fentanyl or other poisons. Kids had died because of this guy and his gang of accomplices. Money and power were all they cared about, and the lives and the families that were torn apart never kept him, or those like him, up at night.

Shaken by the evil of it all, her dad was determined to get the guy off the streets, so he couldn't harm any more innocent people. Callie remembered his passion as he stayed up late poring over his case, his arguments, his evidence, looking for any holes or flaws that might help the drug dealer get off. But in the end, he'd won the case, and the dealer was behind bars for life. Another day at the office, some might say, but for her dad, it was another life or perhaps many lives saved.

He never let what he did become routine, and he never lost his passion, but maybe that passion had driven him too hard, and his body had kept score.

Stroking his hand with her thumb, she tried to will her love and strength into him, directly to his heart, hoping to keep it pumping somehow.

"Dad, we need you. They need you." She gestured with her hand to indicate the wide range of his positive influence.

Callie was struck by how she felt cut off from her dad, in a way she couldn't remember ever feeling. His silence was like a chasm between them. Those with sight loss like hers, severe enough to cut them off from most nonverbal communication, need words to fill in the gaps.

Anyone who spent enough time with Callie soon figured out that rolling the eyes, frowning, smirking, pointing, and so on were useless efforts. And so, a unique language had developed between her and her closest group of friends and family. They had learned that they had to tell her what their face was saying with words, saying things like, "I'm not sure about what you just said" or "You're confusing me." Rather than pointing, a descriptive phrase like "It's at the back-left corner of the counter" was needed.

Callie and her family spoke this language fluently, and Lee had often laughed that he and their dad even spoke like this to each other when Callie wasn't around because they'd become so accustomed to it.

A few weeks before, Lee and Callie had laughed over a story Lee told her about taking a girl from his class out on a date. He had taken her arm to lead her into a restaurant, "which wasn't so weird or unusual," Lee said, smiling. "What she did think was strange, however, was when I warned her to step up at the curb."

Evidently, the perfectly sighted girl had laughed and told him she didn't need a play-by-play, which then required an explanation on Lee's part. Luckily, the girl had been kind and found the gesture endearing, which was probably why Lee had considered a second date with her.

Despite all the noise of the machines, it was too quiet in the cold hospital room without her dad's voice. Even the comfort of being able to focus on his familiar face was denied to her now. With all the sensors and tubes, she couldn't get close enough to see him clearly without worrying about knocking something loose.

"Cal." Lee stopped his pacing, once again resting his hand on her shoulder. "Have you eaten anything?"

"No, not since this morning," she admitted. "But I'm not sure I'm hungry."

"Well, I might as well put my nervous energy to good use. I'm going to go get us something to eat. I hear hospital food is terrible, but since I don't have a car, and you don't have a car..." Lee paused expectantly, but she was too drained to laugh at his not-so-subtle attempt at humor. "I guess we'll just take one for the team," he finished, resignation in his voice. "Will you be okay? I mean, I'm not going far."

"The floors and my nerves will appreciate the reprieve from your pacing." She tried for a teasing tone, feeling bad for her brother, whose sole purpose in life often seemed to be making her smile.

"Be back soon," he promised, squeezing her shoulders and then heading out the door.

When he was gone, Callie couldn't help but relax, not

because Lee had left but because his unrelenting pacing had ceased with his departure.

Can't he just sit and pray and...

Her thoughts drifted as she realized she wasn't sure what she was supposed to be doing either. If she talked to her dad, would he hear her? Probably not. She had already poured out a dozen silent prayers, and now she felt emotionally drained.

A sudden wave of weariness washed over her, and she leaned down and placed her cheek on her dad's hand, closing her eyes. It was a way to connect with him, to feel his presence. Maintaining that posture for several minutes, she began to think she might doze off when a voice from the other side of her dad's bed startled her.

"Callie, are you alright? Um, it's Ben."

Surprised, she lifted her head to look in his direction. For no reason that Callie could understand or imagine, his voice flooded her heart with warmth, like hearing the familiar voice of a long-lost friend.

"Ben? You're still here?"

"Yes, but if you'd rather be alone, I understand."

"No, it's fine, as long as you're not prone to pacing." She smiled weakly. "But it's been like an hour or more. You've been around all this time! That's incredibly kind but totally unfair to you."

A chair squeaked across the floor, telling Callie that Ben had taken a seat, evidently ignoring her arguments.

"I'm so sorry about your dad. I know neither you nor your brother have a ride, so whenever you want to head home for the night, I'd like to help."

"Ben!" Callie let out a long sigh, feeling too grateful and admiring this kind stranger too much to argue anymore. She smiled and then her face shifted to a puzzled expression. "How did they let you in here? They told me only family."

"Well…" Ben paused, and Callie could hear the amused smile in his voice as he continued. "Your brother has taken to calling me 'Uncle Ben.' That and the fact that they saw me come in with you, so I guess they just figured I was family."

Callie couldn't help but laugh, which flooded her heart with much-needed strength. She'd had a feeling that Lee had had something to do with Ben still being around.

"That's my brother! You'll be stuck with that nickname forever now, you know. He'll never give it up."

Ben chuckled, the sound light and refreshing. "That's fine. I don't mind, though I'm hardly old enough to pass for his, or your, uncle."

Smiling, Callie suddenly wondered how old Ben was. From the brief glimpse she had caught when she was near enough to see his face, he looked to be older than her but not by much, maybe in his late twenties.

"Lee comes by it honestly. My dad is a big one for nick-names. I can't remember the last time he called either of us by our real names." Callie smiled at the tender memories.

A nurse entered the room and read the information on the machines. Her pen tapped against her clipboard as she recorded the results. It brought Callie back to the somber-ness of their surroundings, and the light moment passed, like a coveted cool breeze on a scorching hot day.

When the nurse left, they sat in silence for a few comfortable moments. Ben didn't fidget or pace. Instead, he sat peacefully like a pillar of steadfast support.

"He had a terrible stroke. They're not sure he'll ever be himself again, the dad I knew, if he wakes up at all." She dropped her head into her hands.

"Yes. Lee told me on his way to the cafeteria." Ben's voice was pained and full of empathy. "Don't give up. Amazing things happen all the time. Doctors are often proven wrong. He looks strong, and from what you've told me, he's a fighter. He knows you and Lee need him, and he won't give up easily."

Ben's voice held a confidence that Callie didn't feel, though she wanted to. She nodded. "I hope he can fight this, that he has enough left inside, in his conscious mind and heart, to fight his way back." Dropping her hands to her knees, she shifted back in her seat.

"Well, if he's anything like you, I'd say he's got plenty of strength to fight with."

Ben conveyed a confident understanding about her that she didn't know how he'd come to possess. She wasn't feeling strong at the moment, but she knew that her dad would want her to reach down deep and draw from everything he'd taught her about courage.

"When you're different and don't quite fit into the world's, well, the world's mold, I guess, you learn to be tough."

Ben chuckled, a sound that didn't convey humor but seemed to be expressing real understanding, like he knew exactly what she meant, though she didn't know how that could be possible.

"Fitting in is overrated," he said with a resolute sigh.

"Now you sound like him," Callie said as she motioned toward her father's unresponsive face. "He's always told me that what the world thinks of as weak can confound that which it considers to be strong, that there's strength in weakness, strength that the strongest people might never be fortunate enough to discover because they've never had to reach out for it. It's like building muscles. The heavy lifting, the difficulties we face, can make us stronger if we let them."

Ben didn't respond right away, and Callie guessed he was pondering her words. When he spoke again, his voice was heavy with emotions that Callie could feel in the core of her being, even though she didn't know where they came from.

"That is a beautiful truth, but most people don't or can't grasp that at all. They rely on feeling whole and self-sufficient for their strength. When they can't accomplish wholeness, as I'm not sure anyone really can, they give up and give in to being broken and damaged, which is a dark road to walk."

Though she had no idea of the specific circumstances that prompted his words, Callie could feel the pain and sadness behind them. Her heart ached for the experience of obvious hardship Ben had endured. A strange yet intimate moment of shared understanding passed between them that left her feeling connected to him through some unknown yet common reality.

"I'm so sorry," she said, her voice barely audible over the noise of the life-support machines. "Whatever brought you to that, caused you that pain, I'm truly sorry."

BEN'S HEART pounded in his chest. How did this woman see right through him, and what was he doing?

He couldn't remember anyone who had opened his heart like that, causing it to spill out of his mouth so impulsively. What he said shouldn't have made sense to her, yet she'd gotten it, known it came from pain, from his past and the ghosts that still haunted him because of it.

Looking across the hospital bed at her, Ben stared into

her exotic green eyes, which now shimmered with unshed tears; eyes that physically didn't see much but which saw more about him than anyone had been able to see in a long time.

Alarmed, he recognized that this stunning woman was quickly tearing down his walls, brick by brick. He was good at protecting himself and his secrets, having had lots of practice. So, why were his defenses crumbling as if he had none at all?

He'd never known anyone like Callie. She seemed contented, despite her tough circumstances and inabilities. Not that she was happy about it, but she had made peace with it, and that peace filled the space around her so completely that it overcame the lack of contentment that he felt toward his own fate.

Callie waited for a response so she could read more in his voice and his heart and he might have spilled his soul out to her at that moment, recklessly trusting her with way too much, but then, Lee entered the room carrying a tray full of assorted food items. Setting it on a small table near the hospital bed, he turned to study the serious faces in the room.

"I sent you in here to cheer her up, Uncle Ben. You're not doing your job very well." Lee flashed a wide smile, then offered Ben a cup of coffee, which he accepted gratefully.

"And for you." Lee approached Callie and placed another cup of piping hot liquid into her hand.

Lowering her nose to the slit in the lid, she inhaled. "You didn't!" She raised both eyebrows and then took a long, satisfying sip. "How in the world did you find chai tea in a hospital?" she inquired with obvious pleasure.

"Every desert has an oasis or two," Lee said with a grin, proud of his achievement. "My sister's not much of a coffee person," Lee explained, looking at Ben. "But she loves her chai tea, lots of cream, and a teaspoon of sugar. She's high maintenance, but I still love her." Lee patted Callie's head as he turned back to the tray of food and began taking inventory.

"High maintenance, huh?" Callie retorted. "Who's the one who has to have his coffee just the right temperature, or he won't touch it? Too hot and, nope, won't drink it. Too cold and down the sink it goes, even a whole cup that's not been touched."

"That's just good sense," Lee defended. "Room-temperature coffee is stupid."

They both laughed and Ben couldn't help being amused by their sibling banter. He had no siblings of his own and had never seen siblings who seemed anywhere near as close and loving as these two. It was like being inside a warm blanket, the comfort of it blocking out the pain in the room and beyond. Ben was thankful they had each other in such a difficult moment, and he felt fortunate that, through some weird twist of fate, he was there as a witness to this special bond.

Over sandwiches and chips, Callie and Lee spoke lovingly about their father. Neither of them seemed uncomfortable whatsoever with having Ben around. On the contrary, it appeared that telling Ben about their dad, sharing stories and some of his wisdom, brought them some solace. A few of the memories even came with hearty rounds of laughter.

By the time the doctor checked in, Ben almost felt like he knew Ronald LeVray, and he could tell that the man was as warm hearted and open of spirit as his son and daughter. A man of integrity, full of faith, and devoted to justice, he was a protector of the innocent and a shield around his family. As Ben stared at the man, a genuine sense of respect and admiration grew, and again he hoped, though he knew it was highly unlikely, that he would get the chance to know Ronald LeVray himself.

When the doctor came in, Ben stepped out into the hallway. Though he doubted Callie or Lee would have asked him to leave, he still recognized that he was not actually part of this family, and he didn't want to impose.

Ben wandered back into the waiting area, carrying his coat and gloves, which he had never felt the need to put back on. He'd remained on the opposite side of the hospital bed from Callie, and Lee stayed out of Ben's personal bubble, though it wasn't nearly as consequential with him as it was with her.

Most people sensed that Ben liked to keep a large area of personal space around him, though no one knew the real reason for it. By and large, people respected that and didn't impose.

Though emotionally open and available, Lee maintained a good sense of other people's physical boundaries. It was interesting, however, to watch him interact with his sister, as the personal space issue played out differently with her. They had a language, birthed by necessity no doubt, that was like a well-rehearsed dance. Ben had studied it while they told stories about their dad.

When Lee offered Callie something, like her sandwich, he touched her arm, so she would know he was there and offering it. He seemed to know what she could or couldn't see.

Sometimes she reached out and patted Lee's arm or slapped his back in jest, demonstrating she knew where he was. But there were other times when she seemed unaware of something he was offering or that he had moved to a different position. Lee always did something to clue her in whether patting her, describing something to her, or speaking to her.

Ben watched the whole unconscious system they had developed over time with great interest. It was almost as though when Callie was with Lee, she wasn't visually limited because he had learned to counter such limitations. If Ben asked Lee how he did it, he doubted Lee could have described the system. It was like a baby learning to walk, learning little by little, step by step until he could walk across the room. If Ben was going to be around Callie...

The thought was cut short as Ben remembered the truth of his reality. What was he thinking? He couldn't be around Callie. Over the last few hours, he had let his guard down, and he'd almost made a big mistake, almost revealed too much.

Though Callie was like refreshing water that his thirsty soul needed, he couldn't be around her because of who he was. The old familiar walls began to rise again around his wrecked heart. If he cared about this girl, the best thing he could do for her was stay away.

"Everything alright, Uncle Ben?"

Looking up, Ben was startled to find Lee beside him, Callie on his arm.

"Um, sure," Ben stammered, rising to his feet. "Are things okay? I mean, with the doctor and your father and all?"

"Same, same." Lee shrugged, pushing his free hand through his red curls. "The doc told us to go home and come back tomorrow. Nothing will likely change for a while. It will take time, and Dad is being carefully monitored. Callie doesn't want to leave, but, well, I'm making her, and since you're our only way out of this prison of bad food, small spaces, and offensive smells, I guess we're here to impose upon you some more. If that's okay."

"Yes, of course, only it's not imposing. I'm happy to help."

Ben led the way back down the elevator and out to his cold SUV. Lee offered an admiring whistle and a teasing comment about Uncle Ben's good taste in vehicles before making sure Callie was settled into the backseat. Then, he surprised Ben by jumping, unabashedly, in front next to him. Ben smiled at the gesture, which spoke of Lee's affection for him beyond just being a hired driver.

"Do you two need to stop anywhere on the way home?" Ben asked as he started the SUV. "Make a grocery run?"

"Nope," Lee replied. "We're all set for food. My car should be fixed in a couple of days, and I can use my dad's car till then. I'll have to retrieve his spare keys from the house. Callie might need some rides with my dad not here and all. Can we request you specifically? That way when Callie is on her own... Well, you already know how to help and all."

As the voices of caution in his mind protested, Ben pulled out his phone and brought up his contact information. He set it on the middle console, so Lee could see it.

"Just call me directly."

Lee entered the information into his phone, looking back and forth from his screen to Ben's.

"Ben Sawyer," he said, articulating each syllable. "Cool name. Sounds like an explorer or a traveler or something."

Ben chuckled under his breath at the hidden irony in Lee's words as he backed out of the parking space.

The drive to the LeVray house was quiet, everyone lost in their thoughts. When Ben pulled into the driveway, Lee broke the silence. "Thanks for your help today, man. Like, sincerely, thanks for hanging around and all."

Pulling cash from his wallet, Lee held it out to Ben, but Ben raised his hands in protest. "I'll just put it on your tab. We'll settle it later. Callie..." Ben turned back to direct his voice toward her. "Please call me if you need help, a ride, or anything. I'm sure, well, I mean I'm hopeful that everything is going to be alright with your father."

"You were like my guardian angel today. Thank you for being the nicest stranger I've ever met." Despite her weariness, she beamed a devastatingly beautiful smile at him as Lee took her arm and helped her out of the car.

CHAPTER 6

THE PREDICTION

As Ben pulled away from the LeVray house and turned back toward the main road, he noticed a black car parked on a side street. It was a classic, maybe an old Dodge, from the 1960s or '70s, large and boxy. At one point it had been restored, but it did not look well maintained, having some noticeable scratches and a few small dents. Its tinted windows made it hard to tell if anyone was inside, but Ben thought he caught a glimpse of movement behind the windshield as he passed.

It caught Ben's attention because it looked out of place in that upper-middle-class neighborhood and because it was a rare and unusual kind of vehicle. If it were a classic that someone was fixing up, parking it on the street and not in a driveway or a garage seemed strange. The sight of it initiated in him an odd feeling of dread that had no reasonable explanation.

Perhaps it's someone visiting a home here, Ben thought, dismissing his suspicion as his mind drifted back to the events of the day. He decided to head home, as it was getting late, and he didn't feel up for any more pick-ups.

As he put miles between himself and Callie, he felt keenly empty and alone. The interactions between them had been surprisingly meaningful, and watching Callie and Lee's close bond had renewed buried desires and needs for the same within him.

Though Ben wasn't sure he'd ever experienced the same level of connection as what he witnessed between Callie and Lee, there was a time in his life when he'd been loved and cared for by another. He'd felt important and needed, back when he still thought of his curse as more of a gift. Though he had no idea how he had become who he was or why, the fact that he could give her something that no one else could, made him happy and gave him a sense of purpose.

But then he grew up and had to go out on his own and be away for long periods. He'd been unaware of the void his absence had left in her life. Like a drug, it had become an addiction of sorts, but she refused to let him see how much his absence destabilized her. He'd been young and, like many people his age, self-focused as he plotted his future. She'd put on a good face when they were together, assuring him that she was fine. By the time he realized she was lying, it was too late.

That was when he realized that who he was wasn't good. He didn't have a gift, but he carried a kind of weapon, a power that, because of its limitations, ended up more harmful than helpful.

From that moment forward, he began to hate it, and self-loathing became his constant companion. The feeling protected others but kept him isolated. It had been a long time since he'd had anyone in his life who truly knew him, all of him. Though loneliness weighed heavily on him, he'd learned to live with it. When he questioned his path, all he had to do was think back to the pain of what had happened to her and how he knew for sure it was because of him and what he was. That knowledge kept him from daring to make the same mistake again.

But Callie had awakened something in him. She didn't seem to need him, not that part of him anyway, only an arm or some guidance, but she could have asked anyone for that. Comfortable with who she was, her need for others filled them more than it helped her.

Somehow Callie could see into him, which was the height of irony given her physical limitations. Because the help she'd asked for could be given from the part of him that was just Ben and not the other, giving it had opened a door inside that had been locked for a long time.

If Ben hadn't helped her, Callie would have been fine, but he had the feeling he would not have been. Her small hand around his arm guided him toward something he'd forgotten, a part of him he'd left behind. But in opening that door, the walls that protected that other part of him, the part he hated and needed to hide, weakened, and that frightened him.

Perhaps after all these years of running and hiding, he had only managed to push aside but not cure his addiction. He wanted to help others, needing to give what he had. It was the only way he could make sense of any of it, the only way to assign any purpose to it.

But what if he did end up helping her, by accident or intent, with every part of who he was, and everything changed? Her trusting nature, her acceptance of who she was; what if he changed all of that and turned her into a different person because of giving her a gift that he kept retracting? Her sweetness might turn bitter, and her warmth might grow cold. He'd seen it happen before, and he couldn't bear to watch it happen again.

Rain began to fall as he pulled up to his high-rise apartment building, and his internal walls began to grow once again. He couldn't take the chance with this kind soul because of his own needs, attractions, and impulses. It would lead to the destruction of the very thing he cherished.

Ben glared resentfully at his bare hand on the steering wheel. *Why?* he fumed. If he was just Ben, nothing more, he would call Callie, take her out, and get to know her. The only fear would be the normal first date kind of nervousness that came with getting to know another person. How small such fear felt to him compared to what he faced!

It was difficult to separate and identify the part of him that was just Ben. He shook his head as he realized he could barely recall the time before the curse had taken over his life. He'd been so young, just a kid. His entire adult life had been defined by the part of him that he didn't understand or want.

How was he supposed to continue running and hiding? Would he forever be alone and isolated, unable to have or make a real life with someone?

He felt like the rope in a sick game of tug-of-war, his need pulling him one way and his fear wrenching him back. He formed a fist and punched his steering wheel, letting his frustration get the better of him.

It took him a moment to regain his composure, but at last, he took a deep, resigned breath, put his gloves on, wrapped his coat around him, and headed out into the downpour. The entrance to his building was covered, but the rain was coming in sideways, and it soaked him as he fumbled for his keys.

Just as he was about to unlock the doors, they flew open, and his eyes met the kind, round face of Ms. Essie, the building's security concierge.

Ben had met Ms. Essie on his first day in town. She'd been friendly and kind and had eventually convinced him to stay a while, even helping him get set up in an apartment there. A retired police officer with a charming Southern accent, she had an uncanny way of getting people to share their hearts. She knew all the residents by name and remembered every detail of conversations she'd had with them. She always had a pot of coffee, a comfortable chair, and a listening ear, though, at times, she also didn't mind sharing her wisdom.

"Mr. Ben Sawyer!" Ms. Essie boomed with a wide smile. "You're plain soaked, yes you are! Come on in here, and get yourself dried off now, ya hear?"

She gave Ben a towel and he wiped his face and hair. "Thank you." Ben returned her smile, handing back the towel and accepting a cup of coffee.

"Now, you come right in here and sit with me. You look like you've been through it today, surely you do! Nothin' that can't be set right, though, I guarantee."

Ms. Essie led Ben to a plush seating area with a cozy fireplace alive with orange and yellow flames. Clutching her own cup of coffee, she sat across from him in an oversized tan chair while he settled himself on the matching couch.

No one could resist Ms. Essie, as she embodied a sense of love and home that flowed out from her in steady waves, transporting those in her presence to a simpler time and place where people valued and practiced conversation, kindness, and genuine care for others. Ben didn't know why, but with her, he felt at ease, almost normal.

He slipped his coat off and even tossed his gloves on the couch next to him.

"Alright," Ms. Essie started, looking directly at Ben with her dark eyes. "Now, you go on and be tellin' me what happened to you today."

"Um, well," Ben stammered, not knowing where to start. What could he really tell her anyway? Considering her dad's profile in the community, the news about Callie's father would likely be a news story of some importance. Still, something didn't seem right about Ben spreading the information like cheap gossip. "I took a customer to the hospital today because her father was ill. I hope he'll recover, but I know it's a hard time for her and her brother and, well, I wanted to do more to help but..." Ben's voice trailed off as he wasn't sure what more to say.

Ms. Essie leaned forward in her chair, her black spiral curls bobbing as she nodded in understanding. Though she had to be in her seventies, her smooth brown skin and bright eyes gave her the appearance of one much younger, and her boundless energy also rebutted her age.

"Mm-hm!" She smiled again, seeming to be enjoying a private joke that Ben didn't share. "This wouldn't happen to be the LeVray family now, would it?" She sounded confident despite the question at the end.

Ben's mouth fell open in shock. "How did you..."

Ms. Essie laughed, a warm, soft sound that sweetened the air around them. "My husband and me, we been knowin' the LeVray family for years, what with us bein' cops and he bein' the prosecutor. We stay in touch with the department, and, well, word spreads quick 'bout this kinda thing. A great man, that Ronald LeVray! Tough as nails in the courtroom, protectin' the good folk of this community, but soft as butter with everyone else. Lovely family too.

Callie is a special girl, yes she is! Brave and…" She paused and raised an eyebrow as she focused her gaze on Ben. "Lovely inside and out. Yes indeed, she's a magnificent girl. Were ya knowin' that she plays the cello with a music group 'round here?"

Ben was still trying to process the fact that Ms. Essie had, seemingly, figured out all the details without him having to open his mouth.

"No I didn't, but I'm not that surprised. She seems, well, talented and special in many ways."

Laughing again, she slapped her knee with delight. "Oh, ya got it bad, now don't ya, Mr. Sawyer? You surely do!"

Heat rose to his face, and he looked away from Ms. Essie's penetrating gaze. He was about to protest but then changed his mind, knowing there was no way to hide the truth from this insightful woman. "I guess I got a little more involved than I usually do," he confessed, raising his eyes to meet hers again. "I mean, normally, I just drop people off and never get to know what happens. But Callie asked me to help her, and… well… before I knew it, I was being mistaken for a member of the family and meeting her brother and…"

"Oh yes, Mr. Lee LeVray." Ms. Essie poked her finger toward the ceiling to punctuate the statement. "He's got a fire to match that hair a his, but he's usin' his powers for good, not evil, so it's alright." She beamed with all the affection of a proud grandmother.

"He's already calling me 'Uncle Ben.'" Chuckling, he leaned back against the couch in a gesture of surrender.

Ms. Essie's laugh echoed across the tile floors again like music, and Ben couldn't help laughing along with her.

"He used to call me 'Ms. Essie-Bessie' when he was a young 'un. Made me and Louis giggle like school kids."

"Is Louis your husband?" Ben asked, not knowing if her husband was still alive or not.

"Yes, he surely is. We been married for many years now. He ain't in the best a health, mind ya, but I plan on celebratin' another anniversary with him, that's for certain!"

The last few words were said with a feeling of forced confidence. Though her eyes shadowed, her abundant love for her husband still shone through.

"That's wonderful! What a rare example you two set in a world of lost love these days." Ben dropped his gaze to his lap as the pain of his own broken family gripped his heart.

"Oh, I don't figure love's gettin' lost so much as people do. It's hard to be holdin' on to another person when folks can't rescue their own broken selves. Life's always been hard, Mr. Sawyer, but now people ain't holdin' on to each other anymore. It's like everyone's livin' in their own lonely, broken house, and they can't fix it up for themselves, much less help another with his fixin'. You know what I'm meanin'?"

Though she asked the question, she turned her head away from Ben and focused on the flames leaping up and down in the fireplace.

Ben had to clear his throat before he could speak. "Yes, I do, Ms. Essie. I truly do know what you mean."

They were silent for a moment as they both drifted back into unspoken memories. Finally, Ms. Essie took a deep breath and refocused on Ben's face, her expression confident. "But I'm knowin' that Miss Callie and that LeVray family are pretty good exceptions to that rule. I'm knowin' they've learned the secret of lovin' and healin' broken places. Some might see that lovely girl and think she's, well, that she's broken in some outward ways. But that girl's got it together, and it ain't 'cause she's fixed things on her own. No, sir! That family's knowin' how to be a team, to be doin' life, with all its hardships, together." Ms. Essie chuckled softly as she finished. "And Lord knows she's probably keepin' those two men in her life in one piece, much more than they're doin' for her."

Smiling, Ben nodded in agreement. "I just hope they don't lose their father." His eyes fell to the floor. "That might change things for them, for Callie. She seems to draw a lot of strength from him."

"When God's closin' a door, He's always openin' a window, Mr. Sawyer." Ms. Essie grinned, lifting an eyebrow and winking at him. "You fixin' to take that lovely girl on a date?"

Shifting awkwardly, Ben wished he could tell this kind woman all his hopes and fears. "I can't."

"Why in heaven's name not?" Ms. Essie gazed at Ben like she could see deep into his soul.

"You know that whole thing we just said about being broken?"

She nodded, though her eyes still held the question.

"I'm broken, and I can't be fixed, and I can't be, well, a helper for anyone else. My house is unfixable, and anyone who enters will get damaged in the collapse." The words came out so fast that it sounded like he'd been holding them in for a long time, as though he had finally exhaled after coming up from several minutes underwater.

To Ben's surprise, Ms. Essie didn't respond right away. Instead, she touched her palms together in front of her, lowered her head, and closed her eyes, like she was offering a prayer. After a moment she fixed her gaze on Ben, sincerity and conviction showing in her eyes.

"Now, you listen here to this truth from an old Black woman who's seen her share a broken people. Nobody's unfixable. Heavy burdened, heavy hearted, bent down with sorrows, oh yes! Many a people are fittin' that description. We're all lost sheep needin' someone to come after us. But not a soul in this great big world can be walkin' alone, Mr. Sawyer. We gotta be trustin' someone, takin' a risk sometime. The surest way to get healin' is to heal someone else. We can't be helpin' everyone, but we can be healin' someone, goin' after a fellow lost sheep, takin' a hand, and walkin' together. People say it's more blessed to be givin' than receivin' 'cause givers are always gettin' more than they're givin'. Givin' is a real gift, and I'm knowin', just knowin', that you, Mr. Sawyer, you got a lot to give, but you gotta be trustin' someone first."

A lump stuck in his throat, and for a moment he couldn't speak. This was the second time that day that a virtual stranger had reached straight into his frozen heart and filled it with the warm light of acceptance, though they had no idea what they were accepting.

Sucking in a deep breath, he smiled at the kind woman sitting across from him. "Ms. Essie?" Ben asked, lifting his eyes to meet hers.

"Yes, sir?" she answered, meeting his gaze.

"When are you going to just call me 'Ben'?"

Slapping her knee again, she let out a belly laugh that rang through the high-ceilinged room like wind chimes. "I'm just an ol' southern girl at heart, Mr. Sawyer. Besides, you're feelin' like a Sawyer to me more than a Ben. 'Course I could always adopt 'Uncle Ben' from Mr. Lee LeVray," she teased.

Ben chuckled as he stood and grabbed his coat and gloves. He didn't want to leave the compassionate woman's presence as she filled a mother-shaped hole in his heart as no one had since, well, since he actually had a mother. But he was tired, and he was afraid that if he stayed much longer, he would tell her more than he should.

Ms. Essie took his empty coffee cup and tossed it into a nearby trash can.

"You're one of the kindest people I've ever known."

She placed her hand on his back, and Ben didn't flinch away. "You're good people, real good people. And 'cause a that, I'm bettin' it's already too late."

Ben frowned, feeling puzzled at her statement. "Too late for what?"

"Too late for you, Mr. Sawyer. I'm bettin' Miss Callie's already seen that good heart a yours and already knows who ya are. I'm bettin' ya already seen that good heart a hers and have already fallen for it too. Ya mind me, it's too late." She smiled with confidence, like she'd already seen the future.

Ben returned her smile, but as he turned to head toward the elevators, he whispered softly, "I hope not. For her sake, I sincerely hope not."

CHAPTER 7

THE LEARNING

Callie's phone had been ringing off the hook all evening. Several of her dad's coworkers had called to check on his condition, and Aunt Peggy, her dad's younger sister, who lived out of state, had wanted to know if she should come to town. Callie had encouraged her to wait, assuring her that they would know more in a few days.

Just as she thought she had reached a lull in the well-wishers' inquiries, her phone vibrated again. It was her best friend and fellow strings player in their locally popular trio group, Grace Sophia.

"Gracie, hi," Callie said as she accepted the call.

"Cal, why didn't you call me? What's going on? Is your dad—"

"He's stable for now," Callie interjected. "He had a serious stroke, and he's unconscious. They're treating him the best they can, so we'll have to wait and see. But, Gracie, I'm so scared."

A sob caught in Callie's throat, and suddenly she wished she hadn't left the hospital, that she was still sitting by his bedside holding his hand.

"Cal, I'm so sorry! How absolutely terrible! Your dad's like a dad to all of us, you know. Even Lobster loves him."

Lobster was the pianist in their group. His real name was Roberto Salvador, but a while back Grace had taken to calling him "Robster," which after a short time evolved into "Lobster," mostly due to Callie's dad's tendency toward using affectionate nicknames. The name had stuck, and now nearly everyone who knew him called him that.

Though Lobster was a couple of years younger than Callie and Grace, he was immensely talented. Short and stocky, he didn't care much about his appearance. He walked with a distinct limp, the result of a bad accident he'd suffered years ago that he didn't like to talk about.

Apart from Callie and Grace, Lobster kept to himself and was quite "musician odd," possessing an artistic focus that made him socially awkward at times, but somehow Callie's dad always managed to coax a smile from him when he came to the house to practice.

Callie's was the only house with a baby grand piano in its own room with plenty of space for Callie and Grace to play alongside, so her house was their trio's unofficial headquarters.

Ronald LeVray loved the music and would often sit in as they all played. He had been and still was a good pianist in his own right, though his job had left him little time to play in recent years.

When she was younger, Callie had also learned to play basic piano, but, in the end, she had fallen in love with the cello, the instrument known to be closer in its sound to the human voice than any other. She loved the cello's range, how it could play high notes and sound like a viola or a violin but also ring with low tones that reverberated right through the bones.

Though Callie had taken private lessons when she was young and learned to play complicated classical pieces by ear, she preferred to play more modern melodic ballads that people knew and loved to hear. Their trio, known as Heart-Strings, played in hotels and restaurants and at charity events, weddings, and other events, playing an average of ten performances per month.

Callie had already received a brief call from Lobster, which consisted of him saying he was sorry, followed by an awkward silence.

"Thanks, Lobster," Callie replied. "I'll let you know when we know more, okay?"

He'd hung up then, forgetting to say goodbye, but Callie thought she detected a sniffle before the line went dead. Lobster cared; he just wasn't great at expressing it. He'd probably sit at his piano and work out his feelings in a beautiful rendition of some Beethoven classic.

"Cal!" Grace's voice brought Callie back to the present. "Why didn't you call me? I could have helped you get to the hospital or sat with you."

Grace's kind words communicated the beauty of this friendship, which had long blessed Callie's life and heart. Gratitude for her friend filled her with warmth, like breathing in pure oxygen after being out of breath.

"I'm sorry. It all happened so fast. I knew you were working, and they told me I had to get to the hospital immediately, so I used a ride service. They wouldn't let anyone in the room except family anyway, well, except Ben, but that's a long story." Callie knew her words were coming out jumbled, but it was hard to make sense of all the day's events in a few summarizing sentences.

"Ben?" Grace asked, curiosity and a little touch of betrayal leaking out.

"Well, yes. Ben was my driver, and I asked him to walk me into the hospital, but he ended up staying around, and Lee, well, you know Lee. He sort of adopted him and started calling him 'Uncle Ben,' and the hospital thought he was family."

Grace erupted with a girlish giggle that made Callie wish she hadn't brought up the topic.

"Ugh!" Callie groaned. "We took up his whole day. We didn't have a ride home, and he, well, he was really kind, but I'm not sure why he cared enough to stick around and help us."

"I know why," Grace said, unleashing another giggle.

"What?" Callie was confused. How could Grace know anything about Ben?

"Look, Cal, I know you can't see well and all, but let me clue you in, girl. You're gorgeous, inside and out. I know why he stuck around. Is he cute?"

Stunned, Callie was slow to answer. "Um, well, yes, but I don't think that's why. I mean, he just sort of got roped into staying and he's a kindhearted person."

"Did he leave his number?"

"No. Well, I think he gave it to Lee, but—"

"Thought so," Grace exclaimed, sounding satisfied.

"Gracie!" Callie let out a defeated breath of air. "I think he just wanted to be helpful. You know, like, he could give me a ride again if I needed one, and it would be nice because he already knows I need help, and he knows what to do, so..."

"Great idea!" Grace tried for a serious tone, but Callie could hear a suppressed giggle behind it. She knew Grace had the best of intentions, but Callie was exhausted and emotionally drained and couldn't engage with her in that way at the moment.

"Cal, I know you're tired, so I'll let you rest, but I'll be by to see you tomorrow. And if you need anything in the meantime, just call me, please."

"Yes, my sweet friend. I will."

A FEW MINUTES LATER, Callie rounded the corner into the kitchen to grab a quick snack before heading to bed. She was worn out, and she wanted to be up early to get back to the hospital. She hadn't had much to eat since the hospital sandwiches, and despite her nerves, she wasn't sure she could sleep on an empty stomach. That was if she could sleep at all.

As she entered the kitchen, she heard Lee's voice. "Great, thanks, man! That totally works. See you at eight."

There was a moment of silence, informing Callie that Lee had hung up with whomever he'd been talking to. Lee's hunched form sat at the kitchen island, and he reached up and patted Callie's arm as she passed by, heading for a bowl of fruit that they always kept on the counter. The action threw her off balance, and she bumped her hip on the corner of the island.

"Cal, can't you watch where you're going?" Lee teased.

Though Callie normally loved Lee's good-natured jabs at her, she turned toward him and gave him her best rendition of an "I'm not in the mood" look before grabbing a banana and seating herself on the chair across from him.

"Whoa, touchy! Okay," he said, dragging out the "O" for emphasis. "Hey, Cal, I got things all worked out for tomorrow. Ben's going to pick us up at eight and then—"

"Lee!" Callie interrupted. "You can't do that! He's, well,

we're not his problem, and we already took up too much of his time today."

"It's fine, Sis, seriously. He was glad I called, and anyway, he's just going to drop us off at Dad's work, so I can get his car. I'll drive us to the hospital and stay with you until lunchtime. I've got a big test in the afternoon, so I've gotta get to school for a couple of hours for that, but then I can come back and get you, or whatever you want to do."

"What about practice?" Lee was on the school's wrestling team and, though the season was winding down, he still had daily practices and a few tournaments left.

"Oh, I can miss some. Coach will understand. I don't want you by yourself there too much. You might harass the staff or talk Dad's ear off or something."

"I hardly think Dad will mind, and anyway, he'd like my talking much more than all your pacing any day. I think Gracie may come and sit with me for a while. We'll stay in touch about it, okay?"

"Whatever you say, boss," Lee said as if speaking to a ranking officer.

Yawning, Callie stretched, then stood to toss her banana peel in the trash. "I'm going to bed, little brother. It's been quite a day! I've got a lot of prayers to say tonight. I hope Dad is better tomorrow. I mean, I hope something changes, improves. I can't let myself imagine if..."

Callie couldn't finish, and before a heartbeat had gone by, Lee was there. He wrapped his big arms around her and pulled her close. "It'll be alright, really! I know it's scary to think about, but that's not gonna happen, and even if, well, I'm not gonna let anything happen to you. I mean, I'm here. You're sort of stuck with me, you know? It's like an annoying little brother thing. I'm here to torture you and harass you for life. That's just your cross to bear."

Despite her tears, Callie let out a weak laugh and gave him a playful punch in the chest. "Isn't there an off button for that?"

"For what?" Lee inquired, feigning ignorance. "My charm?"

"Call it what you want, but I'm glad I didn't get that red hair of yours. I think the mischievousness that comes from that hair has soaked into your brain."

Callie smiled, then turned to head out of the room.

"You're just jealous," Lee called after her. "I know because your eyes are green with envy!"

"So are yours!" she tossed over her shoulder, followed by an exasperated sigh. "Love you, General Lee."

"Love you too, Callie Flower," he returned, both of them using their dad's favorite pet names for each other.

Pausing in the doorway, she kept her face turned away from Lee.

Will I ever get to hear my dad call me that again?" she wondered as a deep sense of sadness settled over her heart.

TRUE TO HIS WORD, Ben's SUV pulled into the LeVray driveway at eight the next morning. Lee called to Callie that Ben had arrived as he searched for their dad's spare set of keys. "I texted him to come in for a minute!" Lee shouted as he bounded up the stairs accompanied by the sound of frustrated sighs and pounding feet.

Callie headed for the door just as a soft knock came from the other side.

"Good morning," Ben said in his familiar, gentle voice as Callie opened the door and stepped back, beckoning him to enter.

"Hi, Ben." She smiled warmly. "I'm sorry we're running

behind. Lee can't find Dad's spare keys, and I think he's going to tear this place apart looking for them. Want a cup of coffee?"

"Sure," Ben replied. "And don't worry, I'm not in a hurry."

Callie motioned for Ben to follow her into the kitchen. Retrieving a clean mug, she began to fill it, placing her index finger inside the lip to let her feel when the cup was nearly full.

"Do you like anything in it?" she asked as she turned toward Ben, who had seated himself on the stool at the island.

"No. Black is fine."

As Callie went to set the cup in front of him, Ben reached out his hand, and the cup collided with it, spilling a few drops of hot liquid onto the side of her hand. She heard Ben gasp.

"Oh! Sorry." Chuckling casually, Callie reached for a towel. "Blind Person 101: hand-to-hand transfers can be a little tricky so better to let me set it down and then reach to take it."

"Callie! It burned you!" Though Ben was wearing gloves, he reached for Callie's hand and turned it over to point to the spot where the coffee had spilled. "I'm so sorry!" His voice held so much concern that her heart hurt much more for his unnecessary worry than it did for her slightly scalded hand.

"I'm totally fine, don't worry," Callie said, smiling as reassuringly as she could. "It comes with the territory. Bumped heads, burned hands, stubbed toes, all common occurrences around here. No big deal, really!"

As Ben continued holding onto her hand, Callie became aware that, though they weren't really touching, there was a strange sensation passing between them. Her hand was warming, pleasantly, like it was hovering over a blazing fire. She was bewildered by it, as this was a tangible heat, real and growing.

Abruptly, Ben withdrew his hand, and color rose to Callie's cheeks. The sensation subsided, but she was confused and caught off guard by the experience. She sensed that Ben's quick retreat had been a result of him feeling it too.

A moment of awkward silence hung between them before Ben finally spoke.

"Well, I don't want to be the cause of any of that." Leaning away, he pulled the coffee mug cautiously toward him. It took Callie another second to regain her wits and focus on the conversation.

"It takes a little while to learn the, well, the language I guess you could call it. You know, to learn what I can and can't see and how to work with me in that world. There's no way to explain it; you just have to experience it and get used to it. Everyone does, and I appreciate your willingness to try."

Callie grabbed her mug of chai and settled onto the stool opposite Ben, pushing back a strand of hair as she sat.

There was a pause and Callie sensed that Ben was working up the courage to speak. "Can I ask you, well, what happened? How did you lose your sight?"

Callie laughed lightly. "Oh, it was nothing like that. I was born this way. I've never had full sight."

As Ben sipped his coffee, he pondered Callie's words. "I guess asking how much you can see is a complicated question then."

"Yes, for sure." Callie rested her chin on her hand. "I don't know what normal is, so I can't compare what I see to what other people see. That's why it's so hard to explain to people what I need or don't need or see or don't see. Add to that the fact that different light, shadows, depths, and so on change everything for me, making it better or worse, and, well, it's almost impossible to explain."

"Of course. I understand," Ben replied, and his tone was so sincere that Callie felt that, somehow, he truly did.

Callie lowered her hand, wrapping it around her mug. "Can I ask you something?"

Ben chuckled. "That's only fair."

"Why are you giving up your time, your day, your opportunity to make much more money, to help Lee and me? I mean, don't get me wrong, we appreciate it so much, but it's not fair to ask you to and—"

"Callie," Ben interrupted, raising his hand in protest. "I don't need, well, I mean to say you don't need to worry about that. I'm not working for the money. I'm not even really a driver by trade. It's just something I'm doing now for, well for a temporary job I guess."

Callie frowned in confusion. "So, what do you do for a, well, a non-temporary job?" she asked tentatively, sensing that this was not comfortable territory for Ben.

"I'm an architect, or at least I was trained as one. I love designing structures and then seeing them come to be. It's like being a creator, you know, bringing something beautiful out of nothing."

"That's amazing! What a wonderful gift! So, why aren't you doing that instead of driving crazy people like Lee and me around everywhere?"

Silent for a moment, Ben scooted his mug around in a circle in a nervous motion.

"That's a long and, well, not very pleasant story. I—"

Before he could continue, Lee bounded into the kitchen,

and Callie heard the jingling of keys. "I had to go through nearly every drawer," he stated in an exasperated tone. "You'd think they were valuable diamonds or something with the way he had them tucked away. Sorry to keep you, Uncle Ben. Ready to head?"

Rising, Ben approached Callie but then abruptly stopped in front of her. "I'm going to put our mugs in the sink," he announced. "Just don't want you getting any more burns today."

"Thanks." Callie smiled, then leaned back, raising her hands to show she had no intention of going for her cup. "You're a quick learner," she praised.

"Burned?" Lee asked, the question followed by a knowing smile. "Hmm... I get the feeling I missed something interesting, but it sounds like you're learning the ropes, Ben. I told you she was high maintenance."

"Who's the one who couldn't find the keys?" Callie reminded him. "I'm sure Dad's told you a hundred times exactly where they were. I told you, brain poisoning from that red hair of yours."

Ben stepped between them, standing alongside Callie. "Speaking of which," he said, cutting into the good-natured sibling rivalry, "any word on your dad's condition this morning?"

"I called first thing," Callie said, adopting a somber tone. "They said there wasn't any change. I think that's a bad sign."

Though she didn't really need it for guidance in her familiar house, Ben offered Callie his arm, and she took it, appreciating the support.

"Let's get you two to the hospital, so you can see for yourselves what's going on," Ben suggested, and they all moved toward the front door.

CHAPTER 8
THE CONCERN

As they pulled out of the driveway, Callie seated next to Ben this time and Lee in the back, Ben looked around for the black Dodge he had noticed the day before but saw no sign of it. The night before he had looked up the car on the Internet and found that it was a Dodge Monaco, probably from the 1960s, with custom tinted windows and likely some other enhancements too. He breathed a sigh of relief, not knowing why that vehicle's presence unsettled him but thankful it had moved on.

Ben glanced over at Callie. She sat with her head turned toward the window, seemingly deep in thought. Her hands rested on her lap, and Ben winced as he noticed the small red burn mark on the side of her right hand. Despite her attempts to brush it off, he knew it had to hurt and he chided himself for not being more aware and careful with her. He had watched Lee interact with her the day before and thought he had picked up some good clues as to how to function in her world, but he had been so distracted that morning, caught off guard by how lovely she looked in her fitted green sweater that nearly matched her eyes and her graceful motions and warm-hearted way, that he had forgotten about her vision issue altogether.

He had also forgotten about his own issues, right up until the moment when he looked down and saw himself holding her hand. The action had been so instinctual and immediate that he hadn't even realized what he'd done until he felt the strange sensation of heat in his hand. The feeling was unlike anything he had experienced before, and he was still puzzled and a little unnerved by it.

Regardless of the unexpected consequence, he was alarmed by how easily he'd breached the boundary of touching her. He was so practiced at guarding himself and keeping barriers firmly in place or, at least he had been. If he hadn't been wearing gloves, Ben guessed he'd be running right now.

His recklessness scared him, but at the same time, Ben had to admit he was captivated by the remarkable woman sitting beside him. He stole another glance at Callie. Though he doubted she would notice the attention, Lee might, so he tried to be discreet.

Even with her somber mood, Callie warmed up the space with her presence. She was the loveliest woman he'd ever seen, not only because she was physically beautiful but also because courage, humor, compassion, and grace seemed to glow from her, like a shimmering moon reflecting off the surface of a dark placid lake. These qualities enhanced her external beauty by giving it a rich and enduring depth.

When he was with her, his walls were like wax, melting away in the presence of her open and compassionate heart. Even with how close he had come to ruining his newest "brand-new start" in this town, he still wanted to reach out and touch her again. He wanted to erase the pain of that burn on her hand, and he wanted to know what her skin felt like on his.

Most of all, Ben longed to offer her something of the person he was, without the rest of it, just him. A deep ache gnawed inside as he wished, now more than ever before, that that was possible.

"Is everything alright, Ben?"

Ben turned to see Callie's exotic green eyes focused on him. What had he done or said? Nothing, he thought, but she spoke like she'd been reading his mind.

"Um, yes." He tried to sound confident, but his voice was unsteady.

As Callie continued to look at him with a concerned expression, Ben felt exposed, like she could see right into him. The feeling was scary, but it also thrilled him, as the idea of someone truly knowing him was exactly what he desired most.

"Hey, make this next left turn," Lee said, returning Ben's focus to the task at hand.

A few minutes later, Ben pulled up next to a silver Jeep Cherokee in the parking garage of the city's courthouse. Lee jumped out and opened Callie's door, offering her his arm.

"You're a lifesaver once again, Uncle Ben." Lee smiled and dipped his head in a dramatic bow of gratitude. "We'll be in touch."

"Lee, Callie," Ben said before they could walk away, "Please let me know how your father is doing and, well if I can help further, don't hesitate to ask."

"Glutton for more punishment, are you?" Lee teased as he winked at Ben and then nodded toward Callie.

Feeling a little embarrassed, Ben realized Lee had picked up on some of Ben's attention toward Callie. They exchanged a look, Ben trying to communicate innocence and Lee beaming with unashamed enthusiasm.

It struck Ben as unusual that Lee didn't seem to have the typical protective brother thing going on.

Lee was about to close the door when Ben remembered a message he'd promised to pass along. "Oh, hey, I almost forgot. Ms. Essie Jones, she knows your dad and, well she works as a security guard in my apartment building. Anyway, she found out about your dad and wants to bring dinner over for the two of you tonight. Would that be alright?"

Ben felt awkward asking, but Ms. Essie had been so insistent on it that morning when she caught him on the way out, that he had felt there was no way to refuse her request to pass along the offer.

Callie and Lee both smiled in approval.

"Oh, Ms. Essie!" Callie exclaimed, clapping her hands in delight. "She's wonderful! We haven't seen her in a while, but I know Dad admires her and has kept in touch with her and her husband. It would be lovely to see her."

"Ms. Essie-Bessie!" Lee said in a childlike voice. "Guess I might be too old to call her that anymore. She always gave out candy and bear hugs." Lee looked at Ben and Callie, then shrugged. "Guess both of those would be welcome right now. Plus, her home cooking. That's something Callie and I don't win any awards at." He gave Callie a friendly nudge.

"Alright, I'll let her know then," Ben said, turning back toward the steering wheel.

"Ben." Callie leaned down to speak into the car. "You come too, alright? I know Ms. Essie. She'll bring enough food for an army, and we'll need some help making a dent in it, so we don't hurt her feelings. Anyway, you've at least earned sharing a meal with us after all you've done. I'm certain that was in her plan since she included you in the process of issuing the invitation."

"I shouldn't," Ben started to protest, but he stopped when Lee put up his hand.

"I guarantee you there's no point in protesting." Lee chuckled and shook his head. "No way Ms. Essie is going to let you escape this dinner. You might as well surrender."

Lee's comment brought back the memory of Ben's conversation with Ms. Essie the night before when she had pronounced it was "too late" for Ben and for Callie.

"Well, I'll let her know that you accept her offer and see how the day goes. I sincerely hope things improve with your dad today."

Callie breathed out a soft "thank you" then she and Lee turned to the waiting jeep.

When Ben exited the parking garage and prepared to turn back onto the main road, his pulse quickened as he saw what looked to be the same black Dodge he'd seen in Lee and Callie's neighborhood, only now it was parked across the street from the courthouse. The alarm and sense of dread rose more acutely in him this time, though he still didn't comprehend its cause. This time he caught a brief glimpse of the driver when the sun cast a momentary beam of light directly into the driver side window. He had slicked-back black hair and a shaggy beard. The man's eyes were hollow and cold.

Coincidence? Ben wondered. How many such cars were around? His instincts screamed at him that something was off.

As Ben waited for the traffic to clear, so he could pull in behind the Dodge and investigate further, the car began to move. Ben was trapped by the oncoming traffic, and by the time he was freed up, the Dodge had moved away and turned down a side street, vanishing from view. He circled the area a few times but couldn't find it.

Unease gnawed at him as he drove back to his apartment building. Something was strange, but what proof did he have? He resolved to keep an eye out for the car and for Lee and Callie. There was no need to worry them. After all, he didn't have anything to tell them at this point. Maybe Ms. Essie would be able to help, considering her decades of experience as a cop.

Tucking the worry away for now, he determined to ask for her advice when he got a chance. In the meantime, Callie and Lee didn't need anything else to concern themselves with. They needed to focus on their dad and managing their own lives in light of the new complications they faced. How would Lee continue at school? What about Callie's job and her music performances?

If he could help, he would. He felt connected with this family now, like fate or something better had brought them to him. He needed to be more careful, though, get his feelings for Callie under control.

He looked at the empty seat where she had been just a few minutes ago. The scent of her perfume still hung in the air. He took a deep breath, feeling more in control with her several miles away but also lonelier than he had ever felt before.

Come on, Ben. You've been alone for a long time. Callie doesn't need to carry your burdens as well as her own.

But Ms. Essie's words rang out all the louder, like an ominous warning in his mind. *I'm bettin' it's already too late, too late, too late.*

· · ·

CALLIE AND LEE spent the morning talking to doctors and sitting by their dad's bedside. At least Callie sat; Lee paced. The doctors were concerned as their father's condition hadn't improved, and they believed he may have suffered several additional small strokes since he'd been admitted. The treatments they were administering weren't having much effect, and while Dr. Karl had been kind, Callie noticed a more resigned and somber tone from him as he explained the situation.

"Your dad's stroke was a major one, and I don't know how much can be done. We'll give it a little time. If things don't improve, some tough decisions will need to be made."

Callie and Lee stood in their dad's room, holding each other for a long time after Dr. Karl left. Callie felt like a weight had been set on her heart, and it took her a while to resume her normal breathing rhythm.

Dr. Karl had encouraged them to continue living their lives, to take turns with others to be there with their dad. Callie had a job and her music group, and Lee had high school and wrestling. They couldn't stop living altogether. He assured them that the hospital would monitor their dad and let them know if there was the slightest change. Still, Callie had already let her employer know she would not be working for the remainder of the week, and she didn't have a performance with HeartStrings until the following evening. She did manage to convince Lee to stay for wrestling practice that day.

"I'll come by and get you on my way back from school," Lee said as he finished the last bite of a cafeteria hot dog and tossed his napkin in the trash. "You sure you want to stay here alone all afternoon?"

Lee had lost some of his normal jovial tone, and Callie

could tell that the harsh reality of their situation was starting to sink in for him as well.

"Sure." She shrugged, then sat back in the loveseat next to her dad's hospital bed. "Gracie may stop by, and I can always hit Dad's call button if I need something." She tried for a weak smile, but it didn't reach her eyes.

"You could call Uncle Ben," Lee suggested, a trace of mischief returning to his tone.

"Let's give him a break. I'm sure he has his own life to live." Callie sounded resolute, but in truth, she didn't want to be there alone. Lee's pacing drove her crazy, but the silence of being there with her dad without their usual free and easy conversation was painful.

"Hmm… I love you, Sis, but you're missing it big time."

Lee grabbed his coat, which was hanging over the arm of the loveseat.

"Missing what?" she asked as she shifted her weight to free the sleeve of the coat she was sitting on.

"He kept looking at you in the car this morning. He was trying to be subtle about it, but he's interested, very interested in you, which means…" He stopped and turned toward their dad's bed. "I'm the only one here to give him a hard time and be all protective and father-like about it. Guess that job falls to me now."

"Lee!" Callie stood and grabbed his arm. "Don't you dare, not after all he's done for us and how kind he's been. Besides, I'm sure you're not right. I'm sure he's not, well, 'interested,' as you put it."

Lee turned to face Callie. "Sis, there are some things you're going to need to trust those of us with sight to clue you in on. It's rare, I know, but sometimes I'm right!"

Callie stood looking at Lee, unsure how to respond.

"Silence wasn't exactly the ringing endorsement I was

looking for, but, anyway, I gotta go. We'll talk about it later. I'll work on channeling my inner grizzly bear while I'm gone."

"Lee!" Callie protested again, but he kissed her on the head, tossed her curls with a rake of his fingers, then stopped by their dad's bed and patted his hand before heading for the door. "Oh, by the way, I'm shooting you Ben's contact info, just in case," Lee said as he closed the door behind him.

"Good grief!" Callie mumbled as she circled back to the chair by her dad's bedside. "What am I supposed to do with that kid, Dad?" she asked as she stroked his hand with her thumb.

For the next couple of hours, Callie alternated sitting and standing by her dad's side, allowing memories of him to flood her mind and soul. She had so many for her mind to swim in that it felt like a vast ocean. She remembered her dad pushing her on swings, weekly ice cream dates, playing music together in the piano room, him reading stories to her, and them working together to find solutions to struggles she had at school.

She smiled as she recalled a time when she and her dad had been out shopping together when she was about twelve. They'd been picking out new hair barrettes in the cosmetics aisle of their local department store, something her dad knew little about. Without having a mom around to help, she was mostly on her own. For her to see the colors and designs on them, Callie had to hold them up close to her eyes.

After she'd been looking at various choices for several minutes, a woman stopped in the aisle and stared at Callie. "Forgot to wear your glasses today, sweetheart?"

Callie was caught off guard and didn't know how to

respond. Thankfully, her dad stepped in, grabbing Callie by the shoulders in an affectionate and protective manner. "Ma'am, this is my daughter, Callie. She has to hold things close to see them well, but her heart sees so much more than what her eyes miss. Would you like to help her, since I know nothing about hair doohickies?"

The woman had enthusiastically assisted Callie in her shopping after that, and Callie admired and appreciated how her dad had simultaneously rebuked the woman for her insensitive comment, though birthed from ignorance, and complimented and uplifted his daughter in a potential moment of embarrassment. Her dad was like that. He had taught her how to be at ease with who she was and, in doing so, to help others become at ease with who she was.

"There's a purpose in it all, Callie Flower," he'd said. "People notice you and remember you, which gives you a great opportunity to shine light onto them. Everyone has problems, but yours are right out front and easy to see. That's an opportunity. You can inspire people to hang in there through their struggles by watching the grace and patience with which you bear your burdens. And you'll never have to bear them alone. I'm here to shoulder a good share of them. So, put what you can on me, and I'll carry it too."

Tears streaked down Callie's face as she sat next to this quiet pillar of strength who had been her anchor, her port in the storm.

"I need you, Dad!" Callie whispered. "I'm not done needing you." She buried her face in her hands and cried, her heart aching to hear his voice and feel his arms around her again.

"Callie!" A familiar voice startled her from her private moment.

"Gracie!" Callie raised her head in recognition of her best friend's soft, lilting voice.

Grace rushed over to hold her in a tender embrace, her long blonde hair spilling around Callie's face and soaking up some of her tears. "Oh, my sweet friend! I'm so sorry!" Grace's voice broke as her empathy and love for Callie and her dad caught in her throat. "Is it, I mean, are things worse?"

"About the same." Callie sighed as she grabbed Grace's hand and led her to the loveseat. This room had become so familiar to Callie now that it was almost like being in her own home. "No change isn't really a good thing, though, the doctors say." Callie sat next to her friend and leaned her head on Grace's shoulder.

Grace placed her hand on Callie's cheek, and they sat in silent companionship as Callie attempted to regain her composure and shake off the sweet memories that were ripping her heart wide open. Finally straightening, Callie turned to face her friend. "Hey, I'm so glad you're here, but are you okay missing work today?"

"I just took a late lunch. I can't stay long, but I wanted to stop by to see how you were and to see your dad." Grace let out a sad sigh. "Cal, I don't think I've ever seen your dad's face without a smile on it. It's strange. He does look peaceful though."

Grace stood and went to Ronald LeVray's bedside, and Callie moved to stand beside her. They remained still and quiet, absorbing the silent peace emanating from his presence.

"Your dad is wonderful, Cal. There's no one like him. I hope he pulls through. I hope..." Grace couldn't complete her thought, but Callie knew what she was thinking. She knew that Grace hoped Callie wouldn't be forced to face a world without this fortress of a man who had held her up when she needed him, and been her defender, protector, guide, and so much more.

"You're not alone, you know," she said, turning to look at Callie. "No matter what, you have Lee and me and, well, Lobster, if that counts."

They both laughed at the thought of Lobster being able to help anyone when he could barely handle his own quirks.

"Oh, yes!" Callie chuckled. "Lobster's at the top on my 'call in case of emotional emergencies' list."

"Okay, okay, well, he may not say much, but he cares, you know."

"I know. That sweet soul of his is true blue." Callie smiled affectionately at the thought of him.

Grace brought sunshine into the room as she sat with Callie for the next half hour, recalling memories of her dad and strategizing for their upcoming performance.

"We can cancel tomorrow, Cal. Really, we can. You've got enough on your plate here."

"No, it's alright," Callie assured her. "The doctor says we may have a long stretch, and we can't stop living. They're counting on us to perform, so I don't want to pull out on such short notice. Besides, I think playing cello with you guys might be like medicine for the soul right now." Callie hugged her arms around herself as she recognized her need for something normal and fulfilling.

"Alright, if you're sure. Oh, shoot! I gotta go. Love you, girl." Grace placed her index finger under Callie's chin. "Keep your chin up!"

Callie embraced her friend, and they clung to each other in a lingering moment of comfort that they both needed.

When Grace turned toward the door, she let out a short gasp. "Um, hello?"

Turning around, Callie wondered at Grace's surprised exclamation.

"I'm so sorry to interrupt. I'm Ben."

Callie saw Grace move forward and, though she couldn't see it clearly, guessed they were shaking hands.

"I'm Grace," her friend responded, an amused smile coloring her voice.

"I'm sorry to intrude. I'll let you girls talk. I'll be back in a bit."

"I was actually just leaving, so it will just be a second," Grace replied in a bemused tone. "Nice to meet you, Ben."

"You as well."

When Ben left, Grace turned toward Callie. "Oh my gosh!" she exclaimed, sounding more like a middle-school girl than a woman in her mid-twenties. "That's Ben?" Her giggle caused Callie's face to turn pink.

"I guess it was." Callie shrugged, feeling confused and caught off guard.

"Cal! Do you know he's, like, gorgeous? Like beyond gorgeous, into the realm of knight in shining armor, ooh la la kind of gorgeous."

Callie laughed as Grace's description sent a mixture of odd images through her mind. "Well, I knew he was cute. I mean, I saw him sort of close up and got that much at least. I'm not really one for the outside anyway, you know, Gracie. I'm more of a 'look at the heart' kind of girl, as much because I choose to be as because I'm forced to be."

"Hmm…" Grace cleared her throat as if trying to regain her equilibrium. "Well, if he's got a good heart and also happens to look like *that,* you're one lucky girl! I mean, pot of gold at the end of the rainbow lucky!"

Grace embraced Callie again. "Now, I really gotta go. My late lunch has become almost a whole afternoon. You don't know how badly I want to stay and hear more details, but it'll have to wait. Besides, I don't want to keep you from…" She paused and waved her hand back and forth in front of her as if she were fanning herself. "Other important obligations."

They both laughed again at Grace's exuberance.

Before she left, Grace walked over to Callie's dad and leaned in close. "Get better soon, Mr. LeVray. I'm praying for you."

She squeezed Callie's hand and then headed for the door. "I'll send that hottie back your way if I see him," she teased as she breezed out of the room.

Callie sighed and shook her head as she returned her attention to her dad, wondering what he would think or say if he'd observed the last few minutes of girlish swooning over Ben. She smiled as she guessed his easy-going nature would likely find delighted humor in the situation, though he'd no doubt make it a priority to quickly acquaint himself with the subject of the swooning.

CHAPTER 9

THE PARK

Callie expected Ben to reappear soon after Grace left, but he didn't.

A few minutes passed, and then Callie felt her phone buzz with a text message. She prompted her phone to read it out loud: "Cal, I didn't see Ben on the way out. Maybe I scared him away, LOL."

Callie smiled and then dictated a reply. "No worries. I'm sure he's around here somewhere. You couldn't scare anyone away ever! Thanks for stopping by. You really cheered me up."

Grace returned a smile and a wave emoji. Callie felt her heart fill with gratitude for the gift of such a kind and thoughtful friend.

Turning toward the window, she pushed back the coarse gray curtains. The sun was beginning to set as late afternoon settled over the city.

Callie couldn't make out much of the view except for the faded gray of the cement buildings and parking lots below. She stared up at the streaked blue sky, which seemed to be darkening before her eyes. The life-support machines continued their steady rhythm, marking her dad's vital signs and telling her that he was still there, still with her. Though the continuous sound had become so repetitive and familiar to her that she often no longer heard it, she realized how comforting it was to intentionally tune in to his heartbeat and his assisted breathing, like a beacon in the dark.

As she continued her bedside vigil, Callie found herself wondering what her dad might think about Ben. He was always so intuitive about people, a quality she'd, at least partially, inherited. Her dad would like him; she was sure of that, as Ben had a genuine kindness that made his presence appealing and comforting, even when no words were spoken. But there was something else about him, and Callie wished she had her dad's help to figure out what it was.

When she asked Ben to assist her into the hospital, he hesitated, though she was sure he really did want to help her. Every offer of assistance was like that. He possessed a giving nature, but he seemed to resist it. The unusual thing about it was that his hesitancy didn't seem related to her eyesight issue. Unlike most people, upon meeting Callie for the first time, Ben didn't seem uncomfortable with her visual limitations, just curious. From the moment he took her arm, he seemed to tune in to her heart, bypassing the normal awkwardness of adjusting to the realities of her unique way of life. He spoke with her and related to her as if the issue didn't exist.

So, if the strange hesitancy didn't come from that, what motivated it? As she stroked her dad's hand, she wished she could benefit from his wisdom and insight at that moment.

Callie heard the door open and thought it might be Ben, but a soft female voice announced that it was time to check on her dad.

"We're going to do some tests and clean him up a bit," the nurse said, trying to make an unpleasant situation more palatable. "You might want to step out for a few minutes. Do you need some help?"

Grabbing her purse and phone off the side table, she moved toward the nurse. "Yes, please. Would you mind walking me to the waiting room?" she asked with a weak smile.

The nurse led her to the private waiting area, which was tucked away at the end of the hall. It smelled like someone's lunch, and Callie guessed that there was a microwave in the room that had been put to good use.

She settled into a chair, thanked the nurse, then lifted her phone to check the time. It was nearly 4:00. There was no one else in the room, so she dictated a quick text to Lee. "What time are you coming by?"

A few minutes passed before her phone buzzed with a reply: "I'm running late, so I sent Ben. Isn't he there?"

Callie smiled. That explained Ben's visit. It had been Lee. Somehow Callie doubted that Lee being late was the only reason he had sent Ben her way.

She was about to send Lee another text when the door to the waiting area squeaked open and someone entered. She smiled in relief when she recognized the familiar form and then the voice.

"Callie."

"Ben? I thought you did a disappearing act." She chuckled. "And you definitely had Gracie believing you might not be real after all."

Ben smiled as he sat in the seat next to her, though there was a small side table between them. "I had an errand to run," he explained as he set a Styrofoam cup on Callie's side of the table. "Burn proof," he added as he tapped the lid with his gloved index finger.

Callie offered a grateful smile, then picked up the cup, taking a test sip to check its contents. Then, lowering the cup, she turned toward him, tucking her left leg under her. "You remembered. That's kind, thank you."

The chai tea was perfect, with just the right amount of milk and sugar.

"Your brother had me thinking it was going to be easy to find, but it turns out, there is no chai tea in this hospital. Lee had to go across the street to a little coffee shop to get it." Ben's voice held no annoyance, just a sense of admiration. "I wish I had known his secret," he said with amusement. "It would have saved me time searching the building."

Callie smiled knowingly, as they shared a moment of appreciation for Lee's thoughtful ways. "You know, just because my brother waits on me hand and foot and tries to be a superhero doesn't mean you have to. But I really do appreciate the kindness." Holding her palm to her chest, she expressed how Ben had touched her heart with his thoughtful act.

"He's a great kid," Ben replied. "You're lucky to have such a loving family. And hey, superhero's not such a bad goal to shoot for. I think we've already established that the genes run in your family."

Ben's tone conveyed praise mixed with a dose of humor, but Callie also detected a longing that made her heart ache for him. That mysterious hesitancy and sadness she'd noted before was showing itself once again.

The ache in her heart gave rise to a sudden desire to know him. What was this pain that he carried around like a burden he could never put down, even in moments of laughter? She wanted to understand this kind stranger who had come into her life with such a giving spirit yet a mysterious heaviness that made him guarded and distant. She'd almost broken through his defenses a couple of times, but they'd been interrupted.

Putting her elbow on the back of the chair, she leaned her chin into her palm, looking in Ben's direction. She wished she could see into his eyes, see their color, lock him in her gaze, and study what she found there. In that moment, she would have given almost anything to be able to do so. A sigh escaped her, louder than she intended, and Ben straightened in his chair.

"Callie?" he asked, concern in his voice. "What is it?"

Offering a weak smile, she stretched, working out the stiffness that had settled into her and trying to shake off her thoughts about him.

"I think I'm feeling a little cooped up. I've been here since nine or so this morning, staring at these same walls and breathing the same sterile air." Callie pointed at her face and grimaced. "Bad eyes, good nose."

Though he smiled, Ben was quiet for a moment as if pondering something. Then he stood and positioned himself in front of her. "Come with me," he said, though he didn't reach out his hand.

"Where are we going?"

"You'll see."

She slung her purse over her shoulder and picked up her cup. Ben offered her his arm, and she took it.

They retraced the familiar path back down in the elevator and toward the hospital's front doors, but before they stepped outside, Ben paused near the seating area, then took Callie's cup and purse and set them on a nearby table.

"Ben?" she inquired, raising an eyebrow suspiciously.

"I know your jacket's upstairs, but it's too cold to go without one."

He took off his coat and cautiously, like he was afraid he might break her, helped Callie into it.

"What about you?" she asked as she pushed the too-long sleeves up to uncover her hands.

"I'm good. I'll keep the gloves since those sleeves seem to cover your hands anyway." He grinned, and Callie imagined that she looked like a child wearing her dad's clothes.

Returning her cup and purse, he then offered his arm. She raised her hand and shook back the sleeves, so she could grasp it. When she did, she was keenly aware of how different his arm felt without the thick coat. Ben was wearing a sweater, but it wasn't thick enough to obscure his well-developed muscles. Though less intense than that morning, a similar sensation of warmth moved through her hand, and she was once again puzzled by it.

Grace's giddiness over Ben's appearance penetrated her thoughts, and that, along with the rising temperature in her hand, made her feel shy and dizzy as Ben guided her through the hospital doors and out into the cool afternoon. The air was cold, but as she held onto Ben's arm, her hand remained pleasantly warm.

"There's a park over to our right," Ben informed her. "It has a walking path around it, so we can both stretch our legs. Any more tutorials on Callie's World 101 I need to know?"

Smiling, she appreciated Ben's concern and the thoughtful way he worded the question. "Hmm... well, just let me know of any stairs or major obstacles. That's pretty much it."

"Easy enough."

She marveled once again at how readily he accepted and adjusted to her world.

A cold wind blew Callie's hair around her face as they maneuvered toward the park and began circling it on the wide, smooth sidewalk. They walked in pleasant silence for a few moments, sipping their hot drinks, and she felt some of her shyness dissipate, though Ben's nearness kept her heart rate elevated.

Even if Callie had perfect vision, there wasn't much to see this time of year. The trees were bare of leaves, and the grass was brown and dried up. She heard distant traffic and the cheerful chirping of birds, but she and Ben seemed to be relatively alone in the park, few other people venturing out in the cold January air.

As they strolled, she became aware that the strange sensation she felt as she held onto Ben was expanding, sending pleasant warmth up her arm. It contained within it the feeling of being drawn toward him, like a magnet, this tangible experience entangled with her already strong physical attraction to him, amplifying the feelings. Callie found herself enjoying holding onto Ben's arm not only for guidance but simply for the pleasure of being near him.

Despite the cold, the air felt refreshing and life-giving after the staleness of the small hospital room. She and Ben sucked in a full breath of fresh air at the same time, and they laughed at the irony of the simultaneous action.

"It sounds like you needed to get out too," Callie observed as she squeezed his arm.

"I love being outside. I feel more alive somehow."

She nodded in understanding. "My dad, Lee, and I often go on these champion walks when the weather is nicer. Lee's always pushing for one more mile no matter how far we go. When he was a kid, he used to skateboard or jog ahead, and I think he did double the distance by going back and forth continually. He's never been one to sit still."

Ben let out a laugh that told Callie he'd already noticed Lee's inability to remain stationary. "I can tell that being trapped in a small hospital room isn't Lee's idea of fun."

She sighed in confirmation. "Definitely not. And being trapped in there with him being trapped is, well, let's just say it's not my idea of fun either."

Ben offered another brief sympathetic chuckle.

They walked for a few more minutes. Though she was loath to break the mysterious connection between them, her earlier desire to learn something deeper about him rose inside her again. She stopped, released his arm, and turned to face him. Ben hesitantly mirrored her action.

"So, you know a lot about me and my family, but I know almost nothing about you. Please tell me about your mom or your siblings or something."

When he didn't answer right away, she began to regret her question. Perhaps it wasn't her business, but Ben had become a part of her family's reality, and it felt awkward to know nothing about him.

Ben took Callie's empty cup and tossed it, along with his, into a nearby trash can. Then, he wrapped her hand around his arm and started walking again. She stayed silent, feeling that she needed to give Ben the space to decide what he wanted to share. Her hand quickly warmed again as they moved together. She felt the muscles in his arm tense just before he began speaking.

"Callie, I don't have a family," he began, his voice filled with so much grief that Callie wanted to put her arms around him. "I don't have siblings, a dad, a mom, any of it. All I ever had was my mom, but that hasn't been the case for over six years now. It's not a happy story and not something I would burden you with right now with all you're going through."

Ben fell silent, but Callie didn't speak as she sensed he had more to say.

"You're very blessed, you know, to have Lee and your dad. It's beautiful to watch, and it makes me feel, well, watching you all makes me feel hopeful or alive or something I haven't felt in a long time. I want a happy ending for you and Lee. I feel..." Ben paused to suck in a deep breath. "I feel connected somehow to seeing that happen. I don't know why, but I do. I want you to be safe. I want Lee to be safe too. And I want your dad to be well. I know I just met you all, and I can't explain it, but I need to know that you're all going to be alright."

Ben stopped walking and turned to face her. As she released his arm, the long coat sleeves dropped over her hands. The sky was growing darker, and to Callie, Ben's face was nearly lost in shadow.

"I don't understand it either, but I feel that you should be here too. Like somehow, you're supposed to be here. But..." She touched Ben's arm. "When you offer me your arm, you're carrying some of my burden for me. I'd like to offer you the same. I, well, I can hear in your voice that you've been carrying something alone for a long time. You don't need to do that. I want to be your friend, like you've been for Lee and me." She looked down, nervous to ask the next question but feeling like she must. "I told you about my dad, so many stories and memories. Won't you tell me about your mom?"

He took a slow, deep breath, then took Callie's hand in his. Though he was still wearing gloves, the sensation of heat intensified, feeling more like a light electric pulse between them. She sucked in a quick breath as she adjusted to the feeling. Ben's breathing sped up as well, making her again speculate that the odd experience was mutual.

Though she expected him to wind her hand around his arm, he didn't. After they took a couple of steps forward, Callie saw what they were headed for.

The silhouette of a cement park bench came into focus ahead of them. She shifted her direction to match Ben's as they took a few more steps and then turned and sat together.

The bench was cold, and a shiver rushed through her, though she wasn't sure if it was the cold, the feeling of Ben so close to her, or the mysterious sensation that caused it.

As they sat in silence, Ben still holding Callie's hand, the warmth and pull between them throbbed through her, building like a tidal wave. She wasn't sure what to do with her feelings. They magnified all the longings inside of her, her desire to see his heart and know his pain, and her desire to move closer to him. She fought against them, trying to maintain an appropriate level of distance.

Just when Callie felt her breathing nearly stop altogether from the intensity of it, Ben released her hand and took a deep breath. Part of her wished he hadn't let go, but she wanted to hear him, and she wasn't sure she could think clearly with that wave threatening to crash over her.

As another moment passed, she refocused her thoughts, preparing herself to listen to Ben as he began.

"My mother suffered from extreme depression her whole life," Ben said, deep pain registering with every word. "She never conquered it. Having me in her early twenties, the result of an alcohol-induced one-night stand, didn't help. She did her best, but my mom could barely take care of herself, much less me. I pretty much raised myself and her. I got very sick when I was about twelve, and nearly died. In the end, a bone marrow transplant saved my life, but, well, things changed after that."

Ben's voice shook as he continued, and he directed his words toward the ground in front of them. "When I grew up and moved out on my own, my mom got worse, much worse. I called her often, and even though my college was five hours away, I went home nearly every weekend. She put on a brave face for me when I was home, telling me she was fine and about new friends and the activities she was engaged in, but somewhere deep inside of me I knew it was all a front, though it was one that I really wanted to believe."

His shoulders hunched, and he covered his face with his hands. Callie was sitting so near to him that, although it was nearly dark, she was able to follow the changes in his posture as he told his story for what she guessed was probably the first time.

Though she wanted to reach out to him, she didn't want the distraction from whatever it was that flowed between them. This was what she needed most now, to know him in some way that allowed her to understand where his abiding sadness and pain came from, and she wouldn't do anything to hinder that opportunity.

He dropped his hands and lifted his head toward the sky. The wind blew across them, and Ben shivered, but once again, she wasn't sure it was completely due to the cold.

"Near the end of my sophomore year in college, I became concerned. She rarely answered the phone when I called, and when she did talk to me, it was brief and, well, she never shared anything about how she was doing. Then one week I couldn't reach her at all. I called and called but nothing. I rushed home as soon as I could on Friday, but when I got there, she was gone. Her car was gone, and so was her phone and her wallet."

He turned his face toward Callie. "Something in me just knew what had happened, but I didn't want to accept it. I called the police, and they tracked her phone and car."

When he paused again, she couldn't prevent herself from reaching out and resting her hand on his arm. Though she couldn't see his eyes, she could feel the pain rolling off him in streams of regret and sadness. Her own heart ached as she anticipated where the story was going, and tears welled up in her eyes.

"They eventually found her. She drove her car out into the country, I guess not wanting me to have to find her when I came home that weekend. She overdosed on a drug cocktail." Ben's voice caught in his throat, and she sensed tears forming in his eyes, though he was doing his best to stay in control.

"Oh, no!" Callie raised her hands to her face as tears began spilling down her cheeks. "I'm so sorry, Ben. I'm so very sorry."

"By the time they found her, it was too late. Too much time had gone by for me to be able to see her. I... I didn't even get to say goodbye." Wiping his hand across his face, he took another deep, shaky breath. "I never went home again. I turned the house and everything over to a real estate management company and never looked back. I ran. I guess that's what I sort of keep doing because... because that's simply what I have to do."

The last sentence was said with such finality and conviction that it made Callie's heart ache in sympathy and fear. Was he going to just disappear from her life? The thought of that filled her with an unanticipated feeling of desperate sadness.

"I... I can't imagine. I can't fathom the pain of all that. My own mother died tragically too, but, well, not like that. I'm so sorry."

They sat in solemn silence in the darkening night. She knew they probably should head back soon, that Ms. Essie would be bringing dinner, and she didn't want to be late, but she couldn't move, couldn't break this almost sacred moment.

Callie was sure now that Ben had never shared this terrible story of pain and loss with anyone. It was like the words were foreign, a language he'd never spoken before. Though he kept it locked up inside, it pushed and tore holes in him that needed to be healed. She didn't know if she could help him do that, but she had to try.

"It was... it was my fault," he whispered. "I shouldn't have gone away and left her to deal with her depression alone. I, well, I was helping her when I was home, and when I left, she couldn't cope."

Turning to face him, she grasped his hand with both of hers, struggling to push aside the unexplainable feelings that were now becoming predictable, even if they remained incomprehensible. "Ben, that's not true! You're not responsible. You deserved a life too, and she needed more help than you could've provided. You're only one person, and no one can be everything that someone needs all the time. There must be internal peace and strength. We can help others, but only they can walk their road, accept the help offered, and continue to get up and fight. Trust me. I know."

Callie wasn't sure her words made sense, but as a long moment of silence hung in the air, she hoped they were reaching his heart.

"Callie..." Ben spoke her name so softly that she almost

didn't hear it. The word seemed to be carried away by the wind. "Please tell me what happened to your mother."

The request caught her off guard. She wasn't sure she had the strength to deal with the topic after all the emotions of the day, but she abruptly realized it might be exactly what Ben needed to hear.

Inhaling, she dropped Ben's hand, so she could focus on telling her own story. Turning back toward the park, she set her hands on her knees. Ben seemed to sense the purpose behind her motions and gave her space, though he turned his face her way.

"My mother was an alcoholic. My dad married her before she went off the deep end with her addiction, but not long after they married and had me, her addiction became unbearable. She'd forget to take care of me, leave me places. Eventually, due to my dad's insistence, she went into rehab, and, for a while things seemed to be better. Lee was born during that time." She smiled despite the tears that dripped down her cheeks.

"When Lee was about two, my mom passed out after drinking one day. Dad was at work, and Lee wandered out into the street. I was seven at the time, and I went looking for him just in time to hear tires squeal. I found Lee bleeding on the side of the road. The driver of the car was frantic, and when we couldn't wake Mama, the kind, distraught woman drove us both to the hospital and stayed with us until Dad arrived."

Staring into the darkness, she wasn't sure if she could share the next part. Ben let out an anguished sigh but otherwise remained quiet.

"Thank God Lee was alright, but Dad was so upset that he told Mama to move out until she got sober, for good this time. He wouldn't leave us alone with her, too scared of her irresponsible behavior. He hired a nanny for Lee during the day while I was at school and cut his hours as much as he could to take care of us. Mama spiraled. She drank more and after a while never even tried to see us. A year or so later…"

As her voice faded the only sound was that of the distant traffic and the breeze moving through the barren limbs of the trees around them. Ben's concerned gaze focused on her.

"About a year later, Mama was in a car accident. She was driving drunk and hit a family. She died and she took another family's mom and wife along with her."

Ben blew out a long breath, sounding as if he had been holding it in, hoping for a different end to her story. "I'm sorry, so sorry." His voice was gentle and communicated the acknowledgment of their shared experience of loss.

Sniffling, she struggled to regain control of her emotions. "Dad wouldn't, and still hasn't to this day, told us much about the other family or the details. We were young and, well, Ben," she turned to look at him, "I also thought it was my fault."

Ben straightened in his seat. "How in the world would that be your fault?"

Callie raised her hands, the long sleeves gapping around her wrists. "I thought it was my eyesight. I thought the stress of having, well, a handicapped daughter drove Mama to drink and make stupid choices."

Rising to his feet, Ben paced a few steps away, then returned to the bench and sat facing Callie. He lifted his hand to touch her shoulder but then withdrew it. "Callie, there's no way it was your fault! Your mom's choices were hers alone. You're not responsible for them." The intensity of his conviction took her by surprise. She'd only ever seen his gentle, hesitant side. This was a different part of him, a fiercely protective and confident side.

When she spoke, she softened her voice, hoping to calm Ben's emotions. "I know that now. My dad helped me understand that Mama's choices were hers alone. He told me that having a daughter like me made him a much better man, made him more compassionate, more empathetic, more aware of others' needs. And it gave him purpose and meaning and so many other gifts. He said it could have done the same for Mama, but she made different choices, and those choices were hers alone."

At her words, Ben relaxed beside her. "But you," she whispered, "you haven't had anyone to tell you the same, to remind you of the gift you were to your mom, the blessings you gave her. To tell you that it's not your fault. I've only known you a couple of days, but I know enough to say this. You have a lot to give. Your heart is kind, and you see me, see others, in a way that few others do. You're a good man, Ben, and you didn't cause what happened to your mom. I have no doubt about that."

For a moment Callie couldn't hear Ben breathing, and she began to worry. The air around them was growing colder and Callie's lower lip began to tremble.

Perhaps sensing her chill, Ben shifted closer to her, so close that their shoulders touched, and the warm connection began pulsing anew. They breathed in rhythm with each other as the pull of the strange magnetism and the sharing of their tragic yet similar past experiences weaved a new bonding link between them. Finally, Ben cleared his throat.

"Callie, you, well, you're beautiful and unbelievably strong and special and all those things that your dad said about you. But I'm different. I'm, well, I can't explain it, but

I'm not like that, not good for you, not good for anyone. I don't help people. In the end, I wind up hurting them. I wish I could just be Ben, but there's more, and, well, I shouldn't be in your life, shouldn't be with you."

The loneliness and desperation in his voice made her heart break. Though she didn't understand what he was saying, something in her didn't buy it or believe it. There was something he wasn't telling her; she knew that, but she didn't accept that whatever it was made him a bad person or worthy of the blame he was putting on himself. But she knew this was how he saw himself and that was why he was so guarded. Fair or not, Ben's belief about himself was driving his actions and decisions, and that scared her.

"Are you going to run again?" she whispered, turning toward him and wishing once more that she could see into his eyes. It was so dark that all she could see was the outline of his face.

"I don't know," Ben admitted, lowering his face into his hands. "I should, but I don't know if I can."

Reaching out into the darkness, she boldly set her palm flat on Ben's knee. "Don't," she pleaded. "Please, Ben, don't."

CHAPTER 10

THE DINNER

Ben helped Callie retrieve her coat and check on her father one last time for the night before they headed back to the LeVray house.

They rode in silence as Ben navigated out of the hospital parking lot and onto the main highway. When he reached cruising speed, he glanced over at Callie. Sitting with her hands in her lap, her fingers fidgeted with her purse strap. He recognized the anxious gesture from the first time he had picked her up.

His heart fell as he knew he had made her feel nervous and insecure with his talk of running and being wrong for her. She didn't understand, of course. Ben didn't understand it himself. How could he tell this amazing woman all that he had, spill his heart in a way he'd never done before, and then push her away? Why couldn't he have kept his distance and not let either of their hearts get involved?

He didn't understand the pull inside him that drew him to her in a way that seemed beyond his control. The physical attraction he had for her was easy to understand, at least part of it was, but this went so far beyond that.

Ben had never felt this way about anyone. Being in her presence made him feel alive and known somehow. And when he touched her—well not really touched her; he'd never actually made contact with any part of Callie's skin, but even with the barriers, her closeness caused reactions in him that he didn't know were possible.

Still, none of that explained what had allowed him to feel comfortable enough to tell her all that he had revealed. Ben felt something much deeper, a connection to Callie that his mind couldn't explain but his heart seemed to understand. Now that they knew more about each other's stories though, he wondered if the remarkable similarities in their experiences might be part of it.

He and Callie were alike in so many ways. They each carried a burden, something they hadn't asked for and couldn't change. They each had a painful past that planted doubts and fears about themselves and the burdens they placed on others. The big difference was that Callie wasn't alone. She had great people around to help her and support her with a much healthier perspective.

But then, Callie didn't have a curse. She simply had a human condition that no one would find unbelievable or dangerous. She didn't have a secret to protect, one that, if revealed, might ruin her forever.

Nevertheless, as he drove with Callie next to him, Ben was amazed at how relieved he felt that at least she knew some of it. He was even more relieved that she could empathize with much of what he'd experienced.

His heart wanted to soar in response to her words about him. She found him to be "a good man, warm, and kind." He wished he could embrace her perspective and revel in the praise she offered. But she didn't know the whole story, and he was still convinced that, if she did, she would feel differently.

Callie sniffled, still recovering from the flood of tears she had shed in the park. More than anything, Ben wanted to take her in his arms, to hold her against him and whisper all the things he felt in his heart. His hands nearly shook with the desire to touch her, to really touch her.

"Callie," Ben said as he fought against his instincts. "I'm sorry. I'm so sorry I upset you."

When she turned her enchanting green eyes toward him, it was all he could do to keep his eyes on the road rather than lose himself in the depths of her soul. "No. I'm so thankful that you opened your heart to me. I hope you will feel you can trust me with all of it, whatever you're running from, hiding from, someday."

"I know it's confusing, and I know it doesn't make much sense, but I am trying to protect you. The last thing I want to bring into your life is more pain."

Callie didn't respond immediately, but Ben sensed her mind trying to grasp what he meant, trying to understand the secret he was attempting to protect.

She turned to face him again. "Who protects you, Ben?"

His heart ached as, once more, this woman he'd just met connected directly with a deep wound within him. With his whole being, he needed to have a person who knew everything about him, and, in a moment of rare clarity, he realized, he wanted that person to be her.

Though Callie's heart could discern remarkably well, it was moments like these when Ben was thankful that she couldn't read everything that was in his face, for he was sure if she could see into his eyes, she'd already know all his secrets, and that would mean he would have to run, and he did not want to run, not yet, perhaps not ever.

Gripping the steering wheel with both hands, he willed himself to resist his desire to reach for her hand. He had to stop touching her, even through gloves and coats. She wouldn't understand why there were always barriers and distance. The more he touched her, the more they would both want to connect even more in that way. Her unique situation already made avoiding that hard, and it was beginning to become odd that he always wore gloves around her, even indoors where it was warm. How could he keep up the pretense now that they'd already crossed the safe and broad boundary lines of common strangers? They had shared their hearts today, and Ben sensed she also felt the mysterious pull that was drawing them together. Fear threatened to crush him, even as his heart wanted to soar with happiness.

Ben managed a smile, though he knew there was no way Callie would see it in the darkness. "Callie LeVray," Ben said, letting his smile color his tone. "You are an incredible person. Thank you for letting me take your arm for a while today." Though he tried to keep his tone light, he also hoped Callie caught his sincerity.

She smiled at Ben's reference to her earlier metaphor as she seemed to pick up on his desire to lighten the mood between them. "Well, another several hours of that and a couple of days of driving you around and we'll be even."

Grinning in response, he reveled in the return of their easy back-and-forth. By the time they pulled into Callie's driveway, the tension and anxiety between them had nearly disappeared, offset by the strength of that mysterious connection that kept drawing them toward each other despite the lack of physical contact.

As he scanned the street in front of Callie's home, he saw no sign of the mysterious Dodge. He did see the silver

Jeep and a small white Ford that he presumed belonged to Ms. Essie.

"I think we're late," Ben said guiltily as he opened the door for her and helped her find his arm in the dark.

"I may be in trouble with Lee. He's been texting me, but I haven't gotten back to him. He probably thinks I was kidnapped or something."

Ben and Ms. Essie had agreed upon a six o'clock dinner at the LeVray house, and it was only a few minutes past that now, but Ben felt regret about potentially causing either of them to worry, especially Lee considering everything else he was already going through.

When they approached the door, Callie released Ben's arm to reach for the doorknob, but the door opened before she could touch it, revealing Lee with his arms crossed and a bemused expression on his face. He leaned against the doorframe and stared at them.

"Well, I see you found Ben, Sis. And, Ben, I see you found Callie. Thanks for letting me know." Though he didn't look or sound angry, relief was evident in his eyes.

"My fault," Ben confessed, raising his hands in a gesture of full surrender. "I, sort of, tricked her into taking a walk around the park, and I think the fresh air made us lose track of time."

"Oh no!" Callie wagged her finger in the air in a way that said there would be no arguing with her. "Ben's not taking the blame for this one. He was kind enough to get me out of that stuffy hospital for a few minutes and let me breathe some real air. Losing track of time was all my doing."

Chuckling at their explanations, Lee turned aside, granting them entrance, evidently satisfied with their excuses.

Wanting to speak with Lee privately for a moment, Ben followed him and Callie inside. He was struck by the smell of fresh bread, meat, and vegetables. His stomach growled in response, and his mouth watered. Obviously, Ms. Essie had put together something fabulous for this deserving and hurting family.

Callie moved toward the kitchen, comfortable and more independent in her familiar surroundings, and Ben fell in next to Lee.

"I'm so sorry if we worried you."

Lee stared at Ben, sizing him up, and Ben worried he would uncover more in his scrutiny than Ben wanted to reveal. Then Lee's smile broadened, almost filling his face, and Ben realized Lee already knew a lot more than Ben thought he did. He had noticed the glances he sent Callie's way and maybe even picked up on the connection forming between them. Panic began to rise in his chest.

"Callie's been crying," Lee noted. "I know that 'cause her eyes always get red and puffy. I'm glad you were there for her. I'm glad that she has you, but I hope, and forgive me for being the one who has to channel my inner big brother or protective father here, but I hope you'll be careful with her. Remember how hard things are for her even without all this stuff with Dad going on. She's a special soul, Ben. My sister is one in a million. If you're so lucky as to have captured her heart in some way, treasure it because you'll never be given a more valuable gift."

Patting Ben on the back, Lee moved to follow Callie toward the kitchen, but Ben reached out and caught his arm. "Lee, your sister is the most amazing person I've ever met: beautiful, brave, kind, and so much more. But I'm not, well, I'm not good for her, or not good enough for her. Please, please, understand. I wish I was, but I'm not."

Lee turned back and gazed intently at Ben once more. Then his smile returned, warm and sincere, stretching the spattering of freckles that dotted his cheeks. "Man, Ben, you really put a crimp in my whole 'big brother, protective father thing' here. My next line was supposed to be 'Now you stay away from my sister slash daughter.'" Lee lowered his voice as he delivered his caricatured line. Then he reached out and grasped Ben's shoulder. "Anyone who would tell me they were good enough for her would prove, by that very presumption, that they were not. The fact that you think you're not, well, it tells me my sister has damn good judgment, and she's probably found the one person in the whole world who actually is."

Astounded, Ben stood there, not knowing how to get through to him that, in this case, Lee was wrong, and so was Callie.

"Now, Uncle Ben." Lee slapped him on the back again. "Take off your stuff and stay a while." He motioned to Ben's coat and gloves. "Ms. Essie's definitely expecting you to join us, and I know Callie is too, and I never disappoint lovely ladies if I can help it, especially when they're feeding me pot roast!"

Turning quickly, Lee headed for the kitchen, following the sound of friendly conversation and laughter coming from Ms. Essie and Callie.

Panic overtook Ben. He'd gone too far, stepped too deep. How could he stay here and not be found out? How was he going to continue to be around Callie and never touch her, brush against her accidentally, or worse, give in to his overwhelming desire to connect with her that way?

The more he protested, the more this family reached out, accepted him, and even embraced him. He'd never known such people. They didn't have guards up or walls built; they simply trusted. He couldn't hurt them. If he did, he'd never forgive himself. It would be another heavy burden of guilt that he'd have to carry. But whichever way he went now he would hurt them. If he ran, he'd hurt Callie, and he knew that would crush him. But if he stayed...

"Mr. Ben Sawyer!" Ms. Essie's booming voice broke through his panicked thoughts as she reached out and clasped his shoulders in greeting. Her smile faded when she registered the look of panic in his eyes, but her expression shifted from confusion and concern to sheer determination in a matter of seconds.

"Now, Mr. Sawyer, you're stayin' for dinner, and that's that. You're wanted here, you hear? Come on in here now. Callie's gettin' the table ready for us. Pot roast, potatoes, carrots, fresh bread, all good for the soul,"

As always, Ben couldn't say no to Ms. Essie. Her presence was so warm that it drew him like a moth to a flame. Though he was nearly paralyzed by panic, he removed his coat, hung it on the nearby coat rack, and tossed his gloves on the bench beside it.

"Come on, now," Ms. Essie encouraged, placing her hand on his back and gently pushing him forward. He let her guide him past the front room, which contained a baby grand piano, and into the dining room.

The large floor-to-ceiling windows gave the room a grand, stately look, but the beige paint and soft burgundy curtains that hung from each window, pulled back with fancy beaded rope, warmed the space, making it feel homey.

A rectangular cherry wood table had already been set with four place settings. Each place setting had a cloth napkin set below the fork that matched the color of the curtains. It was elegant but in a way that spoke of a desire to create a feeling of home and comfort rather than merely aesthetics.

Ms. Essie pointed to the second place setting from the left. "Sit!" she commanded, a twinkle in her eye. Ben moved hesitantly, but he obeyed, seating himself in the comfortable cushioned chair.

Whirling around, she headed back to the kitchen. Moments later, all three of them emerged carrying heaped plates full of the delicious food Ms. Essie had made.

Ben watched Callie with admiration, noting how easily she moved and interacted in this familiar environment. She knew exactly where everything was and navigated the room with barely any notable difference from the way a fully sighted person would.

"Ms. Essie, this is amazing!" Callie said after the three of them had sat down, "Thank you so much for feeding our bodies and hearts tonight." Callie reached out and squeezed Ms. Essie's hand, and Ben found himself feeling envious of the easy gesture.

Lee sat to Ben's left and Callie to his right. When Ms. Essie offered a prayer, Ben was relieved when she touched her fingertips together in front of her rather than reaching out for them all to hold hands. She prayed beautifully, offering a plea for Callie's father and her husband as well.

Each time Ben passed a plate to or from Callie, his heart rate increased. The serving plates were large enough and the four of them were sufficiently spaced out at the table to make accidental contact unlikely, but he remained anxious.

"Ms. Essie Bessie?" Lee mumbled through a mouthful of pot roast. "This is delicious, seriously! Can you move in?"

Ms. Essie laughed, and Ben noted that the issue over the use of the old nickname had obviously been resolved.

"Mr. Lee LeVray! That's mighty kind a ya, but I think Mr. Jones might be objectin' to that."

"How long has your husband been ill?" Callie asked, concern in her voice.

"Oh, it's been a slow decline really. He gets weaker and weaker, but his mind's still as sharp as a tack, and we just love swingin' on the porch swing, playin' board games together, or just sittin' in each other's presence. It gets that way after years of bein' together. You just enjoy the presence of the other, their nearness to ya. You don't even need to be talkin'. Not that we don't do our share a that, mind ya." She laughed again, but this time there was nostalgia in the sound.

Glancing at Callie, Ben noticed tears forming in her eyes. "That's beautiful!" she whispered.

"Sitting still all the time?" Lee chuckled contrarily. "Not for me. I'll be climbing mountains in my... How old are you, Ms. Essie?"

"Lee!" Callie scolded. "That's rude!"

Ms. Essie smiled, no hint of offense in her expression. "Old, Mr. Lee LeVray," she said, avoiding a direct answer. "I'm just old."

"Well, you don't look it," Ben chimed in. "And I'm not flattering you, Ms. Essie."

"See?" Ms. Essie triumphed, pointing her fork at Ben. "As I was tellin' ya, he's a keeper."

Ben tilted his head to one side, wondering about the conversation involving him that he had clearly missed out on.

Smiling shyly, Callie looked at Ben as he gazed back at her. Warmth passed between them that elicited memories of their earlier connection in the park.

"Don't," she'd pleaded with him when he'd spoken of

running and leaving her. The plea had grabbed his heart with the force of a vice, nearly grinding every wall he had erected into dust.

Once again, Ben had an almost irresistible urge to reach out and touch her hand as it rested on the table. Instead, he looked down and balled his hands into fists in his lap, willing himself to keep his distance.

When he looked up, he saw that Ms. Essie was staring at him, a puzzled yet understanding expression in her eyes.

He quickly looked away, not wanting anyone else to peel back the layers of his well-constructed armor today. It was needed more than ever in this risky situation.

"How did you and Ben meet again?" Callie asked as she placed her hand back in her lap. Ben wondered if at some level she sensed it was tempting him, so she had mercifully moved it.

"Oh, that's a wonderful coincidence," Ms. Essie said excitedly. "I met him the day he arrived in town, just a few weeks ago. He was tellin' me he was only passin' through, but I talked him right into stayin'. Then 'cause I'm workin' a few hours here and there at an apartment building, I fixed him right up with a place to stay. Yes, indeed. I just was feelin' he belonged here somehow."

Lowering his fork, Lee looked at Ben. "You've only lived here for a couple of weeks?"

Ben nodded, uncomfortable with where the conversation was going.

"I guess I thought you grew up here. Where'd you come from?"

Ben shifted in his seat, and Callie did as well.

"Well," he stalled as he tried to figure out how to answer the question honestly without giving away too much. "I grew up near Boston, actually."

"Wow! What brought you here?"

Now Ben was stumped. He had come there because he was running away, running from the newest "new start" he'd tried. "Fresh start," he replied simply.

"Well, ain't everyone needin' one of those now and again?" Ms. Essie interjected, and Ben was thankful for the help.

Apparently satisfied with Ben's answer, Lee grabbed the plate of potatoes and scooped another giant heap of them onto his plate.

"Usually, my cookin' feeds an army," Ms. Essie teased as she watched Lee dig in. "But it looks like an army ain't got nothin' on one Mr. Lee LeVray."

Rising, she placed the remaining plates of food within his reach, as it looked like Callie and Ben were finished. "You go on now. You're the only one here still growin'. Well, at least in the right direction, anyway." She chuckled at her own joke, and Lee obliged her by putting more of everything on his plate.

"No wonder you have to move around all the time, Lee," Callie teased. "You've got all that extra fuel to burn."

"Blame her," Lee said, pointing at Ms. Essie. "No one around here cooks like this."

"Well, Dad..." Callie closed her mouth and lowered her head. "Sorry, Lee," she whispered, concerned about upsetting him by bringing up their dad.

"Mr. LeVray's a mighty wonderful man, that's certain." Ms. Essie looked off into the distance as if lost in her memories. "Were you knowin' that he and my husband played golf together often in earlier days, back when Louis was healthy?"

"Yes," Callie replied enthusiastically. "Dad talked about that a lot. He cares deeply for your husband. He talks about how he's a great man and was an amazing cop. Dad always told us that Mr. Jones never lost anyone under his care, not a victim, a fellow cop, or even a perpetrator. All those years of serving as a police officer in some of the most dangerous situations and he never lost a single soul. He's quite a legend for that, and Dad really admires him."

"And Mr. Jones is thinkin' the same of Mr. LeVray, yes he is. That man's got a heart for this community and his family too." Pausing, she put her hand across her heart. "You know, when you're good in here and you meet someone else who's good in here, nothin' else matters, not skin color or what your job is or where you come from or anything. Hearts can be bondin' over kindness and love. That's all the ingredients one's really needin'."

Ben shook his head, marveling at Ms. Essie's uncanny ability to say the right thing at the right time. She had a superpower in that regard, but Ben wasn't sure she was right on this one. Goodness, love, and kindness weren't always enough to overcome everything.

Callie stood up and closed the distance between her and Ms. Essie. She placed her hands on the older woman's shoulders and squeezed them affectionately. "I love your wisdom. Won't you please come by more often? You're like a fresh breath of air."

"And bring food," Lee added, still chewing on the last few bites of his dinner.

CHAPTER 11
THE MISTAKE

After dinner, Ben found himself in the kitchen helping Ms. Essie with the clean-up while Lee and Callie were on the phone with the hospital, checking on their dad.

Ben rinsed off the plates and then set them in the dishwasher, though the food had been so good they'd all left little behind.

Humming contentedly, Ms. Essie put the remaining food that had escaped Lee's nearly boundless appetite into containers and stacked them in the refrigerator. Her low, resonant voice made everything she sang sound profound and soulful. Enjoying the sound of it as they worked together, he found that it soothed away most of the panic that lingered inside.

He loaded the last of the glasses, lining them up on the top rack, then reached back into the sink for anything else that remained. The dishwater was murky from the residue of the rinsed dishes, and he didn't realize that a large knife was still hiding below the surface.

The sharp blade sliced deeply into his thumb, but the

pain only pulsed for a few seconds. Instinctively, he yanked his hand out of the water and saw the large cut, nearly half the length of his thumb. It was deep, but as he watched, the bleeding stopped, leaving only a small trace of blood visible in the wound.

"Oh, my lans!" Ms. Essie startled him with her sudden presence next to him and her exclamation of concern. "Mr. Sawyer, you okay?"

Plunging his hand back into the water, panic rose anew throughout his body.

"Yes, fine," he answered way too swiftly to sound natural.

Coming up beside him, she reached for his arm, and Ben froze, feeling like a trapped animal. She clasped Ben's arm above the water line at the spot where he'd bunched up his sleeve to avoid getting it wet. With genuine alarm showing in her eyes, she pulled his hand out of the water.

The cut was still there, but now no blood remained, and as they watched, with Ben helpless to stop the revelation, the cut began to close, like they were watching a time-lapse video.

Ms. Essie looked up into Ben's eyes. Compassion and wonder shone in hers, but surprisingly, there was no sign of shock, confusion, or fear.

Releasing his arm, she walked across the kitchen to where her purse was sitting on a side table. She retrieved a medium-sized Band-Aid and returned to Ben's side. In what felt to Ben like slow motion, Ms. Essie resumed her singing as she grabbed a hand towel and dried Ben's hand, careful not to touch him. She placed the towel on the island next to her and dropped the Band-Aid into his hand.

"You best be protectin' that wound from germs now, ya

hear?" she insisted as she continued to look directly into Ben's eyes.

Ben couldn't breathe. Robotically, he placed the Band-Aid over the wound and lowered his head, averting his gaze.

Ms. Essie smiled, seeming to have resolved the issue in her mind, and moved to take his place at the sink. "Let me finish this for ya."

Taking several steps back, he stood rigidly, not knowing what to do. She'd seen it, right? Surely she had. She had to know that something unusual had just happened.

Or maybe not. Maybe he'd fooled her with the dishwater. Maybe she thought the water had cleared the blood away or that the cut wasn't as bad as it looked. Which was it? If the first was true and she'd seen it and knew something was off, then he had to run. That would be it. He'd pack his things and leave that night.

But if she didn't, if her reaction was simply motherly concern, then he was safe. If he stayed frozen like this, awkwardly still and silent, she'd guess something was wrong, but he needed to know, and he felt paralyzed by the uncertainty.

But if she knew, if she'd seen it, why wasn't she shocked or horrified? Why didn't she start asking questions or become frightened? Why was there no fear or panic at all in her reaction? It didn't make sense.

Taking a seat on a stool at the island, he stared at the Band-Aid he'd placed over a wound that was no threat to him at all. As he struggled to process the reality of the potential exposure, he could barely breathe.

He thought about leaving, never seeing Callie again, never even getting to say goodbye, but he couldn't abide the thought. Just as he was about to burst out and ask her what she had seen, she stopped singing and turned around to face him.

"Mr. Sawyer?" She offered him a warm, reassuring smile. "Everythin's just fine, ya hear? Just fine for sure. Don't ya mind that cut. It won't cause ya any trouble."

It took several seconds for her words to register. If she knew, she was reassuring him; if she didn't, she was still reassuring him. Either way, perhaps everything was alright.

A surge of relief threatened to break him down, cause him to weep like a child, but he swallowed hard and raised his eyes to hers. "Thank you," he whispered.

She resumed her singing, this time an old hymn that Ben knew well. "I once was lost, but now I'm found, was blind but now I see."

Though Ben was relieved that she didn't seem frightened or surprised by what had happened, he didn't understand why or how that could be. The only thing that made sense was that she hadn't seen or hadn't registered what she'd seen, but that didn't seem possible. She had looked right at the wound.

Part of him hoped that somehow she knew and understood. It would be the first time in a long time that he might have someone to share his secret with, someone with whom he might be able to be fully himself, even more than he had been with Callie. But if she didn't come out and say so, he couldn't know what she saw or how she interpreted it. As his heart shrank back from the surge of hope that had begun to spring up in him, he realized he was basically back to where he was before: alone.

CALLIE AND LEE finished their phone call and returned to Ben and Ms. Essie, who were slicing pieces of the homemade blueberry cobbler she had brought and placing them on dessert plates. As the four of them settled into the comfort of the living room couches and chairs, Callie updated them on her dad's condition.

"They said everything is about the same, but there was a small improvement in his vitals that could be a result of some medication or could be a positive sign. They're monitoring it but won't know much more till morning." There was a sliver of hope in her voice.

As Callie sat with Lee on the large couch, enjoying the cobbler and the company, she noticed that Ben was unusually quiet. He hadn't talked much at all that night, but now he said almost nothing, and she felt that his mood had shifted somehow.

Though she hadn't expected Ben to sit by her, he had chosen a seat about as far from her as possible. When she brought up the potential good news about her father's condition, Ben hadn't made any comment, which was unusual for him, as he had always expressed so much concern for their situation.

"Miss Callie," Ms. Essie said, pulling Callie away from her worries about Ben, "I'm really wantin' to help y'all in more ways than just bringin' some food. Anythin' more I can be doin' for you two?"

Callie loved this kind-hearted woman. Her generosity had no limits, and her offers of help came from a deep need to be involved in the healing of others.

"Well..." Callie thought for a moment, pondering the following day's plans. "I think I'll sit with Dad in the morning. I'll bring my laptop and attempt to work while I'm there, but I want to be there with him. Lee, you need to go to school and wrestling practice. You're graduating soon, and you can't miss many more classes. I'll be with Dad until about two or so, but then I probably need to come back and prepare for our performance at the Cartwright Hotel. Gracie is picking me up at about four, so we can get across town in time.”

“Callie,” Ben finally spoke up, but his voice sounded drained of energy. “I'll come at two to get you.”

She'd given up arguing with Ben, so she simply offered a sincere thank you and shot him her warmest smile. He was sitting so far from her that his reactions and expressions, besides what she could gather from his voice and his general silence, were lost to her.

“And I can be with Dad in the evening while you're busy,” Lee added.

“Try not to wear out their floors with all your pacing.”

“No promises!” Lee chuckled.

“Wonderful!” Ms. Essie chimed in, her enthusiasm filling the room. “I have some free time in the afternoon, so I'll visit Mr. LeVray for a few hours after you leave and before Mr. Lee comes. I'll sing him some sweet hymns and pray over him through and through. We'll see if the good Lord won't be doin’ somethin’ incredible, now, won't we?” Her faith filled Callie's heart with hope.

“I know he'd love that,” Callie said with an appreciative smile.

They all finished their cobbler in silence as they thought about the following day.

“Well,” Ben said abruptly, rising from his chair, “I want to thank you so much for including me this evening. The food was out of this world, and the company even better, but I think I'm going to call it a night.”

Before any of them had a chance to react, Ben rushed out of the room toward the foyer.

Rising, Callie followed him, concern setting off alarms

in her heart. Something was wrong. Ben's easy-going way was gone, and his voice held a tenseness that she now recognized as a manifestation of the pain he carried. She'd felt it before when they were in the park, and he'd spoken of running. It scared her. Was Ben about to run; exit their lives without giving them the chance to help him get free of the burden he carried? He didn't like being alone in his pain, but he felt trapped there.

Ms. Essie and Lee didn't follow her. When she entered the foyer and heard Ben gathering his things, she called out to him to keep him from rushing out the door.

"Ben, wait," she pleaded. She needed to say something that she didn't want Ms. Essie and Lee to hear, and she wanted Ben to feel that he could talk freely, so she crossed to the coat rack and grabbed her coat, then opened the front door.

"Can we talk on the porch for a minute?"

"Callie, I—" Ben started to protest.

"Just for a minute," she pleaded again, interrupting his objection.

Ben pulled on his coat and gloves and moved close behind her, grasping the door in a gesture that said he wanted her to go first. He was so near to her that she could feel his warmth and smell his pleasant, subtle cologne mixed with his familiar natural scent.

Pulling herself away from him, she headed out into the darkness as Ben closed the door behind them. The porch light was on, but it didn't help Callie much as the shadows created unrecognizable and confusing images. Her familiarity with her own home meant she didn't need to see much to navigate here, so she took a few confident steps before lowering herself into a wicker chair. The cushions for the pair of them had been removed for winter storage, so the seat was hard and prickly, but she wanted Ben to sit too, hoping to anchor him somehow and keep him from running.

Though reluctant, Ben crossed the porch and sat in the chair opposite her.

"Ben, are you alright? I mean, I know you aren't alright. Please tell me what's in your heart."

He remained quiet, and Callie listened to his breathing, noticing it was irregular. Finally, Ben took a deep breath, then reached out and took her hands in his. The action took her by surprise, as Ben had never reached for her with such intentionality. Most of the time it was either to guide her or out of an almost unconscious instinct to comfort or assist. This was something else entirely.

Immediately, the strange current began flowing between them, as did the strong urge to draw close to Ben. The barrier of the gloves annoyed her, but at the same time, if the reactions were this powerful between them even through that barrier, maybe it was better that he wore them.

Now, she was certain that Ben felt it too. His breathing sped up, and he leaned in so close that she could feel his breath on her face.

"Callie!" Ben whispered, his voice conveying longing mingled with sadness. She felt his desire to close the few inches between them and kiss her. Her heart raced, and her breathing quickened, but she didn't move, not wanting to interrupt the moment. They remained suspended in silence for what felt in some ways like hours, but in other ways like mere seconds before Ben leaned back and dropped Callie's hands.

"I can't. I'm so sorry."

Before she could recover or protest, Ben stood up and

descended the steps. She heard his car door shut, followed by the sound of his engine. She sat still and silent as his car disappeared down the street and faded into silence.

Long after he was gone, she continued to sit there, unable to move. She didn't understand. Ben seemed to care deeply for her, and she could sense his attraction to her. She'd gotten him to open up and share much of his heart with her. Likely, she was the only person in Ben's life who knew the story about his past, his mom, and his pain. Yet he still pushed her away, held on to secrets, and put up walls she couldn't break through. He knew how to give, to help others, but he couldn't fully receive or let himself trust her.

A tear trickled down her cheek as her heart broke for him and for herself, as she wasn't convinced she'd ever be able to break down those walls. He might never let her really know him, even though he needed to let someone in for healing to begin.

As she sat mourning this potential reality, Callie heard something in the yard. Footsteps approached, crossing the dry grass.

"Hello?" she said into the night air.

The front door opened and Ms. Essie's voice penetrated Callie's rising fear. "Mm-hm," she exclaimed, as if seeing something she knew she would see. "He's run off, hasn't he?" It was more of an observation than a question.

Callie lowered her head, and Ms. Essie threw her coat around herself as she took the seat that Ben had just vacated.

"Now, you hear me, Miss Callie LeVray. Don't ya go givin' up on him, ya hear? Don't ya be despairin'."

Callie put her head in her hands, forgetting all about the footsteps that had given her goosebumps a moment earlier. "Ms. Essie, he's hurting, but I don't know why. Well, not all of it anyway. I want to help him, but he's, well, he's scared to trust anyone."

"That's the truth of it, no doubtin'! That boy's broken-hearted in a big way. I seen it before. When a person's carryin' pain alone for a long time, he balls it up inside a him, and ya gotta unravel it bit by bit, like untanglin' a ball a yarn. It'll take time and a lot a patience, Miss Callie, yes it will, but he's carin' deeply for ya, that's certain. If anyone can be untanglin' it, it'll be you, for sure."

Ms. Essie put her hands on her knees and let out a laugh as rich and full of irony as her next statement. "Who woulda ever thought that the good Lord would use a girl with little sight to be seekin' and findin' a soul as lost as that one? He works in mysterious ways, that's for certain, mysterious and beautiful ways!"

Hugging her arms around herself, Callie felt every bit of the night's chill straight through to her bones. "But I think he might run," she said, her doubts clashing with Ms. Essie's faith. "He might not give me a chance."

Ms. Essie leaned forward directing her words straight to Callie's heart. "Oh, no! He can't be runnin' now." She said it with such confidence that Callie almost believed it.

"How do you know that for sure?"

"'Cause he's already fallen for ya, fallen deep. He may be broken, but he ain't forgotten yet what love is. The ones who've forgotten might never be healed, but that ain't Mr. Sawyer. Oh, no! He's rememberin' love very well, and he's stuck right in it, like a fly in honey, he is."

Leaning back, she laughed, a sound of pure joy that split the darkness with its radiance.

CHAPTER 12

THE CHOICE

Callie fell into bed that night, weariness overtaking her. The emotion from her dad's situation, Ben's abrupt exit, and the memories of her past had drained her. She drifted off to sleep but soon opened her eyes to find herself in a beautiful meadow of flowers.

The setting was familiar, but only vaguely, like a long-forgotten memory. As she stared, the scene came into sharp, detailed view, and her heart filled with unspeakable joy. She marveled at the sights around her, focusing her perfect vision on a small orange butterfly that sucked nectar from a pink trumpet honeysuckle. She lingered on every detail, its tiny, wispy antenna and the spots of black that covered its fragile wings. The wind blew, and the creature lifted into the air, its flight graceful and free.

In the blink of an eye, darkness descended, like thick black curtains. Somewhere in her memory, she knew this bleak place too. She coughed in response to the ash that stuck in her throat, and she was startled by the crackle of what sounded like broken glass under her feet. In the distance, she heard her dad's voice calling her. It echoed like it was being spoken in a narrow tunnel.

"Dad!" she shouted, reaching out to grasp him, but nothing was there.

Eerie footsteps approached behind her, crunching dead grass as they drew closer in the night. Panic filled her, and she was about to scream when she felt a gentle hand on her shoulder. At the touch, the darkness vanished, and the field of flowers returned. She turned to see who had touched her, but no one was there.

When Callie awoke and saw the sunlight streaming through her window, she realized it had been a dream. A beautiful and horrible dream. Now, in her conscious mind, she recognized it from the night before her dad's stroke. It was similar but different too. It felt real, just as the other one had, and she lay there in a daze for a few minutes, wondering who was behind the mysterious footsteps and the hand on her shoulder. The presence was familiar yet hidden somehow, like trying to see something that was just beyond her vision.

Her alarm sounded, and she got up and busied herself getting ready for the day, shaking off the confusion that the dream had brought.

At the hospital, Lee helped her get settled with her laptop in their dad's room before heading off to school. Throughout the morning, Callie alternated between working, sitting by her dad's side, and visiting with a few well-wishers who stopped by to offer their prayers and support. The hospital had loosened its "family only" policy, which Callie greatly appreciated.

She talked to her dad about everything: work, Ben, Lee, and Ms. Essie. It felt good to get it all out, but the emptiness of the one-sided conversation soon caused her to fall silent, and she returned to stroking his hand and offering whispered prayers.

Nurses came and went several times, each time asking Callie if they could get her anything. She accepted a few cups of water, but she didn't have much of an appetite. Worry over her dad's continued unresponsiveness and Ben's contradictory behavior plagued her heart and churned her stomach.

Hope for her dad's recovery was fading despite the small amount of optimism offered by the doctor the night before. As far as the situation with Ben, her only remaining solace came from Ms. Essie's words: "He's already fallen for ya," she'd said. "He can't run now."

Callie hoped she was right. She also hoped that whatever Ben felt for her would be enough to keep him in one place long enough to heal, to belong, and to let someone convince him that what happened to his mom wasn't his fault; that he was a person worthy of being known and cared for. The thought of having no family and running so much as to never have anyone to fully understand and know her was unfathomable. The pain he suffered from losing his mom was deep, and he'd had no one to help him through it or to process it in a balanced and healthy way. He carried the whole thing alone. That kind of loneliness had to leave a terrible hole. In his isolation, Ben had lost the truth of who he was, and if he kept running, he'd never get it back. Instead, he'd run farther and farther from the possibility of ever grabbing hold of it.

As she sat, holding her dad's hand in hers, she whispered another urgent prayer, this time for Ben.

· · ·

Ben drove around aimlessly most of the morning, his mind and heart a jumble of emotions. He hadn't slept much at all, tossing and turning as opposing thoughts battled for his attention. The few moments when he'd slipped into shallow unconsciousness, he'd found his mind replaying the moment on the porch with Callie.

He'd not been able to stop himself from reaching out for her, letting himself get so close that he could feel her heartbeat in the air between them. When he sat across from her, he thought that if he could reach out and hold her hands again, his desire to be near her would be satisfied. But when he surrendered to that urge, when he even allowed himself to lean so near to her that he could see the longing in her eyes mirroring his, it was far from enough. He'd desperately wanted to kiss her; fold her into his arms and never let go.

Remarkably, once more she'd sensed his struggle. After the incident in the kitchen with Ms. Essie, he'd been tormented, not knowing what to do. He'd almost run from the house, but he knew it would be rude, leading to questions he didn't want to answer. So, he'd hung in there for a while longer, sitting as far from Callie as possible, knowing she'd see through him if he got anywhere near her.

But he'd underestimated her again. That special vision she had that required no physical sight at all had proven, once again, to be wholly effective.

When she'd pleaded with him in her irresistibly tender way to share his heart with her, he'd wanted nothing else. He almost had. He almost decided it was time to trust her completely. After all, if Ms. Essie knew, it was only a matter of time before Callie would as well.

When he grabbed her hands, he knew the connection between them would topple his walls, and he thought he was ready for that. But when the moment came, he panicked as he realized what it would do to him if he lost her.

If he told her everything and she couldn't accept it, or worse, couldn't live with the reality of it, he wasn't sure his heart could endure losing her. The stakes had shifted now. Before, he had worried about his secret being known and having to run. Now, he worried about how he could ever live without Callie in his world.

But it wasn't just about him. It was about her too. The truth would change her life forever. In a real way, a way that had defined who she was and how she lived for the entirety of her life, he'd flip everything upside down. Though he knew she carried heavy burdens, ones she might think she'd be happy to shed, she likely didn't understand the significance of what those burdens had meant in shaping her character and her inner strength.

Callie's limited eyesight had not inhibited his ability to see into her heart. It had been and still was, a learning process to know exactly how to help her or to understand her needs, but those were just incidentals. He'd easily seen Callie, just Callie, from the moment he'd met her. But now he wondered how much of the heart of the woman he was beginning to fall in love with was rooted in her experiences with difficulty and struggle. Take away the struggle, and would she lose something precious, the very thing that made Callie, Callie?

If he was the cause of fundamentally changing this amazing person in any negative way, he'd never be able to bear it.

Though this thought was enough to send him running, an even scarier possibility existed. If losing the burden didn't change her, the horror of being set free, only to be returned again and again, back and forth, burdened and unburdened, might do it. He didn't know, and even if he warned Callie, and somehow gave her the choice, he guessed she wouldn't know either.

It was that fear and his fear of her rejecting him, her inability to accept something so inhuman, so unbelievable that, in the end, stopped him, though it took every ounce of his strength and willpower to do so.

His soul in torment, he returned to his apartment just before noon. He should text Lee and tell him he couldn't pick up Callie and wouldn't be able to help anymore. He needed time to think. Maybe some distance would give him the courage he needed to run again, as he should.

He was just about to enter the elevator when Ms. Essie caught him by the arm.

"Mornin, Mr. Sawyer. Got a moment?"

"Ms. Essie," he acknowledged, though he couldn't get his face to form a smile. "Well, I was, I'm not sure I can—"

"It'll just be takin' a moment. I promise."

He followed her to the little sitting area near the fireplace, though it was too early for a fire.

He sat down, and Ms. Essie sat across from him, though she didn't settle herself like she usually did. She stayed perched on the front of the chair, leaning as close to Ben as she could manage and looking into his eyes.

"Mr. Sawyer, I want you to hear me now. I'm knowin' you're fightin' yourself a fierce battle right now in that good heart a yours. I'm knowin' you're feelin' like you can't offer that lovely girl any part a ya 'cause ya think you'll be hurtin' her or changin' her somehow. You hear me. Miss Callie ain't good 'cause she is or ain't seein' well. She's good 'cause she's good, Mr. Sawyer. I'm knowin' her for years, and she's just good all the way through, head to toe. Not perfect, mind ya, none a us are. But she's been through ups and downs, lost her mama, had to help with raisin' her little brother like she was his mama, had to face many a struggle. It ain't changed her heart. Only way you'll be changin' her or hurtin' her is if you ain't trustin' her. Ya hear me? You ain't poison, Mr. Sawyer, ya ain't. You're broken, and Miss Callie's real good with broken."

Ben dropped his head into his hands, tears threatening to spill out despite his best efforts. "Thank you, Ms. Essie. Thank you."

Rising, she approached him and squeezed his arm affectionately, then disappeared behind him, leaving him alone with his thoughts. He raised his head and stared at the wall, noticing for the first time a picture hanging there. It depicted a cliff with mountains looming in the distance. On the cliff face was a climber, captured in a moment of strained effort as he stretched for his next foothold. Ben's eyes traced up the face of the cliff, following a rope attached to the top. Holding the rope was another climber, watching and guarding his friend's progress and ensuring the security of the rope at its anchor. As Ben looked into the eyes of the man at the top, he wasn't sure if the man climbing the cliff or the man minding the rope was under more strain. They were in the struggle together, each dependent on the other, unable to accomplish the feat alone.

Pondering the picture, he shook his head at the irony of its connection to his own choices. He was at a crossroads. He could choose to continue to climb the cliff alone, or he could join with another in the struggle. Whatever he decided to do, he knew his life, from that moment on, would never be the same.

At long last he stood and headed back outside to his car. He wasn't sure if he was the one climbing the cliff or minding the rope, but he knew he and Callie, through some unbelievable twist of fate or divine providence, were, at least for now, in this struggle together.

As Ben drove to the hospital, he chided himself for forgetting, once again, to speak to Ms. Essie about the strange vehicle he had noticed hanging around the LeVray neighborhood and then at the courthouse. He had meant to talk with her about it the night before, but with everything that had happened, it had slipped his mind.

Stopping at the local deli, he grabbed a couple of lunch salads. He would be a little early, but that would give him a chance to apologize to Callie for running off the night before.

When he reached the hospital, he parked in what had become his usual spot and grabbed the salads. The weather had turned bitterly cold, and for once he was glad to have his thick coat and warm gloves.

When he arrived outside Ronald LeVray's room, he knocked softly on the door.

"Come in?"

Ben knew she wouldn't be expecting him yet, and after the way he'd acted the night before, she had probably wondered if he would come at all.

Pushing the door open, he said her name as warmly as he could manage, wishing to reassure her of his intentions.

"Ben?" she said hesitantly. Callie was sitting cross-legged on the loveseat with her laptop. Like every time he saw her, Ben had to stifle an awestruck inhale at the sight of her.

She wore fitted jeans and a ruby-red blouse that had ruffles around the edges of a modest but appealing V-neck. The blouse was sheer and fell over her shape in a way that accented all the right things. She closed her laptop and set it aside, offering Ben her full attention.

"Hi," he managed, trying to speak in a humble tone as he pulled over one of the folding chairs and sat opposite her, maintaining his normal unreachable distance.

He set down the bag of salads, took off his coat, and slung it over the back of the chair, then, reluctantly, pulled off his gloves, shoving them inside the coat pockets.

"What time is it?" she asked, stretching with obvious fatigue.

"It's only a little after one. I'm early. Thought you might be hungry." He pulled the two salads out of the bag. "Hope you like avocado salad?"

"Love it!" she smiled, gratitude shining in her alluring green eyes.

She uncrossed her legs, and Ben handed her one of the salads, slowly to ensure she saw it coming. As she took it, she smiled. "You're really getting the hang of this," she teased, though he could still see the questions about him lingering in her eyes.

He took the fork out of its plastic wrapping, turned it so the handle would contact her hand, and then moved it slowly toward her.

"Fork?" he added, just in case.

"Now you're just showing off." She smiled again, and some of the tension eased from her face.

They ate for a few moments in silence. As Ben glanced around the room, trying to decide how to start his apology, he spotted a strange orange stuffed animal atop the storage cabinet on the other side of the room.

"Um, Callie? Do you know there's a crab or some kind of crustacean thing staring at us from the cabinet?"

Callie laughed. "Why, yes, unfortunately, I do. It's actually a lobster."

Lowering his salad to his lap, he cleared his throat. "I'm

going to need a little more information here than simply what kind of sea creature it is."

"Right." Her eyes lit up with amusement. "Well, Lobster came for a visit today, a very brief visit."

Ben shook his head. "Lobster? I'm lost."

Callie laughed again and finished her bite of salad before she explained. "Lobster is the pianist in our trio. That's not his real name, of course, but we've called him that since, well, forever. He's shy and a little awkward with people, but he's got a great heart. He came in to see Dad today, snuck in, and nearly scared me to death when he finally spoke up just a few feet away. He just sort of stood there by Dad for a few minutes and then came around to me and shoved something into my hands. He said he wanted to get something for Dad that would remind Dad of him. Then he pretty much turned and left. Imagine how long I had to stare at that thing to figure out what it was. How in the world did he find a stuffed lobster anyway? I've never heard of such a thing."

A smile remained on Callie's face as she reflected on the memory, and Ben felt appreciation for this odd fellow he'd never met for cheering her heart.

"I'd like to tell you that all of that makes sense now, but, well, I'm not sure I can say that with a straight face."

Callie shrugged. "That's just Lobster. Ever and always unique and unpredictable."

"Well, I'll be interested in meeting him sometime."

Callie's eyes registered a question, and Ben could see that she was ready for his explanation. He wasn't sure what he was going to tell her, only that he had to tell her something to fix the situation and ease her heart and mind.

Before he began, he set his salad on a small side table. "Callie, I'm really sorry about last night." He put his palms together and leaned forward, hoping she could read something in his face.

She set her salad down as well, but she didn't lean forward. "Sorry about almost kissing me or sorry about running away before you did?" There was good-natured teasing in her voice but also a hint of genuine hurt.

Ben glanced over at her father, suddenly feeling self-conscious about having this conversation in front of him, even if he was unconscious.

"Well..." he began, hoping his tone conveyed his sincerity. "At the risk of your father waking up the moment I confess this, definitely much more the latter than the former."

Callie smiled, and the ache in Ben's heart started to ease.

"Yes, I think you might have some explaining to do if my dad suddenly woke up and saw a strange man sitting here with me, confessing he regrets not kissing me when he had the chance."

"We're going to have quite a lot to fill him in on when he wakes up." It struck Ben as sad that this was the only image he had of this incredible man. He'd heard so many stories about him from Ms. Essie, Callie, and Lee that he almost felt like he knew him. But his personal experience was limited to this version of Ronald LeVray, helpless and being kept alive by machines. He wished that wasn't the case, as he'd really like to know the man who was responsible in so many profound ways for the extraordinary woman before him.

"So, then..." Callie interrupted his thoughts as she leaned toward him. "Are you going to tell me?"

"Tell you?"

"What happened last night, Ben? What upset you?" Her tone was serious but warm and full of genuine concern.

Ben looked down and wound his fingers together as his arms rested on his knees. He stared at the thumb that had been cut. Not a trace of a scar remained.

"I will tell you, Callie. I don't know how, but I will tell you about me, about everything. You might not want me in your life anymore when I'm done, but I still have to tell you. I know that now."

Her eyes filled with tears, but they didn't spill down on her cheeks. She shifted to the edge of her seat, so they were only about a foot from each other. Ben thought she might reach out for him, but she kept her hands on her knees even as they both felt the familiar pull toward each other grow as the distance between them shrank.

"Please," she pleaded. "It's okay. I'm not a runner. I've seen your heart, and somehow, in a way I can't understand, I know you." She paused to take a deep breath, then let it out. "Please, Ben, don't be afraid."

They both sat perfectly still, only their breathing and the sounds of Callie's dad's life-support machines audible around them.

Once again her words had spoken to the deepest needs within him. He had no idea how Callie could understand and see what she did in him. Though he hadn't shared his secret, the one he kept locked away, he began to think that perhaps she had already uncovered the most personal and crucial secrets he held.

Finally, Ben leaned back in his chair and let out a deep breath. "I'd like to take you on a date, Miss LeVray, dinner maybe. Would you consider going with me?"

As she sat back as well, surprise registered on her face. That wasn't at all what she had been expecting to hear.

"Well," she considered, "I've got a date across town tonight with a cello, a quirky pianist named Lobster, and my best friend. We won't be done until about eight o'clock, so…"

"That's perfect."

"But it's forty-five minutes away, all the way across town. I won't be back home until nine or so. Then I'd have to change and—"

"I'll meet you at the hotel at eight," Ben said, a note of finality in his voice.

"Ben! That's such a long drive, and I'll be in an evening gown and heels, and you'll have to drive me all the way back and load my cello and—"

"Is this a fancy way of saying 'no,' you don't want to go out with me?" he asked with a teasing smile.

"No!" she nearly shouted. "I, well, I…" She paused, and Ben could tell she was trying to figure out how to convince him not to go to the trouble.

After a moment, she raised her hands in surrender and shrugged. "Alright, Ben Sawyer. You win! You've been going way out of your way for me since the moment I met you, so why should this be any different?"

She slumped back against the couch, her whole body signaling she had given up the fight.

Ben laughed in triumph. "If you think one second with you hasn't been worth whatever 'trouble' you think you've put me through, you don't know. Truly, you just don't know."

Callie smiled then, a different smile than Ben had seen before. This wasn't a friendly smile or a smile birthed from humor. It was more like a shy, flirty smile, and Ben liked it.

CHAPTER 13

THE ANTICIPATION

As Callie and Ben were throwing away the remnants of their lunch and packing up Callie's computer to head back to her home, a nurse entered the room.

"Miss LeVray?" She stopped when she came up beside Callie.

Hearing her somber tone, Callie ceased packing her bag.

"I'm going to note your dad's vitals. Then I need a quick word with you."

"I'll step out," Ben offered, but Callie caught him by the arm, and her eyes begged him to stay. He got the message, turning back and resuming the clean-up. If this was bad news, which she feared it might be, she needed him there. She couldn't face it alone.

A few minutes later, the nurse stepped away from Ronald LeVray's bedside and came to face Callie and Ben, who were standing side by side in front of the loveseat. Ben had tried to get Callie to sit, but her nerves wouldn't allow her.

"Miss LeVray," the nurse began, compassion filling her voice, "Dr. Karl called this afternoon to check on your dad. He asked me to take one more reading and if, well if the readings came out the way they just did, he wanted to ask you and your family..." She paused, and Callie guessed she was probably looking at Ben as the staff still hadn't figured out how he fit in with her and Lee. "He wants you all to meet with him tomorrow morning, if possible. Say, around ten o'clock?"

Callie's knees begin to shake, and Ben surprised her by placing his hand supportively on her back.

"Yes, we can do that," Callie replied, fear and dread spilling out with every word.

The nurse tried to lighten her tone as she continued. "Don't worry yet. Dr. Karl is going to keep you in the loop on everything, so you know what to expect and what your options are. Don't worry," she repeated, which only made Callie worry even more. "I'll let him know to expect you all around ten then." After patting Callie on the arm, she exited quickly, likely happy to escape the sad faces that resulted from her news.

Callie sat, and Ben slowly lowered himself beside her. He sat so carefully that Callie thought he might be afraid of her in some way. She covered her face with her hands, and Ben placed an arm gently around her shoulders. She closed her eyes, and before she could think better of it, leaned into him, her head resting against his chest. Instantly, a soothing warmth began spreading throughout her body, like she was lowering herself into a bath. As she allowed herself to relax against him, she felt an inexplicable sense of familiarity, like she'd been in his arms many times before.

Her heart overflowed with the range of emotions

pouring through it: fear for her dad, fear for Lee, and a pull toward Ben that was irresistible. The emotions came in a torrent, like a downpour of rain that threatened to wash her away. She breathed in and out as she felt Ben's heart pounding against her cheek, reacting to her just as she was reacting to him.

Sitting still and quiet, Ben held her for a long moment, not attempting to come up with some meaningless platitude to diminish the seriousness of the situation. He quietly anchored her heart. The pulse between them moved in a beautiful rhythm that, though it awakened a new and intense kind of desire inside of Callie, also eased her anxiety, filling her with a strange mixture of longing and satisfaction.

After a few moments, as she felt the growing connection threatening to overtake them both, she lifted herself from his chest, and his hands retreated from around her. Only then did she open her eyes and look at him. His face was so close to hers that, although she still couldn't read his eyes, she could see the passion and pain in his expression, pain for her and her family, and the passion of their unspoken connection.

Turning away, in a seemingly difficult yet deliberate motion, he stood and crossed the room to retrieve their coats.

"Callie..." he said, the mixture of emotions evident in his hoarse tone. "If you want to change your mind about all of it today—the performance, the date—I understand, and I'll make calls for you and—"

"No," she interrupted, wiping her hand across her cheeks to clear the remaining tears that hadn't soaked into Ben's sweater.

"There's nothing I can do here right now. Ms. Essie is

coming and then Lee. They'll let me know if anything changes. In truth, I need to get out of here for a while. It's like my heart needs to breathe. I'm no good to my dad if I work myself into a hopeless place."

"Alright. If you're sure." Ben put on his coat and gloves and then stood in front of her, holding out hers. "It's really cold outside. You're going to need this, and be sure to bundle up tonight too. They're saying it may snow."

Callie slipped her coat on and buttoned it up. Then she stopped by her dad's bedside, gripping his hand in hers. She bent down and kissed it. "I love you, Dad."

Her heart yearned to hear the same words from his lips, but she feared she may never hear them again.

AFTER BEN ESCORTED Callie to her door and they said goodbye for the moment, both anticipating their date later that evening, she took her time getting ready. She wished she could untangle the thick web of emotions that gripped her heart. She was fearful about meeting with Dr. Karl the next day and what it might mean for her and Lee, but she was also excited about her date with Ben and the newfound understanding they seemed to be developing. Though he hadn't embraced her again after her breakdown at the hospital, the barriers between them were crumbling, and Ben seemed increasingly resigned to including her in his heart and his secrets.

Strangely, she felt no real concern about whatever Ben was holding onto so tightly. Already seeing into his heart, she was sure of his character, and that was what mattered to her, not his past or the faults and flaws he so easily saw in himself.

The personal nature of what they had already shared

contributed to this feeling of security, but she had to acknowledge that there was more to it than that. A lot more.

Callie had never experienced anything like the feelings she had for Ben. Physical attraction was certainly present, but that alone seemed like a cheap and inadequate way of describing what was going on between them. Whatever it was, it was nearly tangible, like something she could reach out and grasp, yet it was also indescribable. It wasn't a normal stirring of attraction and emotional connection, though those seemed to be the catalysts. It was much more real, as real as someone touching her or the feeling of hot or cold against her skin. It was as if, when she was near him or connecting with his heart, they were both being drawn to the same physical space or their hands were reaching to grasp the same object. That was the only way she could describe it. He seemed to have a direct link to her heart and she to his. It wasn't like reading each other's minds; it was more like watching a play but being able to see what was behind the roles, straight into the lives of the actors themselves.

They needed to talk about it. She was already confident that he was experiencing the same things she was, but somehow it felt too sacred and intimate to discuss it directly. But if it got any stronger, they'd have to. As incredible as it was, the power of it was overwhelming, and if they didn't talk about it, it might push them to cross boundaries or make decisions they weren't ready to make. The thought of talking openly with Ben about it made her nervous, but she was determined that, if necessary, she'd be able to do so.

She put on a little extra make-up, undergoing the

process by touch as she had taught herself to do many years ago. She fixed her hair in an up-do that she hadn't attempted in quite some time and was pleased when her hair complied with her coaxing. After slipping into her nylons, gown, and shoes, she headed downstairs, conscious of the fact that Grace would be arriving in a few minutes.

The conversation with the nurse and her and Ben's subsequent interlude had put her behind schedule, and now, with her extra efforts at dressing to impress, she felt rushed as she gathered her thickest coat and gloves, remembering Ben's warning about the weather. She hoped it wouldn't snow.

Walking around in a nearly sleeveless gown and heels is ridiculous in snow, she mused as she put on her necklace and earrings to complete the ensemble.

She dictated a couple of quick texts to Lee, letting him know about their appointment in the morning and her plans with Ben. Predictably, Lee's teasing kicked into high gear.

Don't let him kidnap you this time, Sis. Remember, he's your uncle, so don't do anything you wouldn't do with an uncle.

Callie huffed at his insinuation, but she loved her crazy brother for all his antics. It wasn't lost on her that he hadn't commented on their appointment with the doctor. Lee was great with the jokes, but it was hard for him to express his deepest emotions. She wished she could hold him close and reassure him, but at the moment she was the one in need of that, and she wasn't sure she had much to give.

Lee let her know he'd be at the hospital for as long as he could stand the confinement. Then he had a video game tournament with some friends. Though she had no interest in video games, Lee liked the camaraderie of competing with others around the world, right from their basement. She'd frequently hear him cheering or complaining loudly from their large-screen gaming/TV room downstairs. The intensity and seriousness with which he competed always made her laugh.

No sooner had she grabbed her purse and cello than she heard a knock at the door.

"Gracie!" she greeted enthusiastically, careful not to disturb their make-up or matching dresses as she hugged her friend.

"Wow, girly!" Grace exclaimed, grabbing Callie's hand and backing away from her to take a good look. "Are you going for model of the year or what?"

"Well, maybe, a little," Callie admitted. "I know we gotta go, so I'll give you the scoop in the car."

"Oh yes, you will, as I have a feeling this has something to do with 'Mr. Ooh la la'!"

Callie laughed as Grace grabbed her cello, and they rushed out into the cold late afternoon wind. A few snowflakes landed on her nose and lips as they loaded up. Then she slipped into the passenger seat next to Grace.

First, Callie updated Grace on her dad and their upcoming appointment with Dr. Karl. Thankfully, she managed to keep her eyes dry, not wanting to smudge her make-up or show up with red, puffy eyes for their fancy engagement. She had to swallow a lump in her throat several times, and Grace didn't push with too many questions, understanding Callie's fragile state.

"What about that boy—Sam, isn't it—that you've been dating?" Callie asked, changing the subject, but Grace clucked her tongue in response.

"Oh no!" Grace said, scolding Callie for her futile attempt at diversion. "Spill it, girl. Let's have it *all!*"

Callie was silent for a moment, temporarily disobeying her friend's request to share in her life. She wasn't sure what to say. So much of what had happened between her and Ben was personal and private, and she would never violate his trust. But she wanted to let her friend in on her life, tell her about Ben, and the possibility of new love.

"Well," she began, realizing they only had about fifteen more minutes until they reached Lobster's house, and there'd be no comfortable girl talk with him around. "It's a little complicated, but Ben asked me out on a date tonight after the performance. He's picking me up from the hotel. I hope that's okay. I probably should've checked with you first."

Grace laughed, a fearless, carefree sound that Callie envied. "Hmm... if the shoe was on the other foot and a Greek god like that asked me out, girl, I love you and all, but I'd probably leave you on the street in the snow with your cello and Lobster."

Callie burst out laughing at the image of her and Lobster and her cello stranded on the side of the road, her in her gown and high heels and Lobster... well, just being Lobster. "Okay, okay," she begged, trying to keep her immaculately made-up face in order.

"Seriously, what happened? Did you guys kiss or something?" Grace's girlish giddiness made Callie feel like she was sixteen instead of twenty-three.

"Well, almost, I think."

"You *think*?" Grace's confusion mingled with her giggles. "You're not sure if you kissed him?"

"Well, Ben is... complicated. His heart is as pure as gold, but he's got a lot of pain, and it's hard for him to trust and, well, I think that makes it hard for him to reach out physically. I guess that's it. I really don't understand all of it myself."

Grace let out a long audible breath, processing Callie's words. "Is he... I mean, do you get the feeling he's interested in *that*?"

Callie smiled at her friend's caring but awkward question, but she understood how what she had said led her to that concern.

"Yes, I don't think a lack of desire is the problem," Callie assured, recalling with a smile the way his heart had sped up in rhythm with hers on the porch or the way it had beat double time when she leaned against him.

"Do tell!" Grace inquired, the giddiness returning to her tone.

"Well, let's just say I've had enough close calls, and my hearing is really good, and, well, let's leave it at that." Drawing a horizontal line in the air with her hand, she let her friend know she wasn't going to go any further. "It's not a desire thing; it's a fear thing, like he's genuinely afraid for some reason, afraid to let anyone touch him in any way, and I don't know why."

Both women fell silent as they processed the little information they had, neither knowing how to interpret the situation.

"But I think we might be breaking through some of that fear," Callie added with a smile. "When I found out about my dad today and I was really upset, Ben held me. He reached out and put his arms around me, and I'm not sure he even thought about it; it just happened, and I think he's alright with it. I mean, he didn't jump up and run for the door or anything."

"And was that nice?" Grace asked, clearly wanting more juicy details.

"Yes, but I wish it wasn't colored by all the terrible emotions of the bad news. It's like I have this terrible thing going on and this great thing going on, and I can't truly feel either one because of the existence of the other, you know? If I feel happy and enjoy this new thing with Ben, then I remember how we met, why we met, and what my reality is, and the joy just drains out, like letting a stopper out of the sink and watching the water flow away. It doesn't feel right to enjoy it, but part of me can't help it." Callie put her hands over her face as if trying to hide from the confusion. "Oh, help, Gracie!"

"Poor thing," Grace soothed, rubbing Callie's back with her free hand. "It's not fair, the timing of all of this. But you need to enjoy it, Callie. How often does this kind of thing happen? I mean, I've been on, like, seven dates in the last month, and nothing, nada, no spark, no connection. I keep looking, but it's not easy to find, you know? Like a generous, kind, person you connect with at a soul level as well as a physical one. I mean, there are plenty of guys who are happy to just connect physically, but that's not for me or for you. If you think you might have found it, or been sent it, or whatever, don't take it for granted, Cal. Find a way to grieve your dad's situation separate from this, but let yourself be happy, and let yourself connect with Ben if that's what your heart's telling you to do. Even if he's, quote, complicated, end quote."

Callie laughed, knowing her friend had probably made the air quotes with her hand but, knowing that Callie couldn't see them, she offered her the verbal description as well.

"I'll try." Callie sighed once her laughter had ebbed. "Gracie, you're amazing! I love you, my friend. How'd you get so smart?"

Grace shrugged. "Hanging out with Lobster?" They both laughed as they pulled into Lobster's driveway.

Ben called and made reservations at a well-rated Italian place near the Cartwright Hotel. He pressed his white button-up shirt and slacks and slipped on his gray sports jacket. If Callie was going to be wearing an evening gown, he wasn't going to ruin the look with jeans and a casual sweater. But he drew the line at ties. He hated them with a passion and had been able to get away without wearing one for quite some time now.

As he exited the elevator at about six thirty, anxious to arrive at the hotel a bit early, so he could hear some of Callie's performance, he almost bumped right into Ms. Essie, who looked like she'd been waiting for him.

"Mm-hm!" she exclaimed looking him over. "I heard 'bout your plans from Mr. Lee. You're a mighty smart man, Mr. Ben Sawyer." She had a twinkle of self-satisfaction in her eye. "A mighty smart man, indeed."

"Yes, I am, Ms. Essie." He smiled back at her. "You know why? Because I listen to mighty smart people who are kind and caring."

Laughing, she slapped him on the back.

"I just hope, well, I hope we're all going down the right road here. It would kill me if I hurt her, if she..." He couldn't bring himself to finish the sentence.

"Be ye strong and courageous," she quoted in a voice that was between singing and talking. "Now you go on." She waved her hand toward the door. "I'll be keepin' an ear out for Mr. Lee and Mr. LeVray, so you two have fun and let all the worry go for one night. I'm knowin' Miss Callie's needin' that."

Ben guessed that Lee and Ms. Essie had caught up at the hospital when Lee came to relieve her from her bedside vigil. She seemed to know about the impending meeting with the doctor and understand the anxiety it was creating in the LeVray family.

"I'll try my best to keep her mind off of all of it, Ms. Essie."

"I'm bettin' you will." She laughed again, a bit of innuendo in her voice.

As he walked to his car, the wind lashed at him. The sky looked like snow was coming, and Ben could smell it in the air.

Poor Callie! He worried about her clothing in this weather even as he pictured what she might look like in her gown.

As he started the forty-five-minute drive to the hotel, he kept replaying that incredible and utterly terrifying moment in the hospital. When Callie heard about the doctor wanting to meet with her and Lee, Ben saw her losing her strength, and his heart gave him no choice but to put his arm around her, even though he felt exposed without his gloves and coat for protection. Every alarm bell went off in his head when she leaned against him. How easy it would've been. Just the lightest contact and that would've been it; his secret would have been out.

Though Ben had accepted that Callie finding out about him was inevitable, he wanted this date, this night first. He wanted to spend some time with her, laugh with her, and make some beautiful memories, just in case that's all he would ever have. Once she knew, he doubted anything would be the same, and he was still convinced that, in the end, he would have to run.

But he would risk it all with Callie. He'd take the chance

of opening himself up to someone, even if it killed him. He couldn't be alone anymore, and he couldn't walk away from her. Tonight, he wanted one good, real, unimpeded date. Just two humans doing human things without anything else in the way. Those memories would be his to hold onto if everything fell apart.

That had been his plan, but when she leaned against him, he thought it was all over, that there wouldn't be a date, not like the one he had wanted. When he survived the first moment, however, and he realized he hadn't touched her skin and that she had her hands over her eyes, something else had overtaken him.

Nearly since the moment he'd met her, Ben had wanted to hold her this way. The sadness she felt for her dad's situation and the comfort they'd shared in telling each other about their pasts had made him want to embrace her. But when it happened, the force of the link between them caught him off guard, though he supposed it shouldn't have, due to their previous experiences. His heart sped up as he tuned in to the feeling of her, warm and soft and everything Callie. Her smell swirled around his face, and her hair brushed against his neck. Somehow, he knew she belonged there, right in his arms, and that though he'd been unaware of it, he'd lived his whole life with the absence of something as vital to him as the air he breathed. As long as he could remember, he'd always had an empty place in him. Now he knew what was meant to fill it. When she finally sat up and he forced himself to move away from her, he became fully cognizant that never again would he be blindly innocent, not knowing the need and, therefore, not craving her presence with him.

Though his feelings and experiences with her were very real, he didn't understand them, but it had nothing to do with his curse, or at least he didn't think it did. They still had never connected skin to skin, and that was the way it worked with the curse. That's what his limited experience had taught him anyhow. Now he wished he knew more about himself, what he was, why he was, and how it all worked. Spending most of his life running from it rather than using it or learning about it had left him with little to go on.

He'd been vaguely attracted to other girls in the past, though he'd never experienced the same level of attraction, both physical and emotional, as he felt for Callie. None of the strange sensations he was experiencing with her had been present in those situations. It seemed that the more they shared and the closer he came to telling her everything, the more powerful the connecting force between them became. He couldn't help but wonder what would happen when he really touched her or kissed her. He needed to talk to her about it, but admitting it and talking openly about such things wasn't exactly where their relationship was at right now.

One crazy secret revelation at a time, he told himself as he watched the first snowflakes smack against his windshield and disappear into the night.

Despite his concern about Callie in a thin dress, he was glad of the cold. They would both be wearing heavy coats and gloves, which would make his desired night of unimpeded normality possible. Instead of her arm, he could take her hand, acting more like a lover than a guide. He could put his arm around her shoulders and brush her hair away from her face. It wouldn't be quite the same as doing all of that with his uncovered hand, but it would be enough, and most importantly, it would give them time to just be themselves and experience a normal kind of date.

When Ben was about halfway to the hotel, the snow started falling harder, accumulating now on the grass and trees. It might be a tricky drive back, but he'd learned to drive in snow, so he wasn't worried. His vehicle had four-wheel drive, and they would take their time. It might even give him an excuse to spend more time with her before everything changed forever.

CHAPTER 14

THE DATE

By the time Ben arrived at the Cartwright Hotel, the snow was almost a blizzard. There was already an inch of snow on the ground, and it looked like there would be much more to come. He parked and buttoned up his coat as he made his way to the front entrance.

People were coming and going from the hotel, and everyone who stepped outside had the same look of surprise as they encountered the heavy snowfall. As he watched their reactions, he chuckled to himself, thinking about how such weather had been a normal, everyday occurrence during wintertime where he grew up.

It was now seven thirty. The drive had taken him longer than he had anticipated because of the road conditions. Callie had told him that this was a charity dinner, followed by an auction. Her trio would perform through the pre-dinner and dinner time while everyone ate, socialized, and drank. That would end a few minutes before eight, the rest of the night being devoted to the auction itself.

The hotel had a fancy, upscale lobby with expensive

furniture and rich dark wood floors and tables. An elegant chandelier hung from the center of the room like a twinkling sun, casting its light on the world below.

As Ben entered, he was captivated by the music. The trio was playing a tune he didn't recognize, but the melody was hypnotizing. He could hear each instrument, the rhythmic chords of the piano, the lilting, almost bird-like sound of the violin, and the deep, resonant tones of the cello

He hadn't told Callie about his passionate love for music. He had sung a little when he was younger, and though he wasn't sure he'd ever want to perform in public like Callie, he considered his voice to be adequate, maybe even pleasant. His mother had loved his voice, and she would often ask him to sing some of her favorite songs from the musicals they sometimes watched together, including selections from classics like *The Sound of Music*, *Les Misérables*, *My Fair Lady*, and many more.

Ben strolled to the open doors of the hotel's large ballroom. Inside, people sat eating around circular tables, but a significant number were standing and wandering around, everyone wearing luxurious gowns or tuxedos and carrying a glass of something that bubbled or fizzed. This kind of scene was quite familiar to him, but it represented a time in his life that he very much wanted to forget.

Just as he approached the doorway, the song ended, and Callie's group began to play a song from one of his favorite musicals, "All I Ask of You" from *Phantom of the Opera*.

It began quietly, and for a few minutes, Ben didn't even look for Callie. He closed his eyes and listened to the cello lead the first verse, mouthing the words along from memory. As the song progressed to the chorus, the violin took over as the melody soared to a higher octave.

Peering through the crowd, he scanned the room for Callie. The piano was tucked into the front left corner. Its occupant—Lobster, he presumed—was hidden from his sight because of the piano's angle. He spotted Grace, however, as she played, but his eyes kept searching as people moved in and out of his way.

At last, Ben caught a glimpse of Callie, and when he did, he forgot how to breathe. She looked angelic. Her hair was up in a flowing cascade of curls that fell in layers around her face. Her arms were bare, and they moved in a picture of elegance and grace as she worked the bow with her right hand and slid her fingers up, down, and across the strings with her left. She had no music in front of her, unlike Grace, whose music stand stood like a metal statue. Callie's eyes were closed, and he could almost see her breathing to the music as she moved. He couldn't see much of her gown, as the cello covered nearly all of her from the neck down, but Ben was mesmerized by the motion of her playing, and he felt increasingly annoyed as people blocked his view. He couldn't go any farther into the room since he wasn't part of the event, and he didn't want to attract attention, so he contented himself with the brief glimpses of this incredible woman with whom he would soon be privileged enough to spend the rest of the evening. He felt sorry for other men who he knew were watching her, noting her beauty and talent, and wondering what it would be like to be with her.

Not a chance, he thought, grinning with satisfaction. For a moment he simply enjoyed the normality of being a man, proud and grateful for the attention of an amazing woman.

When the song ended, the crowd clapped heartily. Those who had been seated stood and offered the group their enthusiastic praise. Now Ben couldn't see Callie at all, so he retreated to the lobby and took a seat, making sure he had a clear view of the ballroom doors.

When the applause faded, everyone took a seat. Those milling about in the lobby headed for the ballroom and settled themselves into extra chairs that were brought in for the auction. There was a lot of commotion, and Ben imagined Callie feeling lost in the midst of it. Such a chaotic situation was hard to handle with perfect eyesight, so it had to be even more confusing for her. He knew Callie had Grace though, and judging by the confidence and trust she placed in her friend, Ben figured she was in good hands.

Eventually, the activity settled, and he heard the auctioneer begin his introduction, explaining the procedure and the rules of the event. Ben's stomach flipped as his anticipation of seeing Callie grew.

A few more intolerably slow moments passed before he heard Grace's giddy, girlish voice echoing from a nearby hallway. Realizing they must have come out a side door, Ben repositioned himself in front of a mirror that covered the back of the lobby.

Grace appeared first, her violin case slung over her shoulder, and beside her was Callie.

Ben stopped breathing and nearly dropped his coat as Callie stepped out of the shadows and into the ambient light of the chandelier. Her long black gown clung to her, showing off her tiny waist and perfect feminine curves. The dress had a slit up one side that revealed her left leg several inches above her knee and its plunging neckline was not nearly as modest as the red blouse she'd been wearing earlier. She wore a black choker with shimmering rhinestones that matched the dangling earrings that sparkled amidst her cascades of light copper curls.

Awestruck, Ben couldn't speak or move. Callie's green eyes blinked, and he wasn't sure if she could see him in the dim lighting and at such a distance, but Grace could. She giggled when she spotted him, the sound of it filling the lobby.

"That's so perfect!" she said as she watched Ben struggle to regain his composure. "And I'm getting a double feature." She gestured toward the mirrors as her eyes twinkled with the delight of Ben's reaction.

Drawn like a moth to a flame, Ben approached until he was only a few feet from Callie. The moment she saw him, a smile filled her stunning face.

"You clean up well," she said, clutching her hands together nervously in front of her.

"Callie!" Ben stammered. "I can't... I can't tell you how incredibly beautiful you are!"

"It doesn't get better than that!" Grace laughed again.

Neither of them laughed or looked Grace's way, so she raised her hands and backed away from them. "Okay, third wheel here. One Callie LeVray, delivered as promised. I'm gonna go help Lobster load the stuff. Have fun, you two!"

Nudging Callie, Grace held out her coat and gloves. Then she kissed her on the cheek, whispered something in her ear that Ben couldn't hear, and disappeared back down the hallway.

Still speechless, Ben struggled to breathe as he stood staring at her. Whatever Grace had said to her had caused Callie to light up with another smile. It made her face radiant, accentuated by her dark pink lips and a small dimple that Ben had never noticed before on her right cheek.

Though he wasn't touching her at all, not even through the barrier of clothing, that mysterious fire began to move between them again, like it was being cycled around and around in a circle, moving from Ben to Callie and then from Callie back to him. Each time it circled it grew and brightened. He almost stepped forward and kissed her, right there in the lobby, unashamedly and without fear, but Callie saved him.

"Um, Ben? You have to talk, you know, the whole bad eyes thing?" She made a sweeping gesture across her face, and Ben suddenly realized they had been standing there for quite some time without speaking at all.

He could get lost in her eyes and stare at her all night, but she couldn't see everything that was processing in his. Now, impulsively, he wanted to touch her, so she could see exactly what he felt for her as it poured out of him.

"How about dinner?" she asked, laughing at the fact that Ben still wasn't speaking.

"Um, yes, dinner. I'm sorry. I'm, well"—he fumbled for the right words,—"I don't know what I am, I'm... I'd be willing to stand here and stare at you all night, I guess, but yes, let's do dinner."

She laughed again at his jumbled sentence. "You know, Ben, you can still stare in the restaurant if you want, though watching me eat might not be nearly as, um, well, enchanting."

He breathed deeply as feeling began to return to his extremities. He put on his coat and gloves and then reached for Callie's. "It's pretty much a blizzard out there, and with that dress..." He paused and sucked in another deliberate breath. "You're definitely going to need these."

She turned around, so he could help her into her coat, and Ben's heart stopped again as he saw that nearly half of her back was visible above the low scoop of the dress. He stared at the beauty of her pale, flawless skin.

This dress is going to be the end of me! Ben thought as he, once again, tried to regain his sense of equilibrium.

Callie was a conservative dresser. She always looked beautiful and feminine, but this dress was in a whole different category, nowhere near conservative.

"Ben?" she inquired, pulling him out of his trance.

"Right, dinner," he managed as he helped her into her coat, sad when the bulk of it covered everything. After pulling on her gloves, she reached to take his arm, but Ben grasped her hand instead, intertwining his fingers with hers as he enjoyed the familiar rise in temperature.

She turned to face him, smiling shyly, as she squeezed his hand.

"So, that's how we're going to play it now, is it?" she asked, satisfaction in her tone.

"Yep," he replied. "After seeing you in that dress, I'll never be able to simply be Ben your driver and guide again." His voice carried the humor in his smile, but he sincerely wanted to convey that there was no going back for him or for Callie.

Callie laughed, a soft and contented sound. He was doing his job. Ms. Essie would be proud. For a while at least, she was forgetting all about her sorrows and troubles. And he wanted to keep her there, at least for one night.

As they exited the lobby, hand in hand, the snow hit them like hundreds of tiny splinters lashing their faces. Callie shivered next to him, and he put his arm around her shoulders, trying to shield her from some of the driving snow.

"Good gracious!" she exclaimed through chattering teeth. "It's like the whole world changed while we were in there."

Callie's high-heeled shoes slipped on the snow-covered

asphalt, and Ben used his other hand to hold her up. She slipped and slid, and Ben kept catching her by the arm, the shoulder, and even once under her armpit. Laughing, she clung to him, but no matter what she did, she couldn't keep her feet firmly on the ground.

Finally, about halfway to the car, Ben swung her up into his arms, and she gasped in surprise.

"I think this is easier," he announced.

She giggled in delight and clung tightly to his shoulders as they made their way, much more fluidly now, to Ben's SUV. Setting her down in front of the passenger-side door, he reached to open it, wanting to get Callie out of the cold, but when she went to step up into the car, her foot slipped out from under her again, and Ben had to grab her with both hands around her waist.

"I'm sorry!" she offered, but the apology was mostly lost in her laughter. Ben laughed with her as he scooped her up and set her firmly in the seat. He couldn't help it. Her smiles and laughter were contagious, and the feeling of her in his arms made him deliriously happy.

Once he'd settled in the driver's seat, he started the SUV and turned the heat on to full blast. When he had latched his seatbelt, Callie put her gloved hand on his arm.

"I'm so sorry," she said as giggles escaped past her words. "This is ridiculous! If I'd known it was going to be like this, I would've brought some other shoes, so you wouldn't have to carry me like a hopeless damsel in distress all night."

"And ruin all the fun?" Ben replied with a playful smile. Then they both laughed again, joy filling their hearts to the brim.

The drive to the restaurant consisted mostly of strategizing how they would deal with Callie's shoe issue to get her safely inside.

"I'm going to stop at the front entrance, lead you inside, and get you seated in the waiting area," Ben said. "Then I'll park the car and come get you." He struggled to focus on the problem as he glanced at her irresistibly stunning face.

"Alright. That works for me," she agreed, holding in another giggle, then letting it play out in her smile.

Fortunately, the restaurant had a covered entryway, so Ben was able to escort her inside with no problems. After parking the car, he walked back into the restaurant, only to find two young men gathered around Callie. They were asking her casual questions, but Ben recognized their intentions immediately.

Rushing up beside her, he spoke her name so she would know it was him, then pulled her away, glaring with a fierce warning first at one and then the other young man.

"Thank you," she breathed out in a relieved whisper.

"I can't leave you even for a second looking like that. It's like chumming the water for sharks."

Callie smiled, but Ben could tell the incident had shaken her up.

"I guess we're back to me carrying you as our only option," he teased, though he was pretty sure that really was their only option at this point.

Callie squeezed his hand. "No choice, I guess." She sighed, feigning annoyance.

He gave the hostess his name and soon he was leading Callie through the tables and chairs. After they were seated, the waiter set menus in front of them and then left them to make their choices.

"Ready for more Callie 101?" she asked as she held up the menu and waved it from side to side.

"Hmm… let me guess. I'm going to be putting my Italian language skills to good use," Ben deduced, turning the menu over to get a feel for the various categories.

"You have Italian language skills?" she asked, sounding impressed.

"You'll see."

Ben earned several rounds of laughter from Callie as he did his best to read the choices in an exaggerated Italian accent. The sound of her laughter filled his heart so full that he felt that he'd be willing to do anything to keep her laughing and hold the sadness at bay.

It took several moments for them to warm up enough to remove their coats and gloves. Ben had to suck in another halted breath when Callie took off her coat, and it took all his manners and discipline as a gentleman to avoid letting his gaze follow the line of her dress as it descended.

Against all his instincts and desires to reach for her hand, Ben kept his hands on his side of the table. He wanted time with Callie, time to laugh and talk, and he wasn't going to change it all sooner than necessary.

After the waiter brought out salads and bread, Ben spoke up as he enjoyed the sight of her from his side of the table. "Your cello playing is, well, there are no words. It's just like you are: beautiful, graceful, and captivating. I was mesmerized."

Callie looked down, color rising to her cheeks. "Thank you. How much did you hear?"

"Pretty much all of the last two songs. That song from *Phantom of the Opera* is one of my favorites. How do you remember it all without sheet music?"

Callie took a bite of salad before answering his question. "Well, I learned how to read music first, but it was too hard, visually. So, I'm not sure if I learned to play by ear simply out of necessity or if that was just in me all along. It's hard to tell sometimes, you know, what we become because we have to and what we just are. Though I think who we are in here"—Callie pointed at her heart—"is just who we are for sure. Maybe some of what we end up doing is a little harder to determine that way though."

When he chuckled, Callie gave him a puzzled look.

"It just sounds like something Ms. Essie said to me."

"Well, if I'm channeling my inner Ms. Essie, there must be some truth to what I'm saying. That woman is incredibly wise."

Ben nodded. "Yes, she is." He thought about how much that woman's wisdom was responsible for him being there at that moment with Callie. As he looked at her, though, he got a strange feeling that the same might be true for her.

"Um, can I ask you something?" Callie said, her tone turning serious. "If you don't want to answer, that's fine, no pressure. I don't want to spoil the night."

Ben felt a few bricks of the old walls threatening to rise in him, but he couldn't refuse her anything as he looked into her bewitching eyes. "That's fair. What is it?

"Why aren't you living your dream, using your gifts? You said you were an architect, and when you spoke about it, you were so passionate. So, why are you a driver? Not that I'm not grateful," she quickly added. "After all, we never would have met if you hadn't been."

He relaxed at the question. Though this kind of inquiry would have usually made him panic, she already knew the answer, even if she hadn't put it together yet.

"Callie, I run a lot. Getting in with an architectural firm, building a client base and all of that, takes time. Running, moving, constantly changing my whole life isn't conducive to that."

She lowered her head, and his heart dropped, realizing he had done the very thing he didn't want to do. He'd replaced her smile with fear and worry.

"Hey," he said, trying to undo the damage, "I'm not running this time, not unless you tell me to, alright?"

She raised her eyes again, and as always, Ben felt like she could see right through him.

"And why in the world would I ever do that, Ben Sawyer?"

A pause hung in the air for a moment before Ben answered. "Bad Italian accent?" he said with a teasing smile, trying to evaporate the tension between them.

She laughed as she picked up on his desire to keep the night joyful.

"Or," she pondered with a serious expression, "maybe it will be your tendency to stop talking to me when I'm wearing a fancy dress."

"Oh no!" Ben raised a hand in objection. "You can't blame me for that one. That's all your doing. No woman should look, well, so incredible, Callie. It's totally unfair to do that to a man."

Callie dipped her head in a feigned apology. "I'm so sorry for the trouble I've caused you. You know, I've worn this whole outfit lots of times, and no one's ever stopped speaking to me because of it."

"Well..." He leaned back and rubbed the scruff on his chin for a moment as he thought. "Did any of them have the privilege of taking you out to dinner? Did they know they were going to get to sit with you, talk with you, share a little of their soul with you? Or were they trying desperately to talk their way to that opportunity?"

"Why, Mr. Sawyer!" Callie exclaimed, a sly smile raising

the corners of her lips. "Is that your sneaky way of asking me how many men I've dated?"

Ben stopped stroking his chin and waved his hand in the air as if to dismiss the assumption. "Well, if that's what you heard. But you don't have to answer if you don't want to."

"How about this; I'll talk if you'll talk. Deal?"

"Deal," he agreed.

"Alright," she said hesitantly, trying to think of how to proceed. "Well, I had a boyfriend in high school for about a month. He finally worked up the courage to kiss me on the cheek after about that long and then"—she took a deep breath—"he started dating my best friend about a week later."

"Ouch!" Ben grimaced.

"I went on a few dates here and there in college, but, honestly, I was pretty much a bookworm and studied or played cello most of the time, so nothing to write home about."

"And...?" Ben coaxed, feeling like there had to be more.

"Well," Callie laughed, "I think Lobster had a crush on me for a while."

"Hmm... I think I need to meet this Lobster character."

"He wanted to meet you tonight after he loaded our equipment, but I'm guessing that after your whole 'stunned into silence' routine, Gracie probably dissuaded him from that, for tonight anyway."

Ben chuckled. "Probably a good idea. Especially since I barely remember Grace even being there, and then only because she handed you your coat and I was concerned about you being cold." Ben paused, suddenly feeling bad for both of Callie's friends. "I'll have to make it up to them. I don't want them thinking I'm not interested in getting to know them."

"Oh, don't worry," Callie said, smiling in amusement. "Gracie certainly gets it, and I have no doubt she'll explain it to Lobster."

Ben had the distinct feeling he was missing out on some private joke between them.

Callie opened both hands and pointed them toward Ben. "Okay, enough stalling, I've spilled all of my not-so-interesting secrets. Your turn."

Ben resumed rubbing his chin with his thumb and index finger. "I did not date in high school. Taking care of my mother was pretty much a full-time job. In college, I went on about five dates total, nothing serious and nothing real. I'm not interested in casual dating, Callie. I find that a waste of time, and when, well, when you're who I am, that's not really possible anyway. But even if it was, I wouldn't want it."

Ben read admiration mixed with confusion on Callie's face.

"Oh," Ben added, raising a finger in the air, "and I met this amazing girl just a few days ago, and I'm serious about her, really serious about her."

Callie smiled. "And...?"

Looking intently into Callie's eyes, he leaned closer. As they focused on each other, the pull of the connection between them grew, and Ben's desire to touch her, to kiss her, and to embrace her nearly overtook him.

Remembering the purpose behind their time together sobered him, and he drew back to dull the effects of the connection.

"And if I'm smart, I won't miss another opportunity to

kiss her when it comes my way, even if her wicker chairs are the most uncomfortable things I've ever sat in."

Callie broke into an unbridled laugh, and Ben grinned at her reaction to his truthful, yet intentional joke.

"They're not meant to be sat on in the wintertime," Callie said, trying to get the words out around her laughter. "And besides," she swallowed, attempting to control another outburst, "I think they beat a freezing cold cement park bench in January anytime."

Ben tilted his head. "We really must do a better job with our seating choices," Ben noted with mock seriousness. He was rewarded with a fresh round of giggles.

"Yes, we must," Callie agreed through her laughter.

The waiter brought their main courses and cleared their salad and bread plates. Inwardly, Ben cursed the gesture, feeling like his time with Callie was going by way too quickly, draining out like sand in an hourglass.

"Ben…" Callie forced herself to adopt a more serious tone., "How old are you?"

"Twenty-seven," he replied, a question in his tone. "And you're twenty-three, right?"

"Yes," Callie responded, though Ben could tell that she wanted to say more.

"So, you're twenty-seven, and that's all the dating you've done? How is that possible?"

Remaining silent, he waited for Callie to come up with the answer on her own. He saw it in her face when, at last, she did.

"Running," she sighed in defeat.

"Right."

She lowered her chin again. No matter how much he reassured her, until she knew, until she understood, this reality would frighten her. And once she knew, well, she might be thoroughly frightened then.

Silence lingered, and once again, Ben had the almost irresistible urge to hold her in his arms to comfort and reassure her. They each ate a few bites of food, but Ben noticed that Callie was mostly just moving pasta around on her plate or twisting it around her fork.

"And now you're not running, because…?" Callie looked up at him for an answer.

"Because I'm tired of it, Callie, and because…" He paused and lowered his voice to almost a whisper. "I found something here that I think is worth risking everything I have and everything I am for."

Her eyes sparkled like green pools of water in sunlight. The corners of her mouth lifted, and she breathed out a sigh. "That's a pretty good answer," she said with more contentment in her expression.

They ate for a few moments in silence before Ben broke it.

"I hope you don't mind if I ask you something. Same rules apply here—you don't have to answer if you don't want to."

Callie nodded, encouraging him to go on.

"If there was a way to get your full eyesight, would you want it?"

Callie laughed, apparently much more comfortable with the question than Ben had anticipated.

"Why, do you know about some new scientific breakthrough of which I'm unaware?"

"No, just purely hypothetical."

Setting down her fork, she put both hands in her lap and stared at Ben as best as she could. "Yes."

Ben contemplated her simple answer, wanting more

but unsure if he should continue with his line of questioning. Callie seemed so comfortable with who she was, and he didn't ever want her to think that her eyesight was a focus of his thoughts because it certainly wasn't, except, of course, in the way it related to his own issue.

"Do you want to know why?" she inquired, raising her eyebrows as if she was surprised he hadn't asked.

"Yes, if you want to share."

"Because I want to see into people's eyes and connect in that way with their souls. You know how people always say that the eyes are the windows to the soul? I wish I understood that, that I could share in that. I'd like to know the color of people's eyes and the truths that hide there." She laughed lightly before continuing. "I'd like to have seen the expression on your face when you saw me tonight and fell speechless. When you miss the eyes and much of the details of the face, you miss a lot. It often leaves me feeling like I'm on the outside of the world, instead of in it."

Ben's heart ached. This amazing woman didn't want sight so she could do more things or be someone else. She wanted to see so she could connect with people, see into them, and feel like she was a part of their emotions and experiences. Ms. Essie was right. Callie was good through and through. He shook his head, honored to be sitting at a table with someone so profoundly beautiful, inside and out. Suddenly, all he wanted was to give her everything she desired, forever and ever.

"But, I'm always amazed at how you seem to know exactly what others, and me in particular, are feeling and thinking. You don't seem to be lacking in that way at all."

She hugged her arms around her, as if chilled. "Well, with you..." Callie looked down shyly. "Well, that's something different. Normally though, I sometimes think people are seeing me, so they think I'm seeing them. I believe in the theory that when one sense is lessened the others are heightened but..." She left the sentence unfinished, seemingly afraid to face some hidden pain that flashed in her eyes.

"I'm sorry," Ben said softly. "I shouldn't have asked."

"No, no, not at all. I'm glad you did."

Her statement was sincere, but the air hung heavily between them for another moment before a heart-stopping smile filled her face, eventually reaching her eyes. "I will tell you this," she said. "I'm quite often not the least-sighted person in my house."

"What?" Ben was caught off guard by her change of tone and by her statement, but he smiled at the return of the humor between them.

"Ask Lee to find anything—his socks, his keys, his backpack, anything—and I'll wager I could find it ten times faster, even if I closed my eyes."

"I'll stand as a witness for that one." Ben chuckled and raised his right hand, remembering Lee's frantic search for their dad's spare keys.

"I bet he'll find Ms. Essie's leftover pot roast though," Ben added confidently.

Callie chuckled in agreement. "Now *that* he'll be sure to find."

Much too soon for Ben, the waiter came and removed their empty plates and left Ben the check. He glanced at his watch and was shocked that it was already a little after ten.

"The last thing I want to do is even think about this night ending," he said as he placed his credit card onto the small plastic tray. "But I know the weather is only getting worse, and if we stay here much longer, we may have to get rooms for the night in that fancy hotel you performed in."

Raising an eyebrow, she sent Ben a teasing yet slightly suggestive smile that made his heart race. Ben laughed and held up both hands, as if to halt that thought completely before either of them allowed it to develop.

"Oh no! I definitely don't need to hear Lee channel his inner protective father again. To tell you the truth, that was a little frightening."

Callie gasped. "He didn't!"

Ben chuckled in confirmation.

"Well, I shouldn't be surprised. After all, he reminded me tonight that you're just 'Good old Uncle Ben,' and he thinks I should behave accordingly."

"Hmm. I'm going to have to work hard on losing that nickname somehow."

"Good luck with that!" Callie said sarcastically. "Poor Ms. Essie hasn't been able to shake hers even after all these years."

When the bill was paid, Ben reluctantly slipped on his coat and gloves.

"Ready for some more adventure, Miss LeVray?" he asked as he stood up and stepped to her side of the table.

"Are you referring to the snowstorm outside or just life with you in general, Ben Sawyer?"

"Both," he replied, smiling. "Definitely both."

CHAPTER 15

THE KISS

Ben helped Callie into her coat, and she slid on her gloves. The restaurant was nearly empty now, so they moved easily to the front door and outside.

The snow was much deeper now, looking like at least three inches had accumulated, and it was still coming down hard. Callie shivered next to him, and he figured that no matter how thick her coat was, the lack of material in the dress was inevitably going to leave her chilled.

"Alright, Miss LeVray," he announced, scooping her into his arms again. She let out another girlish giggle that made him happy, all the way through to his bones. He carried her nimbly to the car, but this time when he set her down, he braced her between the car and his body to keep her from sliding while he opened the door.

It only took a fraction of a second for Ben to realize that was not the best plan. Bright swirls of light filled his vision as the force of the pull he felt toward her shocked him. It was like being caught in a raging current and resisting it was like swimming upstream. He struggled to breathe, much less get his hands to work properly. Callie also gasped, confirming again that the phenomenon was mutual. He tried to keep himself from looking at her, knowing his already intense attraction for her would only magnify the experience and make it impossible for him to pull away. The only thought that kept him from giving in, taking her in his arms, and kissing her passionately was his concern for her freezing to death, right here in the restaurant parking lot.

It took several tries before he managed to open the door. Then, in one quick motion, he picked her up and set her in the passenger seat.

After closing her door, he stood in the cold, trying to regain control of his thoughts and emotions. The mysterious connection between them was incredible and exciting, but without understanding its source or intention, it was bewildering and disorienting as well. And it seemed to be growing parallel with the deepening of their relationship. He needed to be more careful, ensuring he stayed well in control of his actions with Callie.

When he finally settled himself in the driver's seat, he heard Callie let out a long breath. As he started the car, he chuckled to himself. "I know, wow! I know," he mumbled.

They sat in stupefied silence as Ben tried to refocus his concentration on driving in the snowstorm. Whatever was happening between them, there could be no doubt that it was not normal. It was many times stronger than typical attraction or infatuation. And now, he was convinced that it had to have something to do with him, who he was, though he didn't understand how. But, since this had to be because of him, because of whatever inhuman thing he possessed, it was yet another reason why she deserved to know the truth about him. She had to be confused as to why she was experiencing something much stronger than the normal kind of attraction she would have been expecting at this stage of a relationship. Even if he told her everything he knew about himself though, he still had no explanation to offer her about this, as he had none for himself either.

"Ben?" Callie finally spoke up, her voice barely above a whisper.

"Yes?"

"Um, well, I've never really been in a relationship quite like this one before, but, well, is this... is this normal?"

Ben let out a long sigh, grateful that Callie had brought up the elephant in the room but also unsure how to answer her. He was glad that he needed to keep his eyes on the road and couldn't look over into her captivating eyes, as he needed to think clearly about how to respond.

"I've never felt this way either, but... No, I don't think this is, well, the way it usually is, not for..." He was about to say "normal people" but changed his mind. "Not for everyone anyway."

Taking a deep breath, he willed himself to continue, recognizing that she deserved at least as much as he was about to say. "Callie, there are things about me that, well, aren't like everyone else, and I don't know how that's affecting me or you. I can only tell you I've never had this experience before either, and I don't understand it or know what it is. " He couldn't keep himself from smiling as he finished his thought. "It's absolutely incredible, though a little overwhelming for sure!"

Callie also let out a sigh of relief, apparently somehow comforted despite his woefully inadequate explanation. She followed the sigh with a sarcastic laugh. "That's one way to describe it."

A moment of pleasant silence went by as they processed

their thoughts and feelings. Despite the confusion it brought, they smiled at the mutual experience. Then Callie turned toward him and spoke hesitantly. "Can you help me understand something?"

"Sure, if I can," he replied, trying to communicate openness despite his instinct to shut down about anything related to his secret.

"What do you mean when you say you're not like everyone else, that there are things about you that are different? Can you help me understand what you mean by that?"

Her voice was gentle, and Ben knew she was trying to reassure him that she'd be okay if he shared his secrets with her. It was a fair question. Between what he'd already revealed and the fact that she was experiencing something that shouldn't be possible, it was only natural that she wanted to understand. He knew what he would ask of her next wasn't fair, but he wasn't ready to give up this sacred time yet.

"I will, I promise I will. Please, just give me the rest of tonight. I want to enjoy this time with you before you know and it all comes crashing down around us. Please."

Callie was silent for a long time, and Ben worried that perhaps he had really scared her this time.

"Alright," she said softly, "but please, please don't run. Please give me a chance to, well, to know you, really know you."

Despite his need to keep both hands on the wheel in the conditions, he reached over briefly and interlaced his gloved fingers with hers, squeezing reassuringly. He had already promised to do that, and he would. Though the consequences frightened him, he longed for her to fully know him, more than anything.

They were about halfway home, and the snow was falling in blinding waves, like thousands of pieces of confetti being shot from a cannon.

"It seems pretty bad out there," Callie observed. "Are you comfortable driving in this?"

Though he felt confident driving in snow, truth be told, the weather was testing even his limits. Visibility was only a few yards, and though there wasn't much traffic, he worried about others who weren't as used to driving in the snow and might make reckless choices.

"I've driven in this kind of weather often," Ben said, trying to sound as reassuring as possible. "This is crazy but beautiful. Can you see all the flakes hitting the windshield?" He paused, watching the tiny flecks, lit up by the streetlights, plunging toward them. "It's like hundreds of shooting stars whizzing at and around us."

From the corner of his eye, he saw a smile spread across her face. "I can see it a little, though I'm sure my star show's not quite as spectacular as yours. After your description though, I can kind of fill it in and see it in my mind."

Smiling, he felt satisfied that he'd been able to broaden the experience for her.

Suddenly, a new fear rose in him. What if, when he told Callie who he was, all of it, she was angry with him? What if she felt that little moments like this, when he could have helped her see, helped her experience what she was missing, but didn't, were moments she felt he stole from her, holding back when he could give?

In truth, he wanted to give whatever he could, as limited as it might be; he'd give it all to her gladly. But once the genie was out of the bottle, there was no going back. Once she knew, and all the consequences of knowing all of it descended on them, they could never be like this again, just Callie and Ben.

But Callie might not see it that way. To her, it might be dozens of moments where he refused to give what he could, and that might change her mind about him.

Though undesired and unasked for, he had a power that could radically alter moments for others in unbelievable ways, but he was the only one who could decide when to give and when to withhold. The responsibility and consequences of giving what he had made him feel heavy and unworthy, and watching the limitations of it play out wrecked him inside in ways he wasn't sure anyone could ever understand.

Shaking his head, he tried to clear away the doubts. He'd already been down this road. He'd decided not to run this time, not again. He'd chosen to risk trusting Callie, even though he knew if his reality destroyed her, destroyed them, it would ruin him for good.

"Can I ask you another somewhat serious question?" Callie asked, her inquiry startling him.

"It seems to be the night for that," he replied, trying to keep his tone light.

"Why doesn't this seem to bother you at all?"

Ben glanced over as she pointed at her eyes.

"I've had a lot of experience with people's reactions, and, well, the truth is, most people are scared of it. They don't understand it, so they shrink away from it, which pretty much means retreating from me. It's rare for someone to react like you have. You don't seem afraid of dealing with it or learning about it." She shifted to face him as best she could within the seatbelt's restraint. "You seem to be able to look right past it and see just me. How is that?"

Her question stunned and dismayed him. She really didn't understand or see herself for who and what she was.

They were traveling on city roads now, and Ben spotted a gas station turnoff, so he maneuvered into the parking lot, thankful no one else was in sight.

He put the vehicle in park, unbuckled his seatbelt, and turned to face Callie's puzzled expression, no doubt wondering why they had stopped. Ben grabbed both of her hands tenderly with his. "Callie," Ben began, the strength of his deep conviction in his voice. "Your goodness, beauty, joy, strength, sense of humor, care for others, open heart, and so much more, these are all the things you are. Whether you can see or not see, hear or not hear, walk or not walk—high-heeled party shoes notwithstanding..."

Callie laughed despite her emotions.

"None of that matters. If someone can't see those things when they're with you, they're the ones who are blind, Callie."

She smiled, but Ben noticed a tear forming in the corner of her eye before she looked away from him.

"Thank you, sincerely, but most people don't look at things that way."

He'd never seen this part of her, the painful part, the part where the burden was, where hurt gathered like a muddy puddle in a low area after a rain.

Despite the power of the reaction he knew they'd experience, he reached across, unbuckled her seatbelt, and pulled Callie toward him, resting her head on his shoulder.

"I'm sorry, so sorry," he whispered.

Shifting her weight toward him, she tried to maneuver across the middle console. As she did, her forehead touched the skin of his neck, which sent panic throughout his body.

Within seconds he felt the draw begin, a sensation of

suction pulling from the spot where their skin touched. It was followed by the kickback, a sense of euphoria that came with the giving. It was like being filled with something that his soul craved. The kickback was never as potent as the draw, but it offered a slight counterbalance.

Stiffening, he expected Callie to scream or cry out, but nothing happened. She rested silently against his shoulder for several minutes, her breathing becoming more and more even.

What's happening? he panicked.

Maybe it was gone, not working anymore. But the draw from him was undeniable.

When Callie sighed contentedly, he understood. Her eyes were closed. Realizing that could change at any second, he sat up straighter in his seat, sliding her head an inch downwards, which broke the contact point.

Ben's body relaxed, and the drawing ceased, as did the kickback. The only thing that remained was the familiar fire between them.

At his motion, Callie lifted her head and looked at him. "Is everything alright?"

He didn't know what outward reactions all the inward turmoil had elicited, but he was sure there were some. He had to tell her soon. This wasn't working anymore. They were growing too close, too intimate. He didn't want her to find out by accident and be shocked and afraid.

He looked out the window at the falling snow, now more vertical since they weren't moving. His time was almost up. They were only a few minutes from her house.

Placing a gloved hand on her cheek, he wished he could feel the softness of it. She leaned into his hand, smiling shyly.

"I'd better get you home. It's getting late. Lee will, for sure, think I've kidnapped you this time."

As he pulled back onto the road, they both remained quiet. Ben felt drained from the torrent of sensations and emotions, dreading the end of their one "normal" date and the knowledge that he would soon need to reveal his secret to Callie.

By the time they pulled into her driveway, the snow had slowed. Ben put his car in park, unable to accept the ending of the evening.

Callie reached for his hand and Ben gladly obliged.

"I hope you can be there tomorrow with Lee and me. I don't know if I can face the day without you."

"If you want me, I'll be there," Ben assured her.

"Thank you, and thank you for this magical, dazzling, beautiful night. It was perfect!"

Ben couldn't have agreed more.

"Would you consider giving me another opportunity to dazzle you, Miss LeVray? Maybe wear those shoes again, and I'll arrange another snowstorm, just so I can carry you around."

"You got it!" she agreed, beaming. "I might need to wear something else though. This is strictly a concert dress."

"Then I'll take you to a concert," he replied quickly. His humor was rewarded with another of her beautiful laughs.

"One more question." He held up one finger like a promise not to exceed it. "And again, it's one of those you don't have to answer, as I respect the whole friend-to-friend confidences thing."

"Okay," she said a little dubiously.

"What did Grace whisper in your ear tonight just before she left?"

Looking down, Callie fidgeted with the purse in her lap. "Hmm… Well, that's a tough one. Are you sure you want to know?"

Ben nodded. "Definitely."

"Well, she said, and I'll quote Gracie directly here so as not to incriminate myself in this situation in any way, 'Now *that* is the look of a man completely and irrevocably in love.'"

Her cheeks turned pink, and she stared at the floor. After a moment of awkward silence, Ben let out a slow whistle. "You have some very smart and observant friends, Callie."

Callie lifted her head and offered him a shy, insecure smile, clearly feeling bad for sharing something that might have made him uncomfortable.

"I better get you inside. It's so late, and you've got an… eventful day tomorrow. I'll meet you and Lee at the hospital in the morning."

"Thank you." The sorrow in her voice matched his. Neither of them wanted the night to end.

Turning off the engine, he walked around the car. When he opened her door, he placed his hand behind his back and bowed at the waist, though he wasn't sure Callie would see the gesture.

"My lady," he teased. "Your carriage awaits."

"You're going to have a bad back tomorrow," she said as he lifted her into his arms and started toward the front porch.

"Not a chance. I'm not even getting workout credit. You're too light."

To prove his point, Ben leaped up the two stairs leading to the porch, though he did so a little more cautiously than he wanted to because of the slick snow. The porch was covered, so only a little drifting snow spilled in along the edges.

He set Callie down, not trapping her this time as he was confident that the ground would be safe enough for her shoes to grip. She dropped her purse on one of the now infamous wicker chairs and smiled.

"I guess asking you to sit is out. Do you want to come in? I think Lee's in the basement, but..."

"I'd love to, but I'm going to be a gentleman and let you get some sleep. I've already kept you up late."

As Callie took a step toward the door, Ben caught her hand, noticing that it was already trembling despite the gloves. He turned her around to face him.

"Callie, would you do something for me?"

"Maybe," she replied with a flirtatious smile.

"Would you close your eyes and not open them again until I say so? Scouts honor, no cheating?"

Callie laughed. "But, Ben, I can't really see anything out here in the dark anyway."

"Please, just humor me. Don't open them. Just trust me."

Callie stepped back so that her back was against the door frame, like she was trying to anchor herself to a solid reference point. "Alright," she agreed, her voice shaky.

Callie closed her eyes and stood there, trembling, though Ben didn't know if it was the cold or the same eager anticipation that was causing him to feel dizzy and warm despite the cool temperature. She had to know he would do this. He'd promised not to miss another opportunity, but now that they both knew about and had experienced the intense reactions that resulted when they drew close to each other, the expectancy of the moment was overpowering.

After removing his gloves, he shoved them into his pockets, feeling like chains had been dropped from his wrists. He lifted his hand to Callie's cheek, which was pink with cold.

When he intentionally touched her without barriers for the first time, she sucked in air and trembled again as they both felt the cycling of warmth and light begin anew. She did not feel the gentle drawing sensation or the release of an inner filling that signaled to Ben that whatever was inside him, be it a gift or a curse, was being transferred to Callie.

Breathing deeply, he got lost in the pure pleasure of touching her face. Soft and smooth as silk, the warmth of her skin on his gave him a feeling of melting into her.

For a long moment that was all Ben wanted, just to touch her, to enjoy loving Callie in this small but intimate way. But then, he looked at her angelic face, her full lips and her closed eyelids, highlighted in grays and pinks, the curve of her neck as it disappeared into the collar of her coat, and the wispy curls that framed the entire work of art so sensually, and a stronger desire took over.

He leaned in, careful to keep some space between them so as not to tempt him to go too far, and breathed her name into her ear, allowing the longing within him to saturate the word.

She trembled fiercely, and Ben worried her knees might buckle, but she clung to the doorframe for support. He reacted to the intensity of her reciprocated longing as he pressed his lips, tenderly, but hungrily to hers. Her reply came quickly as she matched the action, eagerly crushing her lips against his. They remained there, caught in the current, unable to move or breathe as the mysterious and powerful connection bound them together with an inseparable bond.

The fire between them was a raging inferno now, burning through everything in Ben's mind, filling his heart, flinging open every door that had been locked, tearing down every wall that had been built.

In his mind, he saw every beautiful moment with Callie, every laugh, every smile, and every tear. And he saw future moments that he hoped for, moments when they would hold each other without boundaries, and all of Ben's fears would crumble into dust because of this remarkable woman's acceptance and love.

Motion and time stopped as the universe seemed to contract around them, consisting only of the space that they shared in that extraordinary moment.

Though his body and soul wanted her with a fervor he didn't know was possible, he reached deep down and found that part of him that knew that loving someone meant respecting them, and respect meant limits to protect them.

Like pulling himself out of quicksand, grasp by slippery grasp, and kick by sliding kick, Ben fought to regain control.

Callie needed to breathe, to go inside, to sleep, and he needed to wait, be a gentleman, date her, love her for all she was before...

With a stab of inexplicable pain and a groan that came from the core of his being, Ben pulled away. He removed his hand from her face and stepped back, way back.

Frozen in place, Callie wasn't breathing, and Ben started to panic.

"Callie! Breathe!" he nearly shouted at her.

At last, leaning forward, she sucked in a breath of air. Ben slipped his gloves back on and grabbed her arms, trying to steady her.

Her eyes were still closed, and Ben realized that might not be helping her get her equilibrium.

"Callie! Open your eyes and breathe."

As she obeyed, and Ben gazed into them, her eyes were wild and unfocused. Gradually, as she sucked in breaths of air, they began to return to normal.

"I'm so sorry," he said, his voice conveying a mixture of pleasure and concern. "I didn't realize how long you were holding your breath, and, well, I wasn't quite prepared for all of that, and I didn't mean to…"

Callie held up her hand as if to tell him to stop, and he dutifully fell silent. Moments passed as she fought to return to normal, and Ben noticed she didn't look cold anymore. Small beads of sweat clung to her forehead.

Well, at least the kiss served some useful purpose, he mused.

Finally, Callie leaned back against the doorframe and offered him a wobbly smile. "I'm not sure what to say. I'm kind of speechless."

"Now *you're* the one stunned into silence?" Ben teased.

"I don't understand what this thing is between us, Ben, but it's… it's powerful and a little scary. How did you stop? I'm not sure I could have."

Ben lightly grasped Callie's hands, careful not to restart the wildfire. "I don't know what it is either, and yes, it's something we're going to need to talk about and figure out together. But, I'm never going to disrespect you, regardless. I'm not going to cross into territory that I haven't yet earned."

She smiled at him, gratitude and respect shining in her eyes. "You are a keeper, Mr. Ben Sawyer," she said, quoting a line from Ms. Essie, "and a gentleman too."

Chuckling, he shook his head. "Don't give me too much credit. I'm absolutely sure I've never struggled with anything more than I just did in pulling myself away from you."

"Good to know," she replied with a flirtatious grin.

"Alright," he announced, "it's ridiculously late, and though I know I've sufficiently warmed you up, it's cold out here, and after my charms wear off, you're going to freeze, so off you go."

Ben reached for the door and opened it for Callie. He could hear Lee's gaming booming up from the basement and felt much better knowing she wouldn't be alone.

"Goodnight, Miss LeVray," he said, kissing her gloved hand. "I'll see you in the morning."

She gave him one last, longing smile that almost sent him right back into her arms, but he swallowed hard and turned to go.

"Oh..." He stopped and turned back. "And lock this door, please."

"Goodnight, Ben. Sweet dreams." She smiled as she began to close the door.

As he descended the stairs and headed for his car, he chuckled once more. "Oh, they'll be sweet, alright. Very sweet."

CHAPTER 16
THE RESCUE

When Ben returned to his car and started his engine, he took a moment to savor every happy and life-giving emotion that the night had brought him. He was in love with this extraordinary woman and, for the moment anyway, she seemed to care deeply for him too despite all the confusion he'd caused her.

The kiss had deepened and widened the already strong connection between them. With each step forward in their relationship, Callie was being systematically intertwined with his heart and he with hers. They only controlled the progress of the connection; the strength of it seemed beyond their capability to contain. Though the physical attraction was certainly powerful, it wasn't hard for Ben to separate that from the genuine love he had for her soul, her heart, and her character. He wanted more of simply sitting with her, hearing her voice, plunging into the depths of her pains and joys, and experiencing each moment together, no matter what it brought. His need for those moments rivaled his longing for physical closeness, even though that desire was so intense that every time he touched her, it threatened to evaporate every ounce of his well-rehearsed self-control.

Though a part of Ben wished things could stay just as they were, for the first time since he'd met her, he wasn't overcome with panic at the thought of Callie knowing his secret. He was beginning to know her, the deeper parts of her that few others knew, and what he found there comforted him. Callie might be strong enough. She might care enough. She might just have the right kind of heart to understand and accept him. The possibility sent a wave of peace and hope through him, feeding his starving heart with the nourishment it had needed for a very, very long time.

Shaking his head in wonder, he glanced behind him and then backed out of her driveway. How all of this had happened was incredible! Meeting Callie, her needing his help first, but then him needing her so much more. Amidst the sadness of her dad's stroke, something beautiful had blossomed, like a delicate flower blooming in a harsh, barren desert. For the first time in many years, perhaps the first time ever, Ben's heart was open, the old walls gone.

As he drove away from Callie's house, down Lantern Street toward the main turnoff, alarm ripped through him as he glanced in his rearview mirror and saw the old black Dodge he'd seen twice before. It was parked on Callie's street but facing in the opposite direction from which he'd first noticed it, about half a block behind him. Fear gripped his chest at the same moment that he heard a gunshot split the quiet night air.

It only took half a second for Ben to react as gut-wrenching terror cut through him like a machete, hacking every newborn hope and dream to pieces.

Spinning his car around, he stomped on the gas pedal

as two more gunshots rang out. He pulled back in front of the LeVray house just in time to see a black figure dart for the Dodge. For a split second, he considered running after the man, but the looped track of Callie's name repeating in his head refocused his priorities.

He bolted from his car, not bothering to turn it off, and tore toward her front door, pieces of his breaking heart trailing behind him.

A desperate cry came from the core of his being as the porch came into view, its soft shadowy light dimly illuminating Callie's slumped figure.

"Callie!" Ben's tortured scream exploded from him like a bomb as every fiber of his being protested the reality of what he was seeing.

"No! No! please, no!"

Rushing onto the porch, he knelt beside her, his pants absorbing a small pool of her blood. She wasn't wearing her coat, and blood trickled down her bare left arm, crimson streams on beautiful white porcelain.

Panic surged when he saw blood near her left ear, but he soon assessed it to be from a scrape where her head had probably hit the siding as she fell. Her body shivered, and a flicker of hope cast a dim light in his desperate soul.

"She's alive!" he whispered to his shattered heart.

"Callie!" He lowered his voice as the reality that she was still alive and could possibly hear him took control of his reactions.

He ripped off his gloves, tossing them into the night, and kicked open the front door. As he lifted Callie delicately into his arms, blood splattered onto his clothes.

"Lee!" he shouted as loudly as he could, hoping he'd hear him over the sounds of his gaming, even if he was wearing headphones.

When he'd shoved the door closed, he set Callie gently on the floor. Kneeling beside her, he grasped her arm with both hands. Immediately, he felt the draw begin, much stronger this time, confirming that Callie's condition was serious. In desperate suspense, he waited for her green eyes to open.

As he held his breath, he looked for where she'd been hit, as he knew that soon the blood would stop flowing, and it would be harder to tell. He followed the trail of blood on her arm and saw a torn bit of fabric with thick blood around it on her left shoulder. Careful to keep contact with her skin, he pulled her sleeve down and away from her shoulder, exposing the wound. The bullet had entered above her left collarbone. He set his hand directly over the spot as he heard Lee bounding up the stairs.

"Ben?" he questioned in surprise. Then, a heart-wrenching cry pierced the air, and Lee fell to his knees beside Ben.

"What? What?" Lee stammered, but Ben didn't have time to explain.

"Lee, call 911, then bring me the thickest blanket you have."

For half a second, Lee sat frozen, but then he scrambled to his feet and ran from the room.

Ben continued to search for wounds, but now, with no blood flowing, it was hard to determine as the dress's black material obscured the blood splotches.

Bending down, he softly kissed Callie's lips. "Callie, can you hear me? Sweetheart, I need your help."

Unexpectedly, Callie's lips formed a weak smile at Ben's voice and kiss, and her eyelids fluttered. Ben knew what was coming, but all that mattered was Callie staying alive, staying with him.

As she continued blinking, a look of peace and wonder filled her face. Joy tried to push its way into his consciousness, but the terror of potentially losing her overshadowed most of it.

"Ben!" Callie whispered. He lowered his head, so his face was inches from hers. She blinked again and Ben imagined the disorientation that was playing out in her senses.

"Callie, keep breathing and don't move. I know it feels like you can, but please, please stay very still."

After blinking once more, she opened her eyes wide. He was surprised there wasn't more shock in her expression.

"They're blue!" she exclaimed delightedly, as she focused intently on his face. Her voice was ecstatic, filling the somber space around them with a revival of hope and joy.

A look of pure pleasure filled her face as she stared at him, and he knew she was seeing him fully for the first time.

Though he couldn't help but allow some of her overflowing joy to penetrate his heart, it still mingled with his terror as tears dripped down his cheeks and dropped onto hers.

"What's blue, sweetheart? What are you seeing?"

"Your eyes! They're brilliant blue, like a perfect, cloudless sky. And I can see your soul too, and it's beautiful, Ben! Beautiful and good!"

Though her voice was weak, her eyes shone with radiant love. Ben's heart swelled and twisted inside as he tried to manage the emotions that flooded him as well as the physical demands that drew his strength and focus. It all threatened to overtake his ability to think clearly, so he could do what was necessary to save her life.

"Callie!" He exhaled, and a spark of hope began to break through him, sending a fresh torrent of tears down his face.

Lee returned and set a thick blanket beside Ben as he talked on the phone with the emergency dispatcher.

"She's been shot!" Lee shouted, staring at Callie's bare shoulder. "Hurry, oh please, hurry! Yes, we're keeping pressure on it," he conveyed, noting Ben's hand pressed against the wound.

Lee paced a few feet away as he continued talking to the dispatcher.

Ben leaned in close to Callie. "I need to wrap you up, get you warm, but I need to know if there are any more wounds. I know you're not feeling pain right now, but I need to let that pain come back for a minute, so you can tell me if anywhere else hurts. Do you understand?"

Though confused, she nodded.

"Callie, I'm so sorry." A few more tears escaped as he loathed the idea of letting any pain return to her. "On the count of three, I'm going to let go. Just tell me as quickly as you can where it hurts." His voice came out tight and filled with anguish, though he was trying to communicate comfort and a sense of reassurance.

Nodding again, she continued to stare at his face.

"One, two, three."

He removed his hands and within a few seconds, Callie's face contorted in pain, making Ben feel like a sword had pierced his heart.

"My side!" Callie whispered through desperate gasps of air. She squirmed and squeezed her eyes shut.

As quickly as he could, Ben followed the outline of her body down each side and finally saw it: a hole in her dress, spots of thick blood, and a few drops of fresh blood mingling with it. Grabbing the seams of her dress, he ripped it open. The wound was on her left side at the narrowest part of her waist, but he didn't see an exit wound. That meant two bullets were lodged in her body.

"Okay, sweetheart, I've got it. Is there pain anywhere else? Anything?"

Vigorously, she shook her head, her body beginning to tremble in distress. Though he had heard three shots, it appeared that, thankfully, one had missed its mark.

Callie groaned in pain, and Ben threw off his coat and jacket and unfolded the blanket, wrapping it around her hips and legs but keeping the wounds visible for the paramedics to see and work on when they arrived.

"Ben, please!" Callie begged, arching her back in agony, which Ben could almost feel himself.

With one hand, he covered the wound on her side, and with the other the wound on her shoulder. Though he didn't need to touch the wounds directly, the pressure and direct contact ended the pain and bleeding quicker while also offering an unquestionable pretense for anyone looking on for him to continue touching her.

As he waited for her pain to subside and the draw of strength to resume, he lay down on the floor beside her, tucking his body as close to hers as possible while keeping his hands in position, trying to keep her warm, make as many points of skin contact as possible, and manage his fatigue, as he knew that soon he'd be too tired to even sit up.

As he felt Callie's body relax and his strength fill her with wholeness once again, Ben was indescribably thankful that he had this to give to her. He desperately hoped that this time it would be enough.

The irony was not lost on him that only an hour earlier he had been doing everything possible to avoid the slightest touch, but now, here he was, trying to connect with her skin in every way possible.

As Callie started breathing more easily again, the blood flow from both wounds slowed and then stopped, though his hands and his white shirt were covered in it. Callie's eyes remained closed for several minutes, but when they opened again, they focused much more quickly, never straying from Ben's face. Even in this trauma, the fire moved between them, and, curiously, its presence seemed to be slowing the drain of strength from him.

The euphoric kickback was more intense as well, but Ben's terror over losing Callie eclipsed most of its positive effects though it helped to keep him somewhat focused, taking the edge off the worst of his panic.

Lee came back into the room, still holding the phone but not speaking into it.

"They're on their way," he said, panic still audible in his voice. "Be here in about five minutes."

"Lee, now tell them to search for a black Dodge Monaco." Anger at Callie's attacker overflowed, causing Ben to clench his teeth as he spoke.

"Ben!" Lee bent down beside him and placed his hand on Ben's shoulder, noticing the tears dropping onto Callie's face and the contorted effort he was making to keep pressure on Callie's wounds, but unable to understand or process more than that.

Just then, Lee saw Callie's open eyes.

"Cal!" He breathed a sigh of relief. "Hang in there! Help is coming. Please hold on! I can't lose you too. I can't!" Lee's voice cracked, and tears trickled down his face. Blood was everywhere, and Ben could imagine and relate to the fear Lee was experiencing.

"Lee, hurry!" Ben whispered. "They'll lose the chance to catch the demon who did this to her."

Lee stood, but he kept his eye on them both as he spoke into the phone again.

"Ben?" Callie's breathing sounded labored, and Ben wondered if the weight of him practically covering her was keeping her from breathing easily. He shifted slightly while still trying to maintain maximum contact. He'd gladly give her everything he had inside of him, spill out every ounce of strength to keep her alive, but he knew there was still no guarantee.

This was only temporary, and that was the curse. As long as he stayed here, kept touching her, kept pouring himself into her, she'd survive, but he couldn't heal her. The wounds and the damage remained, and he had no power to change that. He wished with all his might that he could, but she'd need doctors and time for that. They would have to repair the damage, take out the bullets, and sew her back together. All he could do was sustain her until then. By stopping the bleeding and keeping her still and out of pain, Ben desperately hoped he'd buy her the time she needed.

"Shh," he soothed, not wanting her to talk too much lest she begin moving around. "You're alright. I've got you now. Please, Callie, fight hard. Please, please don't even think about checking out on me. You owe me another date, remember?"

"But, I'm fine," she whispered. "I feel normal now."

A fresh build-up of tears threatened to spill down his face and drip into her hair. She didn't understand.

"I know, but I'm going to have to let go. I'm going to have to let them take you, let them fix you up. This"—he increased the pressure on his hands, so she'd understand— "this only works while I'm touching you, but it can't fix you permanently. It's only something I can give temporarily. Can you understand?"

She blinked in response, though he knew there was no way she could really understand it. He didn't even understand it. He had little experience openly helping anyone like this. In the past, he'd just run away from it.

Lovingly, he pressed his cheek against hers, blood from her scraped face smearing on his. "When they come to take you, and I have to let go, you have to fight hard. Please, Callie. I can't live without you."

Tears spilled from them both as the seriousness of the situation finally registered in Callie's mind. As she pressed into his cheek, she offered him a weak smile. "I'm not going to let go of you, Ben Sawyer. I'm going to hold onto you too."

When he placed several desperate kisses across her bloody face, he felt the draw of strength diminish a little more, though fatigue was now causing his hands to shake.

As Lee returned, having concluded his call, Ben heard the wail of sirens. Lee knelt by Callie's right side and grabbed her hand as he stared at Ben.

"How in the world are you doing that?" Lee asked with admiration, not suspicion. "I see no fresh blood at all, not even on her cheek."

But Ben couldn't answer, too overcome by everything that his body and soul were experiencing, the draw of power from him and the intensity of the kickback from the giving, the sorrow over the real possibility of losing her, the familiar pulse cycling between them, and the depth of his love for Callie. All he could do was lie there next to her and give everything he had, transfer every last molecule of this mysterious gift inside of him to keep her breathing and alive and, in doing so, keep himself alive with her.

CHAPTER 17
THE REVELATION

A moment later as the three of them lay in a huddled mass of tears, blood, fear, and hope, they heard footsteps and shouts approaching the front door. Lee jumped up and flung it open, but Ben stayed where he was, determined to remain there, sustaining Callie until the paramedics were ready to take over and begin the process of healing her.

He leaned close to Callie's ear, knowing he had only a moment and then they'd be separated for who knew how long. "Be strong, sweetheart. I promise I'll be here when you wake up. I'll be here, so you need to be too. Deal?"

When she turned her head, she pierced him with joy as he saw the overflowing happiness in her face. "Deal," she said in a soft and intimate tone that spoke of the new level of closeness their hearts had reached. "And, by the way, I like it when you call me sweetheart."

Returning her smile, he kissed her lips one last time. He was amazed that she hadn't overwhelmed him with questions or succumbed to panic as she experienced something that should have been impossible. Most of his previous experiences with helping others had been that way.

Peaceful and calm, she seemed to be in wonder at it all. But then Ben didn't understand how this all worked physiologically for those he helped. Maybe she was in shock from the blood loss and horror of the initial trauma. Maybe that shock was keeping her from reacting like she would otherwise. He wasn't sure, but her calm demeanor had helped him to remain focused while assessing her condition and offering her aid.

Three paramedics surrounded them. One of them, a short, stout man with a kind face, knelt on Callie's right side and checked her vitals. Though Ben slid his hands off her wounds, he kept them in contact with her skin, determined to keep her out of pain and thriving for as long as he could, even if it raised some suspicions.

"She's doing well. Unbelievable! There's no active bleeding here," the paramedic said as he stared at the wounds and shook his head in disbelief. He stared at Ben with an expression of awe and confusion.

A gentle hand touched Ben's shoulder. "We're going to help her now," a woman's voice said softly. "We need you to give us space, so we can prepare her for transport. You've done an incredible job here, but we've got her now."

In what felt like the slowest of motions, Ben let go of Callie and moved out of the way. Drained and disoriented, Ben felt like he was waking from a deep sleep.

Noticing Ben's struggle, Lee came up and put an arm around him, helping Ben to his feet. "Man, Ben, you look half dead. Are you alright?"

Ben nodded but kept his eyes fixed on Callie. Her eyes were closed, and her breathing had become more labored.

Evidence of the pain's return was clear, as her face paled, and her smile withered.

The medics were all around her now, calling out numbers and diagnosing her condition with words that Ben didn't understand. Though he knew she was in good hands, and he understood this was what had to happen, that didn't make watching her suffer any easier. Every time he helped a person in pain, he felt compassion for their misery followed by joy in relieving it, but he'd never felt such personal anguish as he did right now, watching the woman he loved in agony.

Grateful for his strength and support, Ben leaned against Lee. Although Ben was larger than Lee, Lee felt as solid as a rock, and Ben guessed he was channeling the adrenaline of the last few minutes into his effort. Though Lee couldn't help his sister, he could help Ben, and he was doing his best.

As Ben watched, Callie's wounds began to bleed again, but the paramedics addressed the problem as best as they could. As they brought in a stretcher and lifted Callie onto it, the stout paramedic kept glancing at Ben, amazement and respect in his eyes. As the truth of it wasn't at all what the man thought, Ben felt a little guilty for the admiration he displayed.

After they wheeled Callie out the front door, wrapping her in heated blankets, Ben turned to Lee. "You need to go with her. They'll let you 'cause you're family. I'll meet you there. You need to be there with her and keep talking to her. Don't let her give up. Please."

"Hey." Lee looked directly into Ben's anguished eyes. "Ben, you're family! You just saved my sister's life, and anyway, how in the world are you going to drive? You can barely stand up."

"Listen to me." Ben tried to keep his head up so he could sustain eye contact with Lee despite the weariness weighing him down like heavy bricks. "I didn't save her, not yet anyway. I just kept her alive until they"—he gestured toward the retreating group—"could get here. Go, Lee! Please! Stay with her. I'll be right behind you."

Lee caught Ben's urgency, and he helped Ben to a nearby chair, then turned to follow the paramedics. In the doorway, he turned back to look at Ben. "Thank you. You're obviously in love with my sister, and I'm, well, I'm so glad she has you... We have you. I don't understand what you just did, but I know it took everything you had, and I can't express..."

Lee couldn't finish, unaccustomed as he was to conveying such deep emotions. Ben offered him a warm smile, letting him know that he understood, then waved him toward the door.

Moments later, Ben heard sirens as the ambulance raced off, carrying Ben's heart with it into the night.

AFTER THE PARAMEDICS LEFT, a team of police officers descended on the LeVray home. One of them, a jovial African-American man with a bald head and the biggest smile Ben had ever seen, brought Ben a glass of water and sat down next to him. His name tag said "Sergeant Evans."

"Brother, you okay?" he asked, glancing at Ben's bloody hands and clothes and his slumped, lifeless posture.

"I'm not sure," Ben replied, gulping the water like his life depended on it. "That all depends on what happens to her."

"Man, I get it," Officer Evans replied, nodding. "My

girl's my life too. Anything happens to her, and I'm done for. Your girl's in good hands though, and those paramedics were talkin' 'bout you like you were some kinda god or somethin', the way you kept her alive."

He paused, but Ben just shook his head, so Officer Evans continued. "I know you're spent, and I know you want to get goin' to be with her, but we want to catch this bastard, and it sounds like you're the only witness, so I need to get your story. We'll do our best to get him off the streets."

"Do you have any idea who would do this?" Ben asked through clenched teeth.

"Mr. LeVray just busted a major drug dealer, put him away for life. The lowlife was part of a large ring of gangs, drug dealers, and all-around bad guys, the worst of the worst. Our guess is they wanted to take Mr. LeVray out, but with him already in pretty poor shape and hard to get at, they went for the next most precious thing to him."

"Not just to him!" Ben spat out angrily.

Evans nodded. "This is going to be a tough one. When someone is as nasty and as connected as these characters, it's hard to figure out which direction to look."

"Since you didn't catch him tonight, I'm assuming she's still in danger," Ben stated more than asked.

"We're sendin' security to the hospital, and we'll be keepin' it tight 'round her and her brother till we find somethin' out."

Ben had his own ideas about tight security.

For the next ten minutes, Ben told the officer everything he knew about the black Dodge, the figure running in the night, the vague look at a face he'd seen through the windshield, the shots he'd heard, and how he had found Callie on the porch.

"I can't figure out why she came back outside," Ben said frustratedly.

"We found a purse outside next to where you found her. Was that hers?"

Then Ben remembered. She'd set her purse down on one of those wicked wicker chairs. He didn't recall her retrieving it when she went inside. That thug must have been lying in wait for her. Likely, he'd watched Ben leave, and when she stepped back out to get the purse…

But Ben couldn't relive the scene right now. He needed to get to the hospital.

When he tried to stand, he swayed, and Officer Evans caught him by the arm.

"No, sir. You won't be drivin' yourself to the hospital like this."

"I have to go," Ben insisted.

"Course you do. We got some help comin' for you. Be here in a few minutes. Why don't you head to the kitchen and clean yourself up a bit? You alright on your own?"

Nodding, Ben turned and moved sluggishly toward the kitchen. As he walked, he was surprised to feel a little of his strength returning. Usually, after helping someone as seriously injured as Callie, it took him much longer, usually days, to recover.

As he washed his hands and arms, he watched the blood swirl and drain down the sink, feeling wrong somehow, like he was washing off something infinitely precious. With a wet paper towel, he cleaned off his face, though once again he felt saddened by the erasing of what was hers off and away from him.

When he finally turned from the sink, he was greeted by the warm, loving arms of Ms. Essie.

"Mr. Ben Sawyer!"

Despite the blood on his shirt, Ms. Essie held him close, her voice and her presence bringing healing and comfort. Guarded by the truth of his reality, Ben had never been a hugger, but now he sank into the kind arms of the woman who had become like a mother to him. The weight of the last hour hit him hard, and a dam inside broke loose.

Only one other time in his life could Ben remember weeping like that; a night similar to this one, when he had lost someone precious to him.

As Ms. Essie stroked his back, Ben let all of it flow out of him in a flood of tears. "Now, you're alright, Mr. Sawyer," she soothed. "You hear me? You're alright, and Miss Callie will be alright too."

The words were steady and sure, and Ben felt them sinking into him, penetrating his fear and doubt.

Ms. Essie was about eight inches shorter than Ben, so the difficulty of standing comfortably in the embrace finally caused him to release her and reach for another paper towel to clean his face once more.

Ms. Essie grabbed Ben's arm and led him to one of the now familiar stools surrounding the LeVrays' kitchen island.

When she brought him another glass of water, setting it down on the counter in front of him, Ben felt her eyes rest on his hand. It took him a minute to realize what she was looking at. His thumb, the one he had sliced with a knife, was completely healed. No scab, no scar, nothing of the injury remained.

Slowly, she circled the island and sat on the stool across from Ben, placing her elbow on the countertop and leaning her chin on her hand, keeping her eyes focused on Ben. She looked tired, and given that it was about two in the morning, he guessed she'd been awakened from a deep sleep, no doubt by one of the cops who knew about her connection to the LeVray family.

Despite her weariness, a smile worked its way across her unusually youthful face. Her eyes shone with the dawn of new understanding, and Ben interpreted her expression. Ms. Essie knew about him. Somehow, she knew. He didn't understand how that was possible, but she did.

"Mr. Ben Sawyer!" she boomed, but then deliberately lowered her volume. "You are. I knew it; I really did!"

Confused by her words, Ben shook his head, his mind tired and unfocused. "I am what?"

"You are Succouri!" She slapped her palm on the countertop and beamed with delight.

"I'm what?" Feeling lost, he wondered if his weariness was affecting his ability to hear and think.

Ms. Essie let out a laugh that sounded like she had inherited the world on a platter.

"Succouri!"

"Ms. Essie," Ben said, shaking his head again in utter confusion. "I have no idea what you're saying."

"Did you cut that thumb, deep and long, and now that cut's plain gone?"

Ben hesitated but finally nodded.

"Did you just keep that precious child livin' with your touch till help arrived?"

Reluctantly, Ben again confirmed with a nod, releasing a long breath of air as he did.

"Then," she pointed at him in triumph—"you're Succouri! No doubtin' it."

Leaning forward, he looked directly into her eyes,

shaking his head as he tried to convey how confused he was by her words. "I'm truly lost, Ms. Essie. I have never heard that word before in my life."

Now Ms. Essie frowned, also looking bewildered. Obviously, she expected him to know the word and its implications, and she was as baffled as he was that he had no idea what she was talking about.

A moment of silence hung between them, and abruptly Ben realized that right now, he just didn't care. He didn't have the energy for this complex conversation. Callie needed him, and he'd promised Lee he'd be there. The time spent talking with the police officer had delayed him far longer than he had anticipated, and now this conversation was threatening to hold him here even longer.

Looking away from Ms. Essie, Ben raised both hands in surrender. "Obviously, you and I have a lot to talk about. I don't know how you know things about me or what that... that word you said is, but right now I have to get to Callie and Lee. I have to be with them. I have to know if she's—"

"Yes!" she said, with a single nod of her head. "Let's be goin'."

"I can drive."

"Oh no ya ain't," she insisted. "You're needin' to recharge those batteries. Come on." She had already crossed in front of him and was beckoning like he was keeping her from an important engagement.

As Ben followed her out of the house, he stepped around officers who were still examining the scene. Leaving the porch, he spotted Callie's small black purse and wished he could travel back in time and change everything.

•   •   •

BEN WAS the subject of a few wide-eyed stares as he rushed into the emergency room at St. Luke's Hospital. His clothes were still covered with blood, so Ms. Essie had dropped him off, promising to return after retrieving clean clothes from his apartment.

Though he still didn't understand how it was possible, he had mostly recovered, apart from a general feeling of exhaustion and the fact that it was nearly three a.m., and he had hardly slept at all the night before.

As he scanned the nearly empty waiting area for Lee, he couldn't help remembering how many times he'd come in and out of this hospital with Callie on his arm over the last few days. Never in his wildest dreams would he have imagined he'd be coming to the hospital for her. Two LeVrays occupied rooms here now, and, from Ben's perspective, that was two too many.

Ben spotted Lee characteristically pacing behind the seating area. When he saw Ben approaching, he offered him a warm but weary smile. "You're looking better." Lee tried for a teasing tone, but it betrayed his stress and exhaustion.

"I am. Any word?"

"She did pretty well in the ambulance." Lee paused for a breath. "Damn, Ben, you're going to be a legend around here. No one knows how you got her to stop bleeding like that. They struggled with it, and they had all the right, well, medical stuff. But in the end, I kept hearing the word 'stable,' so I think that's a good thing. They gave her some pretty good sleep juice, so not another word out of her after we left."

Knowing that Callie hadn't suffered for long after she left him, brought Ben relief. "And now?" Ben coaxed, trying to get Lee to stay focused on the topic and share more of what he knew.

"I haven't heard much since they took her." Lee gestured down the hallway. "If someone wanted to develop an effective form of torture, this would be it." He chuckled humorlessly, waving his hand at the space around them.

Being forced to sit and wait was about as far from Lee's comfort zone as possible. He'd already had his fill of it over the last few days with visiting his dad.

Ben considered inquiring at the reception desk but knew they would have told Lee if there was any news. As his nerves buzzed energy into his system, Ben didn't feel much like sitting either, but he was too fatigued to pace, so he leaned against the wall as Lee resumed his motion.

After a few passes, Lee stopped and leaned on the wall next to him. "I saw the police as I left. Did they catch up to the car?"

"No." Ben sighed in frustration. "They think this has something to do with that criminal your dad just put away for life. Some kind of revenge thing, but they don't know exactly who yet."

Anger hardened Lee's face with a look that Ben had never seen him express before. As Lee was open and generous by nature, the expression came across as severe.

"Why didn't they target me? Why her?" Lee balled his hands into fists, and Ben set a hand on his shoulder.

"I don't know. Maybe they thought she'd be an easier target because of her poor eyesight. You know, because she couldn't see them coming or wouldn't be able to identify them if she survived. These are evil, heartless monsters, Lee."

"Is she still in danger since they didn't quite finish the job?" Lee spat out the words, and his face turned red as his anger built. Ben knew he needed to calm him down, but he wasn't going to lie to him.

"Yes, probably. But they're going to be protecting you and her. And…"—Ben paused and set his face in an expression of unyielding determination—"Lee, I am not going to allow anything else to happen to her. You can be assured of that."

As Ben thought about what Officer Evans had told him, he became increasingly angry with himself. He should have anticipated the danger. Something about that car had disturbed him the first time he saw it. Then after he'd spotted it outside the courthouse, he'd really felt alarmed, but he'd allowed all the questions and feelings related to his relationship with Callie and the incident in the kitchen with Ms. Essie to distract him from following up on his suspicions. He wouldn't make that mistake again.

Lee was silent for a time, and Ben could tell he was struggling with the flood of emotions brought about by all of this. Finally, Lee turned his tortured face to Ben.

"I could have lost my whole family, you know. I'm not sure I believe that my dad will ever wake up, and, well, I could have lost my sister if it weren't for you."

Ben looked squarely into Lee's eyes. "They are still here. They are both still here."

At Ben's words of reassurance, Lee's face softened and a look of gratitude, mixed with bewilderment, took shape. "It's so strange. When I met you that first time, I just had this weird feeling that you needed to be with Callie, that you just sort of belonged with us. It was like meeting an estranged relative or something and having this unexplainable connection. Despite your protests"—Lee paused to frown at Ben—"that feeling just got stronger. I didn't get it. I mean, I thought you were nice and all, and, well, I knew my sister sort of had an interest in you, but there was more to it than that. It made no sense at all until right now."

Ben nodded in understanding. "I felt the same way about you and Callie."

He paused as he considered how much he should share, given that he and Callie hadn't even had a chance to talk about it, though the secret was obviously no longer a secret between them anymore.

"Lee, I'm sort of a, well, a runner, I guess. I don't stay in one place, and I haven't had anywhere to call home in a very long time. When I met your sister, something in me switched on, like I woke up from years of sleep. I can't explain it either, but I'm grateful beyond words. If I had lost her tonight, and if I lose her now..."

Lee put a hand on Ben's shoulder. "My turn to remind you that she's still here. Thanks to whatever you did, she is still here."

Standing side-by-side in silence, they tried to comprehend the complexities and coincidences of their situation. At last, Lee released Ben's shoulder and leaned back against the wall, letting his gaze settle, unfocused, on the space in front of him.

"When Callie was lying there on the floor, she looked, well, something about the way she looked at you. It was like she was really seeing you. It was... well, it was something very strange that I don't understand. And then the way you helped her, completely stopped the bleeding." He shook his head. "In the ambulance, I saw her condition completely change. I mean, I know they were giving her meds and everything, but she seemed almost worse off. The whole thing is just kind of miraculous."

The old panic that Ben knew so well rose within him. These were the exact circumstances in the past that had caused him to run. Someone would have suspicions, no proof or facts, just suspicions, and he would escape before they could confirm them.

But this time, he couldn't run. His feet were stuck as if they were set in concrete because his heart was now tied to Callie's in a way he didn't think he could, nor would he ever want to, undo.

"Lee, I—"

"Are the two of you with Callie LeVray?" a female voice asked from behind them.

They spun around. A woman, who looked to be in her early forties, stood with her hands tucked inside her white doctor's coat. Her chin-length black hair shone in the fluorescent lights, and her round face displayed a calm expression that put Ben at ease.

"Yes," Lee replied.

"I'm Doctor Lane. I've been taking care of Callie since she got here, and I wanted to give you an update.

"Is she—?" Lee began, but Doctor Lane's smile and the look in her eyes cut off his question.

"Callie is doing well. She's in surgery right now to remove the bullets in her shoulder and her side. Neither seems to have caused significant or permanent damage, but we won't know for sure until we get in there and check it out. Her bleeding is under control, and thanks to the expert care of whoever found her, she didn't lose too much blood."

When Lee looked at Ben, Doctor Lane picked up on the message. She bowed her head in Ben's direction, her deep brown eyes showing admiration. As she looked at him, she seemed to notice the bloodstains on his clothes for the first time.

"Anyway, I need to get back to her, but I thought it good to let you know."

"When will she be out of surgery?" Ben asked.

"About an hour maybe, and then she'll need some time to recover. If you two want to go home and change, you have plenty of time for that. I'll be sure to send someone out to get you as soon as she's in recovery. We have some police officers around Callie for security. I'll point you two out to them as family, so they'll let you in to see her."

After offering the doctor their thanks, she retreated down the hallway, and Ben collapsed into the nearest chair, putting his elbows on his knees and leaning his forehead in his hands.

Callie would survive this. She'd recover and be alright. For the first time since he had found her on the porch, he let himself believe it. He wouldn't lose her. She'd make it. He'd given her everything he had, and this time it had been enough.

Something like fresh light and air flooded his veins, and he let out a breath that felt like it had been trapped inside of him for days. Lee sat next to him, and for several minutes they both breathed deeply, allowing their hearts to absorb the positive news.

At last, Ben looked over at Lee. "You should go home and change," he said. "Ms. Essie is bringing me some clothes from my apartment. She'll probably be here soon. I'll stay and let you know if anything changes. I know sitting around here isn't your cup of tea."

Though Lee looked like he wanted to argue, he nodded. "Alright. I'll tell you what, I'm going to go home, change, and get us something to eat. I'll be back in plenty of time. You sure you're alright here?"

"Definitely," Ben assured him with a chuckle. Leave it to Lee to think about eating the moment the worst of the crisis had passed.

After patting Ben on the back, Lee headed for the hospital's front doors. As he did, Ben remembered that Lee didn't have a car. When he turned to call after him, Ben saw several police officers moving to intercept him. Ben chuckled to himself, confident that Lee would get a police escort back to the house.

CHAPTER 18

THE RECOVERY

Callie was in the meadow again. Warmth and light wrapped around her as she opened her eyes, and the scene focused into pristine clarity. Flowers, birds, trees, and insects filled her vision as their colors and movement played out in the most incredible show Callie had ever seen. Hundreds of butterflies in all colors alighted on purple butterfly bushes and clusters of red asters. She could see it all in dazzling detail, every blade of grass, every petal, and every wing.

Smiling in delight, she took a deep breath. The sweet perfumes filled her lungs and made her feel weightless, almost airborne.

Presently, she realized she was holding someone's hand. When she turned, she looked straight into Ben's vivid blue eyes. His face glowed in the sunshine, and her heart throbbed with delight as she took in every attractive detail: the way loose strands of his dark brown hair fell over his forehead, the shape of his eyebrows, the depth of emotion in his eyes, the slope of his nose, the stubble around his upper lip and chin, the curve of his lips, and the warmth in his smile, which made her heart feel full and at peace.

As he opened his mouth to speak, Callie was mesmerized by how his eyes danced and twinkled.

"You owe me another date, sweetheart. Don't check out on me."

Somewhere deep inside, she knew those words, had heard them before, but where?

The scene abruptly morphed, and now she was standing next to Grace in her black concert dress. Ben was several yards in front of her, a look of stunned admiration on his face, his coat hanging precariously over one arm.

As he approached, she saw another picture of him to the side and realized it was a mirror. Two images of him advanced in slow motion. His eyes shone with something different now, a hunger and longing that mingled with a true expression of love. Grace laughed, but she sounded miles away.

"Callie, I can't tell you how incredibly beautiful you are!" Though the words were spoken with passion, Callie didn't need them to measure his sincerity. His face already conveyed the message. The words took a path through her ears to her heart, but what she saw in his eyes blazed an entirely different trail. They both had the same destination, but the routes they forged left different footprints behind.

Suddenly floating, Callie now viewed herself and Ben from above, like looking at a miniature model of a scene in a glass case. Then, everything went black.

"Callie, can you hear me? Can you wake up, sweetie? Try to wake up for me."

A woman's voice spoke, far away and fuzzy. Fighting

against the blackness, she longed to return to the mirrored room where she could see Ben's face with his eyes full of love and wonder.

The pain hit her first. Her shoulder and side throbbed, and her head felt like it had been struck with a hammer. She heard herself groan, but the sound seemed involuntary.

"Callie, it's time to wake up now," the voice said.

She wanted to sleep, to escape the pain.

"Callie, sweetheart, please," a gentle, familiar voice begged.

Ben!

Callie opened her eyes, expecting to see his face like she had in her dream, in perfect clarity, but instead, she saw only blurry images and indistinct faces. The woman and Ben appeared as dark silhouettes, fading into the unfamiliar surroundings. She knew this kind of vision well. Her heart fell with disappointment as she concluded that the other kind of vision, the full and perfect kind, was a reality available only in her dreams. She took a deep breath, trying to remember, to hold onto what she'd seen.

"That's it. Just take your time waking up."

The woman disappeared, and Ben's familiar form moved closer to her.

"Ben!" she whispered, the pain rising in her like a hot flame.

"It's so good to see those beautiful green eyes of yours." He breathed out a sigh of relief that made Callie feel warm despite the cold that saturated her body.

"Where?" she began, but her throat was too dry, and she could barely make herself audible.

"You're in the hospital. You're going to be alright. Thanks for keeping our deal," he said in a voice barely above a whisper.

Slowly, it all came back to her like a slideshow: gunshots, hitting the side of the house as she fell, Ben leaning over her, being cold, blood running down her arm. Then warmth, light, Ben's face in perfect detail, his gentle kisses, Lee's terror-filled expression, and Ben's body tucked against hers. The memories came fast and confused, terror and pain mixed with joy and relief. She remembered seeing, really seeing, like in her dream, but it wasn't a dream. She was overwhelmed, her mind still cloudy and unfocused.

"Ben, I..."

"I'm here, Callie. I'm here." His voice carried so much joy and relief that it momentarily calmed her confusion.

"I think your favorite dress is ruined." She tried for a weak smile, and Ben laughed, a sound ripe with happiness.

"I'll buy you a dozen more. And a dozen pairs of those terrible, wonderful shoes too."

She tried to hold her smile, but the pain stabbed her like a knife, and her smile turned into a grimace, followed by a moan.

"Callie!" Anguish resonated in Ben's voice, and he leaned in close to her ear. "I'm going to take away that awful pain, but please don't move around too much. You've got stitches, and we don't want those disturbed. Do you remember how I helped you before?"

Her foggy mind struggled to understand. Somehow she was sure she remembered seeing Ben's face like she'd seen it in her dream. She remembered moments of excruciating pain, followed by moments with no pain at all. It was all jumbled together, and she was sure she couldn't be remembering it accurately because what she was remembering was impossible.

"I... I don't know. I think so," she stammered, but she

wasn't sure anymore what was reality and what was just a dream.

"Do you remember being able to see me, really see my face?" Ben whispered, his voice filled with excitement.

What is Ben saying? That can't be right! That's impossible! She wondered if maybe she was still dreaming, but the fact that she could barely stay still as the pain built inside her made her doubt that she was asleep.

"But that wasn't real, was it?"

"Yes, it was real! When I touch you, it will happen again, but there are a lot of people nearby, so we need to be careful to keep this between us right now. Do you understand?"

Callie nodded, though she wasn't comprehending what Ben was saying at all.

"Close your eyes for a minute."

As she obeyed, she felt Ben's hands encircle her right hand. Smiling, she thrilled at the realization that this was the first time she'd felt his hands touch hers without gloves. Warm and gentle, his touch soothed her. At once, the heat from him expanded and spread quickly, like something had been injected into her veins, and it swept into every corner of her being. As it went, it cleared out everything unpleasant, all the pain, all the aches, all the exhaustion, and all the cold. As it flooded her body, she felt the familiar magnetic attraction she'd experienced with Ben grow between them as well. It rushed through her, filling her with a pleasant, comforting fire.

She took in an easy, relaxed breath, not understanding why she no longer felt any pain, not even the smallest twinge. Ben's soft lips brushed hers, sending a fresh wave of soft, soothing warmth through her veins.

It was him! Callie suddenly realized. *Somehow, the relief, the warmth, the fire, it's all coming from Ben!*

"Better?" he asked as his lips lingered inches from hers.

"Much better, thank you," she replied as the cobwebs cleared from her mind.

Ben drew a few inches away from her, but he maintained his grip on her hand.

"Now, open your eyes."

When Callie blinked, her vision flipped, like turning a page in a book. Her surroundings pulled in toward her, drawing everything closer like zooming in on a camera. Then it expanded in every direction, bringing objects into focus that had previously been far beyond the outer boundaries of her vision. The expanded scene brightened, like she'd stepped out of a dark room and into the brilliant sunlight. The hazy fog that had blended colors and edges into an indistinct mass lifted, and each object took on its own distinctive borders, depths, contours, and colors, separating from adjacent objects, and she could perceive distances, now able to determine which objects were nearer and farther from her without difficulty. As she stared in wonder, a gasp caught in her throat.

I know this. I remember this! This happened before when Ben touched me as I was bleeding on the floor. This is from him too! Somehow he's giving this to me.

Her gaze eagerly circled the room as she struggled to grasp the reality of what she was experiencing. She could see the accordion folds in the privacy curtains that hung beside her bed. She could read the bold red print on a sign on the back wall that said "Recovery." She could see the back of a woman through the open doorway, talking to what looked like a female doctor with shiny black hair and wearing a white jacket. She could see the wood grain in the doorframe and the imperfections in the paint on the wall.

And she could see Ben. As her eyes finished their sweep of the room, taking in all the new and amazing details, they found his face. Then there was nothing else that she wanted to see. He looked like he had in her dream, handsome and strong with kindness and love shining in his eyes. She remembered seeing those vivid blue eyes for the first time as he knelt over her, taking away her pain. He smiled at her, rejoicing at her expression as she experienced the world around her in a new and wonderful way.

"Ben!" That was all that she could manage as her heart and mind raced with excitement and disbelief. He placed a finger over his lips, reminding her that they were not alone.

If Ben's touch hadn't felt so real and the fire that moved between them hadn't been so familiar, yet something she'd never experienced in her dream, she could have convinced herself that this was, in fact, still her dream.

As she studied Ben's face, which she had longed to do so many times, enjoying the way his smile warmed the core of her heart, she saw something else in his expression: a note of sorrow that she didn't understand. She could see the fire too, that mysterious connection that pulled them toward each other and fueled a mutual longing. She guessed he could see the same thing in her eyes.

"How... How is this possible?" she asked, trying to keep her volume low despite her exuberance.

Ben glanced behind him, and Callie followed his gaze. The nurse approached the doorway, and a look of surprise filled her face as she saw Callie's wide-open eyes.

"Wow!" the nurse exclaimed, rushing in next to Ben. "When you wake up, you really wake up!"

She checked Callie's vitals on the machine next to her

bed. To Callie's continued amazement, she was able to see the nurse's look of shock.

"Everything looks perfect here." The nurse smiled and shook her head.

Ben shot Callie a subtle smile that spoke of the secret between them, and she smiled back at him.

"A few more minutes and then I'm going to give you something for the pain, so you can sleep for a while. You need rest. Your body's been through a lot of trauma. Oh, and your brother really wants to see you too, so don't hog her," she added, aiming the last statement at Ben.

"I won't," Ben promised. "Just give us another minute."

The nurse retreated into the hallway, but she didn't close the door, forcing them to continue talking in whispers.

When the nurse was out of earshot, Callie looked into Ben's eyes. "This is your secret! You're doing this, giving me sight! You... you saved my life, took away the pain!" she whispered with a mixture of wonder and gratitude.

Before he responded, the look of sorrow she'd seen before took over his features, replacing his joy from a few moments earlier. "Yes," he confirmed, then he paused as his eyes filled with tears. "But it isn't all good. There's a terrible side to it. Do you remember that too?" Breaking eye contact with her, Ben dropped his gaze to their intertwined hands.

Callie didn't understand. How could there be anything bad about the ability to give her sight and rid her of pain? Her excitement and happiness wouldn't allow her to process the sadness in Ben's face.

"I... I don't know. It's all hazy. Am I going to turn into a frog or something?" she teased, followed by a chuckle.

Keeping his gaze lowered, Ben didn't laugh, and for a moment Callie wished she couldn't see the intense pain in his face. As the euphoria, brought on by her newly acquired eyesight, settled, her heart gradually responded to his agony.

"I'm sorry," she said, realizing her joke was ill timed.

As Ben remained silent, Callie wished she could reach out and embrace him, but her left arm was in a sling, and he'd already warned her not to move around. She squeezed his hand instead, yearning to wipe the sadness from his face.

"What I have to give you isn't a cure," he said, raising his eyes to meet hers. "It's not healing. When I let go, everything will come back: the pain, the darkness, all of it. I'm so sorry!"

Such profound regret saturated his tone and filled his expression that, all at once, Callie understood. Ben could touch people and make them whole, which was wonderful and miraculous, but then he had to inevitably let go. Very soon, he would have to let go of her and watch the pain return and her world fade back into shadows. Every touch, every offer of help came with a price that his heart had to pay. All this time he hadn't wanted to touch her, not because he didn't want to give, but because he didn't want to let go and take it all away.

Now she understood the story about his mom, why he had said it was his fault, why he had felt responsible, why he ran, and why he hid his gift from everyone, especially her.

He took great pleasure in helping her; she could see that in his eyes, see how he loved it, how he even needed it. But then when the pain returned, it would feel like he was the cause. No longer would he feel that her near blindness was simply a random happening of the universe that had no connection to him. Instead, he would feel responsible for it.

That wasn't the truth, of course, but she could understand how he would see it that way.

As Callie's heart and mind filled with understanding and compassion for the heavy burden that his extraordinary gift placed on him, a surge of warmth passed between them, leaving Callie's skin tingling as it ebbed. They both sucked in a surprised breath, and Ben looked at Callie with alarm.

"Are you alright?"

"I think so. What was that?"

Ben chuckled. "I wasn't hiding anything when I told you I had no idea what this thing is that we feel between us. I really don't know."

As the feeling faded, the look of misery returned to Ben's face. She knew he was thinking about how short the time was before the nurse returned, and he'd need to let go of her and let her rest.

Callie waited until Ben's eyes locked on hers again before she spoke, trying to communicate as much compassion as she could. "It's okay to let go, Ben. I truly understand. I'm sorry about how painful it will be for you and has always been for you. Thank you for helping me, for taking away my burdens for a while, but please, please hear me. You don't own the burdens I carry, and you're not responsible for them. You have an incredible, wonderful gift, even if it's only temporary. And never forget, it saved my life, and that's permanent."

A faint expression of relief crossed his face, but it was still shadowed by sorrow and fear.

"But you might not feel that way after you get used to seeing and enjoying all that comes with that. And when I keep ripping that away from you, you might..." Ben looked back down at their hands. "Well, you could grow to hate me for that, and I would understand if you did."

Callie's heart broke. He didn't understand at all how she felt about him. Pulling her hand out of Ben's grasp, she placed it on his cheek, ignoring the flash of pain and darkness that blinked in and out of her consciousness. With her thumb under his chin, she lifted his head, forcing him to look into her eyes.

"That's impossible! Ben Sawyer, aren't you the one who told me you saw *me*, just Callie, whether I could see or not see, hear or not hear, walk or not walk?"

He nodded, hope flickering in his eyes.

"So, don't I get to feel the same about you? Don't I get to love you whether you make me see or not, cure my pain or not, just *you*, just Ben?"

A tear traced down Ben's face as relief and long-desired peace filled his eyes. He reached up and grasped her hand. "Miss LeVray," he whispered, emotion making his voice hoarse and heavy. "I love you. I truly do."

Callie smiled. Though his words filled her heart with a new kind of joy, for once, they weren't her only means of reading his heart. She could see love shining in his eyes.

CHAPTER 19

THE ANSWERS

For the next two days, Callie slept peacefully as her body worked to heal. Whenever she awoke, Ben held her hand, easing her pain, but they agreed that she needed to rest and let her body heal naturally as much as possible, so he often simply sat with her, watching her as she slept.

Still, her recovery was remarkable. The doctors couldn't understand how her vitals stayed so strong and how she was healing so quickly. Ben was surprised as well.

He knew he didn't have the power to heal, but after the strange surge of energy they both felt in the recovery room, Callie had never suffered the same intense level of pain, and her healing seemed to accelerate.

On the third day, Callie woke up feeling alert and rested. As she was in minimal pain, Ben gave Lee and her friends some space to visit her while he made several phone calls, arranging private security for Callie and Lee to augment that which was being provided by the police.

In the late afternoon, he returned to the hospital. As he approached Callie's room, carrying a fresh cup of her favorite chai tea and a cup of coffee for himself, Ben heard Lee call his name from behind him. Turning, Ben was immediately concerned when he saw Lee's distressed expression.

Over the last few days, Lee and Ben had bonded over their mutual love and concern for Callie, though Ben hadn't shared any more of his secret. Lee's teasing nature had returned, and Ben appreciated the feeling of being fully included as a member of the LeVray family.

Now, Ben was alarmed at the look of anguish on Lee's face.

"I'm on my way up to talk to Doctor Karl," Lee explained. "We were supposed to meet with him the morning that, well when all hell broke loose, but of course that never happened."

Ben nodded, remembering how he had planned to meet Callie and Lee at the hospital, but fate had taken them down a different road.

Nothing had changed with Callie and Lee's father. Callie had asked about him several times and wanted to go see him, but the doctors hadn't given her permission to get out of bed yet. Lee had bounced back and forth, and Ms. Essie, Grace, and even Lobster (though Ben still had never met him) had rotated schedules, sitting at Ronald LeVray's bedside. Callie felt better knowing he hadn't been abandoned.

"I think he's going to tell me there's no hope. Dad's only alive because of those machines. They've done everything for him, but there's been no change. I think we're going to have to choose whether to keep him alive like a vegetable, decaying before our eyes, or let him go." Lee bowed his head, and Ben set the drinks down on the floor so he could place his hand on Lee's shoulder.

"I'm so sorry!" Ben said compassionately. His heart ached for the days of stress and turmoil that this young man had had to face. Now he was carrying the burden alone because Callie couldn't help him.

"Do you want me to come with you?"

Lee looked up at Ben, gratitude in his eyes. "You need to be with her," Lee said, motioning toward the door. "But, somehow, could you prepare her for this? I know she's still weak and all, but I can't make this decision without her."

"I'll try," Ben replied, wishing the task could be avoided but knowing it could not.

"Thanks. Really, thanks." The gratitude Lee expressed carried far beyond this one task.

Turning around, Lee plodded down the hall, looking like a man heading to his execution.

Sighing, Ben considered what he would tell Callie. Though he didn't want to set back her recovery in any way, he understood that this was a decision they needed to make together.

Retrieving the drinks, Ben nodded at the warm smile of the security guard outside of Callie's room, then took a deep breath and headed inside.

"Hi," Ben greeted when he saw that Callie was awake and propped up in bed.

"Hi, yourself," she replied with a smile.

Ben bent to softly kiss her forehead before placing her cup on the tray near her right hand. Her left arm was still in a sling to keep her from disturbing the stitches in her shoulder. "One chai latte for the most beautiful patient in the hospital."

Callie laughed as she picked up the cup. "Well, I'm certainly the most spoiled one."

Pulling a chair up to her bed, he sat, sipping his coffee. Callie's adjustment to and acceptance of his secret astonished him. She seemed relatively unfazed by the constant changes that occurred for her now as the effects of uninhibited contact with him shifted her world back and forth, like having a light turned on and off. Though he couldn't imagine the difficulty in adapting to that, Callie was taking it all in stride.

The smile that came across her face when he touched her and her vision brightened and expanded thrilled him, but when it diminished again, he didn't see the unbearable pain and loss in her face that he had expected.

Callie lit up whenever he entered the room, and they had a chance to be together regardless of whether he was touching her or not. But every unimpeded touch felt like a gift to Ben. The pleasure of taking her hand or kissing her as she slept, without barriers or fear, filled him with happiness and a sense of wholeness he'd dreamed of having but never thought possible.

Because she had slept almost constantly over the last few days, they'd had little time to talk about everything, and Ben knew that the reality of it would take a while to sink in. A small part of him still worried that perhaps in time she'd grow weary of the burden and begin to resent him.

Callie leaned back into her pillows, cradling her cup like a treasured prize. "Thank you. I needed this. I thought hanging out for a few hours a day in Dad's room was confining. Lying here for nearly three days is downright cruel and unusual punishment. What I wouldn't give for one of our freezing cold walks in the park right now, cement bench and all."

Ben chuckled. "Now you sound like Lee. Just a little

longer and then I'll happily escort you anywhere you want to go, Miss LeVray."

Callie offered him an amused smile. "Why do I get the distinct feeling that you're going to continue to live up to your statement that life with you will be an adventure?"

"Of that, I have no doubt," Ben replied with another light chuckle. "But I think you've had quite enough adventure for a little while."

He glanced out the window, thinking about the pleasure it would be to walk with her outside in the cool fresh air, when he spotted the stuffed rust-orange lobster staring at them from the windowsill, like a disgruntled onlooker. He laughed despite the weight of his heart, and Callie gave him a puzzled look.

"The lobster?" he questioned, pointing at the window.

She laughed with him, then grimaced when it caused a stab of pain. "Oh, yes. Gracie and Lobster stopped by while you were out, and Lobster thought it was only fair that it stay here with me for a while. Evidently, it's going to be on a rotation, Dad gets it for a day, then it's my turn. Lucky me!" she said sarcastically. "Let's hope there's not many more rotations to go before I'm out of this place."

Callie paused to smile and sip her tea before finishing. "Despite your wonderful gift, I'm glad that most of the time I can't see that thing staring at me. I think it would creep me out."

"I could always hide it under the bed if you'd like. I don't know how I keep missing Lobster. It's uncanny."

"He doesn't stay long. I think he'd rather sit with Dad in a quiet room where he doesn't have to talk to anyone, or at least where no one is talking back to him."

Ben fidgeted with his cup as the topic of her dad reminded him of Lee's request. After a moment of silence,

Callie lowered her cup and looked at Ben. "Okay, out with it."

"What?" Ben was confused.

"Whatever's stirring around in that handsome head of yours. Let's hear it."

Ben shook his head, amazed once again at her ability to see right through him without the need for physical sight at all. "How do you do that? I can't hide anything from you, can I?" He grinned at the irony in his statement.

Tilting her head, she returned his smile. "Well, not for too long anyway," she teased. "I think it has something to do with that mysterious, well, whatever it is, that keeps us both, shall we say, a little off-balance. I know we've got a lot to talk about, and I have, um, only about ten thousand questions for you, but I get the feeling this isn't about *that*, is it?"

Ben leaned toward her. "I'll tell you everything I know whenever you want to know it, but I have to warn you, I don't know much. How I came to be this way, what it is, I'm nearly completely in the dark. But you're right. This isn't about *that*."

As Callie waited, Ben pondered his approach. He set his cup on the side table, then reached for Callie's hand, wanting her to see his face when he gave her the bad news.

"I just saw Lee in the hallway before I came in here. He, well, he—"

They were both startled by a soft knock at the door.

"Come in?" Callie questioned, caught off guard by the unexpected interruption.

"Evenin', you two," came the cheerful voice of Ms. Essie as she entered the room carrying a large bag.

"Ms. Essie!" Callie greeted enthusiastically. "Come on in."

As Ms. Essie approached, a delicious smell filled the air. Setting down her bag, she pulled out bowls, spoons, and a large container.

"I couldn't leave you all eatin' this terrible hospital food for days, so I brought you some soul food, yes indeed, food that'll warm you right down to your soul."

"Alright, Ms. Essie." Ben laughed. "You're really showing me up here. All I brought her was tea."

"Well, you ain't barely had a chance to leave this dreadful place in days, so don't you go comparin'.'"

She served up a full bowl of steaming chicken noodle soup and brought it to Callie's bedside. When she'd set it on the table next to Callie, she stepped back and placed one hand on her hip, giving Callie a good once-over. "You almost completely got your color back, Miss Callie, yes, you do. You're lookin' lovely!"

Laughing in disbelief, Callie put her hand on her head of loose curls. "I haven't had a shower in days, I've barely combed my hair, and I'm wearing the same gorgeous gown they put me in when I arrived. So, I think you're flattering me, Ms. Essie, but I love you for it!"

"No, no. You're just a lovely girl, and that's the truth of it," Ms. Essie replied with conviction.

She prepared a bowl for Ben, and he moved to retrieve it and pass out spoons. Then Ms. Essie served herself and sat contentedly in the recliner.

After a few bites, Callie let out a satisfied sigh. "This is like food from heaven! You're a lifesaver."

Ms. Essie boomed one of her contagious laughs. "Oh no, Miss Callie! That job's already belongin' to Mr. Sawyer here, for certain. He's the one with that magical touch."

Callie's expression shifted to surprise and alarm.

"It's alright," Ben reassured her, raising a hand and

chuckling under his breath. "I have no idea how, but Ms. Essie knows about me. We had a strange conversation about it after the ambulance took you away, a conversation we've never been able to finish."

Callie set her spoon down, concern still evident on her face. "How'd you find out?" she asked, directing her inquiry at Ms. Essie.

"Well, somethin' inside a me's been suspectin' since I met him, but nothin' I could figure. I've known enough of them to kinda know their way, if you know what I'm meanin'." She leaned forward and looked at Ben. "Then he cut himself real good with a knife that night we were at your house, and when I saw him again, there was nothin', just nothin'. After that, I heard those paramedics talkin' 'bout how he kept you alive, almost no bleedin', and strong. So, I knew it for certain, and I knew you'd be knowin' it too, Miss Callie. Mr. Sawyer here, he's Succouri." She finished her statement in triumph like she'd done that night in the kitchen.

"Let me stop you there," Ben said, raising a hand. "I don't know what that is. I know you think I should know, but, Ms. Essie, I've never heard that word before. What in the world is that?"

"How can you be one and not be knowin' it?" she questioned, shaking her head in genuine confusion. "Didn't the one who made you tell you?"

Setting down his bowl, Ben leaned toward Ms. Essie, feeling stunned and disoriented. "Made me? Someone made me like this?"

"Of course!" She laughed. "You wasn't born like that, Mr. Sawyer, magical life-givin' touch and all."

"How did…" He paused, trying to wrap his head around this new revelation. "How did someone make me like this?"

"You really ain't knowin', are you?" Bewilderment dominated her expression. "That ain't normal, not at all. That ain't the way it's supposed to be." She continued to shake her head in disbelief.

"What *is* the way it's supposed to be?"

"When a mature Succouri gets near the end of his time, he reaches a stage called 'the ripenin'. Only during this short window of time, he's able to be passin' along his gift by givin' away a piece of himself to save another. It might be a kidney or liver donation, sometimes bone marrow, even a blood donation can be doin' it. As a great final act, he's passin' the gift on and renderin' the receiver physically whole as the ability of healin' oneself rapidly is part of bein' Succouri. The giver is keepin' a small bit of strength after that, but it gradually fades. The mature Succouri will be careful with his choosin', wantin' someone who can fathom the gift and the responsibility that's comin' with it but still young enough that he's strong and can be managin' a full term himself and reachin' the ripenin'. Someone in his thirties or a little older is usually a good choice, but I've known one young as you, Mr. Sawyer. Acceptin' the gift is a matter of choosin'. It ain't done without the receiver's full knowledge and permission. It's the giver's job to teach the new one all he'll be needin' to maximize and manage the gift. It's the commitment he's makin' in the passin' of it."

Astounded by her words, Callie and Ben sat in silence for a moment. Then Ben spoke, his voice low and flat, tinged with bitterness. "Well, that would have been nice. No one told me anything at all."

Anger rose in him, yet Ben also realized for the first time that his life had been saved by someone just like him.

"When I was about twelve, strange things started happening when I touched people. It was horrifying, and I thought that maybe I was born, well, inhuman or something, and it had just taken a while to manifest."

"Twelve!" Ms. Essie gasped and recoiled into her seat. "You been Succouri since you was twelve?" Shock and disbelief widened her eyes, and for a moment she was speechless. "That ain't right! Not at all right! I've never heard of such a thing. Who would be puttin' that on a child?" She crossed her arms and shook her head repeatedly.

Overcome by the new light being shed on his reality, Ben sat back in his chair and exhaled. Callie cleared her throat.

"Ben, didn't you tell me you were sick about that time and had a bone marrow transplant?"

"Yes, I had leukemia."

Again, Ben's emotions tossed back and forth from anger to appreciation as he processed the facts of where this strange ability had come from and the true reason he'd recovered so completely as a child.

"Ms. Essie," Callie said softly. "What exactly is a Succouri?"

Ms. Essie's smile returned, clearly happier about answering this question. "A Succouri's a helper, a sustainer, a person to assist others in times of dire needin'. He can't be givin' life or takin' it; he can only temporarily be fillin' someone else with what's in him for the givin'. It's like..." She paused, then unfolded her arms, demonstrating her point as she continued. "It's like if you had a balloon and you were blowin' air into it, fillin' it up. That's what the touch of a Succouri's doin'. He's fillin' up another's physical holes with what's inside a him—well, with himself really. Nothin' changes on the outside. His touch ain't healin' or curin'. He can pause the hurtin' and sufferin' for a time, but he has no way a tyin' the balloon closed to be holdin' it in. When contact is broken, what went in is flowin' back out, and the person's back to where he started. But as you're well knowin', Miss Callie, often all it takes to be savin' someone's life is a little help, buyin' them some precious time. It's a beautiful gift. Succouri are like guardian angels, maybe here to be balancin' out all the sufferin' that goes on. There's no doubtin' it's a gift, but it's a heavy weight too. And if one wasn't knowin' what he was or how he came to be, not to mention bein' so young…" She paused and shook her head as she looked at Ben, her eyes full of compassion. "Well, I can imagine it's been a terrible burden on ya."

Ben let out a huff that indicated the gravity of her understatement. As he stood and began pacing, his mind raced through memories, times when he had needed this clarity so badly. Throughout his life, his identity had been shaped by this strange ability that he never knew how to categorize or use. The choices he'd made, even with Callie, might have been radically different if he'd understood who he was and the purpose of it all. Such knowledge would have saved him years of self-loathing and isolation. But, even as he thought that, he realized his path, as difficult as it was, had brought him to Callie, and that tempered the sting of it.

"Why do you think a mature and experienced Succouri would do that, put such a burden on Ben when he was so young and without help?" Callie asked in a tortured tone which spoke of her pain for his confusion and suffering.

"I'm not knowin', Miss Callie. I'm really not knowin' at all. I never heard of it, wasn't even thinkin' it could be done like that. I never heard of a child becomin' one."

Ceasing his pacing, Ben sat down in front of Ms. Essie. "How do you know about this?" he asked, almost in a whisper. "Are you... Are you one?" Ben's mind searched through all his previous encounters with her.

Ms. Essie laughed. "No, sir, not me. But I married one, Mr. Sawyer."

There was silence for a breath.

"Your husband Louis?" Callie said, her words coming out in a sigh. "He's Succouri?"

"Mm-hm," Ms. Essie said, leaning back in her chair and crossing her arms again.

Ben remembered how Callie had referenced the stories about Ms. Essie's husband and how he'd never lost a life on his watch.

"And," Ms. Essie continued, looking at Callie, "bein' married to one of 'em is surely a remarkable adventure, I can be tellin' ya that! Especially with the special bondin' that goes on." She smiled in a way that spoke of treasured secrets and memories.

Callie and Ben lifted their eyebrows at the same time.

"Bonding?" Callie spoke up first.

"Oh, yes!" Ms. Essie chuckled with delight. "When one's becomin' Succouri, he's gainin' much, this power to touch and sustain life as well as healin' himself too. It's marvelous, truly marvelous! But there's a loss that's comin' with it. An emptiness, a deep lack that's powerful. It's partly in his body but mostly down deep in his soul. The emptiness is drawin' the Succouri to helpin' others, makin' him want to and givin' him some feelin' of fullness when he does, but it ain't enough, ain't nearly enough. What's drawn out from him is always gonna be greater than what's poured in."

 Ms. Essie smiled knowingly as she looked at Ben and Callie, who were engrossed by her words. "That's where the bondin' comes in. Somehow a Succouri's knowin' just the person who can be fillin' the rest of that hole. Not up here, mind ya," she said, pointing to her head, "but deep inside a him, he's just knowin'. Sometimes, it's someone who's needin' him, his gift, but also someone with their own enormous capacity for givin'."

Ms. Essie laughed again at the gaping mouths before her, then shifted her gaze to Ben. "What you're feelin' between ya is an exchange, a sharin' that's bondin' ya together. It's givin' somethin' to her, but it's also fillin' ya up. In time, as the bond's growin', what you're givin' to her won't draw anythin' from you at all. Instead, she'll be helpin' you recover your strength, after you've given to others. The connection is sacred and beautiful, and it'll be gettin' stronger, changin' and showin' itself in unpredictable and wonderful ways that, well, I'll just be lettin' you two experience it for yourselves and not be spoilin' the fun."

Ben recalled how quickly he'd recovered after helping Callie and how he hadn't felt the same intense level of draw from her despite her severe injuries as he'd experienced in previous similar encounters.

"Now," Ms. Essie continued, directing her attention at Callie this time. "He can't be doin' what he does without ya, Miss Callie. He can do some amazin' things but not alone anymore, no he surely can't. The gift is meant to be shared, the burden too. Yes, that's surely the way it's meant to be." Pausing, she lifted her eyes to the ceiling. "And it was not good for man to be alone, so the Lord God provided a helper," she quoted with a sigh of satisfaction.

Though still frozen in stunned silence, Ben felt relief at finally understanding the mysterious connection between them but also convinced that it wasn't just the Succouri in him that had drawn him to Callie. He recalled with a smile how he had felt after holding Callie in his arms for the first time, like she belonged there, and how he somehow knew she always would.

"So," Callie said, savoring the irony of what she was about to say, "he needs *me?*"

Ms. Essie laughed with Callie as they marveled at the truth of their shared situation. "Mm-hm. There'll be many a time when he'll be needin' ya for his very life. How he's gone this long all alone without any helpin' is miraculous. I never seen a Succouri able to be endurin' that long without the bondin', but now that he's got it, he won't be able to continue alone anymore."

Ben sat on the edge of Callie's bed, grasping her hand tenderly in both of his and smiling as he saw the light in her eyes strengthen.

"Well, I already knew that one. Honestly, I didn't need to find out that I was Succouri to know I needed you desperately."

A radiant smile came from her in response to his words.

"Givin' is such a powerful thing," Ms. Essie said solemnly, "whether you're Succouri or not. Sometimes one might feel that because they can't be fixin' it all, healin' it all, it ain't worth much, but that ain't the truth of it. Whatever we have for the givin', it's enough." She looked at Ben, and he got the feeling this was one of the basic lessons he should have been taught years ago.

Callie's brow wrinkled in thought. "But, Ms. Essie, your husband, he's Succouri, but he's, well, he's not well, right? I mean, if Ben can heal himself quickly with no trace..." She let her question hang in the air.

A sad sigh resounded from her that spoke of her wish for things to be different. "Mr. Jones already passed along his gift a while back. Succouri ain't immortal or invincible,

Miss Callie. Like I was sayin' before, once they pass the gift on, they weaken."

She bowed her head, and Ben and Callie saw the pain this reality caused her.

"How long does it last?" Ben whispered, fearing her response.

"Well," Ms. Essie pondered for a moment, "with a good bondin' in place, about forty or forty-five years till the ripenin'." She looked at Ben before adding quickly, "But I ain't knowin' 'bout you at all, Mr. Sawyer, seein' as you got it so young and all. Full human maturity has always been in place with Succouri I'm knowin', so I can't be sayin' 'bout you."

Ben's heart dropped, and he shook his head, realizing he'd already lost fifteen years, time spent in total confusion, and that, if the trend held true for him, he faced the real possibility of a shortened lifespan. The thought made him feel ill, both for himself and for Callie, but once again, he also had to acknowledge that he may well have died at age twelve or shortly after if he had not been given this new identity.

Callie squeezed his hand in a gesture of encouragement and comfort, and they both felt the connection flowing between them, though it felt warmer and more meaningful now that they understood what it was.

"Ms. Essie," Callie said, breaking the silence. "What happens if a Succouri never bonds? I mean, what if he never finds someone or he loses them?"

Turning to look out the window, she sucked in a deep breath before answering. "I'll just be sayin' that it's a mighty sad thing, Miss Callie. The loneliness and emptiness will be drivin' him to, well, to a very dark place."

Overcome with gratitude, Ben bowed his head. He'd

been very nearly in that place, filled with a consuming emptiness he didn't understand, isolated and running. Then he met Callie and almost lost her. Whatever terrible fate Ms. Essie was trying hard to obscure, he'd come dangerously close to it. If not for Ms. Essie's kind words and encouragement and Callie's and Lee's love and acceptance, Ben had no doubt he'd still be walking down that dark path, maybe already reaching its ominous and inevitable end.

CHAPTER 20

THE GOODBYE

Ben, Callie, and Ms. Essie were quiet, lost in thought. Ms. Essie gazed out the window, sweet memories carrying her back in time. Callie and Ben stared at each other as everything they'd learned in the last few minutes sank in. With their new understanding came a sense of awe and wonder that left them speechless. None of them noticed when Lee slipped into the room.

"Well, these aren't the looks I expect to see on the faces of those privileged enough to be enjoying Ms. Essie's cooking."

All three of them abruptly turned to focus on Lee. Though his words were light, one look at his face told them a different story.

"Lee?" Callie questioned, her voice full of concern.

"Mr. Lee LeVray," Ms. Essie greeted. "I got plenty a this soup. I'll fix you right up."

Lee shut the door, but when Ms. Essie passed him a bowl of soup, he held it limply in his hand.

"Alright." Ms. Essie sighed, reaching to retrieve the

bowl from Lee's loose grasp. "Now I'm knowin' somethin's really wrong when you ain't eatin'!"

Lee shot Ben a questioning look, and Ben shook his head. "Sorry. We got a little sidetracked."

Ben slid off the edge of Callie's bed and touched Lee's shoulder as they exchanged places.

"Lee?" Callie asked again, concern rising in her tone. "Dad!" she gasped as understanding dawned.

Tears began rolling down Lee's face, and his shoulders shook. Ben came up beside him and placed his hand on Lee's upper back where a point of contact could be made near his neck, hoping to offer something to him, but he felt no draw at all. Ms. Essie placed one hand on Callie's shoulder and one hand over her heart.

"Cal," Lee sobbed, "he's not coming back. There's nothing more they can do. He's too far gone."

When Callie put her hand over her face as if to hide from the ugly truth, Ben was torn, wanting to ease the pain for them both.

"No!" she exclaimed, tearless for a moment as the shock worked through her heart and mind. Then the tears came in a torrent as she and Lee mourned the painful truth together. Ben and Ms. Essie stroked their backs helplessly. Ben was frustrated that he didn't seem to be able to do anything else to ease their pain. They cried for a long time, expressing a deep sorrow that filled the room with darkness.

At long last, Callie's sobs eased enough for her to speak. "Is he... Is he already gone?" she asked, a fresh streak of tears tracing lines down her cheeks.

"No," Lee replied, fighting for control. "They said we should be there and hold his hand when they... when they take him off the machines. They said he won't feel any pain.

He'll just pass peacefully. I'm sorry. I'm so sorry. I wish I had said something to him that morning. I wish we'd had the chance to say goodbye. I never would have thought—"

"Maybe he just needs more time," Callie protested. "Isn't there still a chance?"

Lee shook his head. "No. Dad had a 'do not resuscitate' order and a clear mandate in his file. He did not want to rot away on machines, Sis. He really didn't want that."

"But I don't know if I can... I don't know if..." She fell silent as more tears flowed down, landing on the sheets that were tucked in around her.

As Callie was still recovering from her injuries, Ben worried about the stress on her. This couldn't be good for her. But what could he do? Lee couldn't do this alone.

When Ben shot Ms. Essie a concerned frown, she gazed back at him with a strange expression that Ben didn't understand at first. Her face displayed sadness and compassion, but something else too.

"Mr. Sawyer?" she said, the strange look now filling her expression as she focused on him and crossed her arms.

Still confused, Ben blinked at her, trying to understand the look on her face.

"I think you can help this precious family that's now as much yours as any will ever be," she said with confident resolve.

"How?" Ben asked, but a small notion of what she might be thinking began to grow in his mind. Alarm set in as Ben wasn't sure it was possible, and he didn't want to crush them if it was only false hope.

Gradually, a light dawned in Callie's eyes as well, and her crying ceased. "Ms. Essie? Do you think? Is it possible?"

Lee looked up in confusion, glancing between Callie, Ben, and Ms. Essie. "Is what possible?"

"Tell you the truth, I'm not knowin'," Ms. Essie replied, directing her answer at Ben. "It would be very difficult, no doubtin' that. It'd take a lot out a ya. You'd be fillin' that balloon all the way up, givin' everything ya had."

Turning, she looked at Callie. "He'd be needin' ya, needin' your help for sure. And it would only be for a short time, ya understand. Remember, it's just helpin', not curin', and he can't be bringin' him back from the dead, so there's gotta be a spark a life left. No way a knowin' if there is or if what's inside Ben for the givin' is enough. No way a knowin' till you try."

"Back from the dead? What in the world are we talking about?" Lee stood, causing Ben's arm to drop from his back.

"But I've never done anything like *that*," Ben protested. "I've barely used it at all. I've been running from it, hiding it, remember? I've avoided it at all costs. I'm not sure I know how to..." Ben's protest hung in the air as a new kind of panic rose in him.

Ms. Essie laughed. "Well, no time like the present, Mr. Sawyer. This is what you are, what you're meant to be doin', the purpose and meanin' in it. No way a knowin' what you can do till you try."

Ben didn't like this. It was everything he hated about who he was. Even if he could work a miracle and give them one last moment with their dad, he'd still have to let go, and so would they. Then he'd always feel like it was his fault. "I... I don't think I..."

Callie reached out and took his hand.

"Callie, I..."

"No, Ben. No! I'm not going to ask you to," she said emphatically. "I understand how awful it would be for you and how it would make you feel. I wouldn't ask that of you. I won't. Please don't worry. I promise it's okay."

Lee started to pace, his hands balled into fists, frustrated at the odd conversation and that he seemed to be the only one in the dark. "Will someone please tell me what's going on? What are we asking Ben to do?"

Ben focused on Callie's face. He believed her. She'd never ask him to do this, but how could he not try? Wouldn't he regret that too? Wouldn't he hate himself if he could have given them a last moment, a chance to hear their father's voice, ask his wishes, offer a last touch, and say goodbye?

There was clear resignation in Callie's eyes. She wasn't going to ask this of him, and she wouldn't resent him for not trying.

And then, Ben knew what he had to do.

"I'll try," he whispered.

"Ben!" Callie pulled her hand away and grabbed his arm instead, but Ben had made up his mind.

"It's alright," he said softly, placing his hand on her cheek, covering the scrape that lingered there. "I have to try. You're part of me now, remember? And Lee is, well, he's like a brother. I have to try. I want to try."

Lee threw his hands up in the air, frustration overtaking him. "Please! I'm begging here! What in the world are we talking about?"

Laughing in delight, Ms. Essie led Lee to a chair, practically shoving him down into it. "You'll wanna be sittin' for this one, Mr. Lee LeVray. You got a lot a catchin' up to do."

Lee took the news about Ben surprisingly well, though he didn't completely believe it until Ben held Callie's hand, and she described where individual freckles were on his face from across the room. Then he made her read a sign on the back of her hospital door. He'd already had questions after watching the scene the night Callie was shot, so that helped him accept the reality of Ben's extraordinary gift. In the end, Lee whistled in amazement and threatened to change Ben's nickname to "Magic Ben" instead of "Uncle Ben," but Callie quickly dissuaded him from that.

Though Callie tried again to change Ben's mind, he was determined, knowing the regret of trying and failing would be less than the regret of never trying at all and always wondering if it might have worked.

A day later, when the doctors finally gave Callie permission to leave her room in a wheelchair, the three of them waited outside Ronald LeVray's hospital room while the doctors removed all of the life-support devices.

As it turned out, Doctor Karl was a friend of Louis Jones. While not knowing everything, he knew enough to not ask too many questions when Ms. Essie requested that he give the three of them a private moment with Mr. LeVray as soon as possible once the devices were removed.

Ms. Essie had given Ben as much help and advice as she could. She'd cautioned all of them again that it might not work at all, since none of them knew whether there would be enough of a spark of life left in Ronald LeVray and enough within Ben to give to make it happen. If it did, she reminded them to keep it short, as it would take everything Ben had to fill their dad with enough temporary wholeness to make communicating with him possible.

As they waited, Callie in a wheelchair and Ben and Lee leaning on the wall, they all felt anxious. Callie was afraid for him. She'd already informed him that she wasn't going to let him be harmed. "I'll tackle you to the ground myself if I see it's hurting you," she had said, her tone serious and resolute.

Ben laughed at the thought, but he could see that she was sincerely worried, so he tried to reassure her while still being honest, letting her know that it would be hard, even painful, and that she should expect that, but he'd be fine. In truth, Ben had never tried to use his gift in a situation this extreme, and he wasn't sure what to expect, even after talking with Ms. Essie about it, but he promised Callie that he'd let her know when it got to be too much.

Ms. Essie had informed Callie there wasn't much she could do for Ben until it was over. Their bonding hadn't reached the stage yet where her touch no longer drew anything from him, so she'd need to avoid touching him and adding to the draw while he was helping her dad.

"But after it's all done," Ms. Essie said, "just wrap him up in those arms of yours, and let the magic do its magic."

As for Lee, Ben could only imagine how fast his head was spinning with everything that had happened in the last couple of weeks, how life had changed for all of them. Certainly, much of it was good. Ben and Lee had grown to love each other as brothers, and Lee seemed pleased, especially knowing what he now knew about him, that Ben was with Callie. It was heartbreaking, though, that it had all started because of his dad's stroke and that, this day, whether Ben's gift worked or not, would be the last time Lee would ever see his father.

Looks of love and understanding passed between them as they waited. Then Lee approached Ben and put his hand on his back. "I feel like all I've done is repeat this to you lately but, thank you. I mean, no matter what happens I know, well, I sort of know how hard this will be for you, so, thank you. I wish there was more I could say or do, but that's all I got."

Ben turned affectionate eyes to Lee. "You and Callie

have given me everything. A place to call home, love, support, and acceptance, even with all my, well, brokenness and uniqueness. What I give you, or try to give you, today is very small compared to all of that. Trust me."

Lee was about to say more, but before he could, the door opened, and a rush of medical personnel left the room. At the end of the line was Doctor Karl. He waved them toward the door, offering a compassionate but puzzled look as he went.

As quickly as they could, Ben, Lee, and Callie flowed into the room, Lee closing the door behind them.

It was eerie inside with no sounds of machines chirping or oxygen flowing in and out. Ronald LeVray lay still and silent, and Ben panicked as he focused on his motionless form. "I don't think this is going to work," he warned, even as he swiftly approached the bed and placed his hands around Ronald LeVray's left wrist. Lee helped to get Callie next to Ben, then walked around to the other side of the bed.

Within seconds, the draw hit Ben hard, like nothing he'd ever experienced before. It felt like his whole body was being sucked with the force of a jet engine into a dark hole, and he had only a single hand with which to try to hang on to solid ground. A tortured groan involuntarily escaped his lips as the full force of it slammed into him, and Callie gasped.

"Ben! Stop! You don't have to do this. Please! Stop!"

"Just give it a second," he begged her through clenched teeth as he waited for the kickback to ease the pressure. Though it came a few seconds later, the effects were negligible, and he continued to fight fiercely to hold on.

"Is anything happening?" Callie yelled, her anxiety

verging on panic. Since she couldn't touch Ben, she was relying on Lee to see if their father's eyes opened.

Several horrifying seconds passed as they all held their breath. Ben struggled with all his strength against the draw, straining to keep himself anchored, as it felt like it was trying to suck his heart right out of his chest. Closing his eyes, he tried to focus on the kickback. Usually, it was nearly as strong as the draw, but right now it was like attempting to counteract a flood with a small trickle.

Seconds felt like hours as they watched, waiting, and hoping. Callie's panic for him rose, and she put her hand over her chest as if she could feel his struggle. Her face paled, and tears glistened in her eyes.

Finally, Lee leaned over his dad. "Dad, can you hear me?"

Silence hovered, and Callie held her breath.

Then, in a moment of unspeakable joy, a whisper broke the silence.

"Lee?"

"Dad! Yes! Lee exclaimed with a relieved and ecstatic laugh. "I'm here. Callie's here too."

"I can't move," he said, so quietly that Callie and Lee had to lean closer to hear him.

Callie began to cry, tears of joy and sadness mingled together.

"Dad, you had a stroke," Lee started. "You're... you're not well. We don't have much time, but we wanted to tell you, to let you know..." Lee's voice failed as tears flowed down his cheeks.

"We love you!" Callie continued for Lee, and their dad's head turned her way. "We love you so much. You're everything a wonderful, giving, selfless father could be. Thank you for giving everything you had to us and for us, for loving me and helping me and teaching me how to accept who I am."

Rising out of her wheelchair, she kissed her dad tenderly on the cheek. He smiled at her, but his confused eyes looked from Callie to Lee and then to Ben.

Ben could only watch from the corner of his eye, no longer having the strength to lift his head as he focused all his energy on holding some small amount of territory in his invisible battle.

"Callie Flower, who...?"

"Dad," Lee spoke up. "This is Ben. He's keeping you alive. It's a long story, but he's part of this family now, and he's giving us this moment with you, but it's only a moment."

Ronald LeVray's expression shifted from confusion to resigned understanding, and he sucked in a deep breath of air.

And Ben felt it. It sent a shock wave through him, like he'd been struck by lightning, and his hands began to shake.

Ronald stared lovingly at Lee and Callie. "I love you both with all I am. I don't know this one," he said, looking at Ben as a smile filled his face, "but I get the feeling he's pretty special."

Despite her distress and tears, Callie smiled in response. "Dad, he's very, very special."

Ronald caught her meaning, and his smile grew.

Callie looked anxiously at Ben. Ben saw in her eyes that she could feel him losing the fight and sensed the need to hurry. She turned back to her father. "I'm sorry, Dad. I'm sorry we can't hold onto you, keep you here for longer, keep you alive."

"Shh," he soothed. Then a look of deep concern

furrowed his brow. "Callie! What happened?" he asked, noticing she was in a wheelchair and staring at the scrape on her cheek.

"Nothing. It's alright. I'm totally fine. Just a little accident, but I'm okay."

Concern filled his eyes, and he looked again at Ben. "Is this young man watching out for you?"

"Yes! And Lee is too. I'll be alright, Dad. You don't have to worry. You've always taken care of me, but I'll be alright now."

The trembling spread to Ben's arms as he felt himself losing his grip and sliding into the void. Lee came around and put an arm around him, trying to boost his strength.

Ronald watched their faces, seeming to grasp the urgency of the moment. "I'm so proud of you both. It has been my greatest joy and privilege to be your dad. I've loved you here, and I'll love you there." He turned to look at the ceiling. "I know where I'm going, and I know I'll see you both again. You're doing the right thing, letting me go. I'll miss you, but I'll be waiting. Please, take care of each other, and never forget how much I love you! And remember, just do today. Just today!"

A tear trickled down his cheek, and Lee and Callie cried softly as well.

Now, Ben's whole body shook furiously, and he felt his knees buckling. He wanted to, needed to hold on somehow, but he was nearly out of strength.

"Callie!" Ben gasped. "I... I..."

She reached for him, then drew back, remembering that her touch would only hurt him.

"Ben!" she cried, the sound resonating with his pain.

Ronald looked directly at Ben, his eyes conveying sorrow at the pain that keeping him alive was causing him.

"It's alright, Ben," he said with such love that Ben felt he'd known him all his life. "Thank you. Thank you for letting me love my kids one last time. Please take care of them. It seems that, well, it seems like you can."

Pulling together the last drop of strength inside of him, Ben raised his head and looked Callie's dad in his green eyes for the first and last time. "I will," he promised with trembling lips. "I promise with everything I am that I will."

Ronald LeVray took one last loving look at all three of them and then, to their surprise, he pulled his arm away from Ben. Ben dropped to the floor, but Lee caught him on the way down. Ronald placed his hand on Callie's and smiled, closing his eyes for the last time.

Ben awoke on the loveseat in Callie's arms. He had no idea how he had managed it, but somehow, Lee had put Callie in the seat so her injured left side was away from Ben and then tucked Ben up next to her on her right. His head leaned against her shoulder, and her arm was wrapped tightly around him, clinging to him for dear life.

Ben felt terrible, like the worst aches of the worst flu he could remember from his early childhood, but he could feel life and strength pouring back into him as the bond they shared cycled warmth and energy between them. Though he felt a small draw as well, now the flood and trickle scenario was reversed, and he was happy to be on the winning side of the battle this time.

As he blinked and tried to lift his head to look at Callie, she leaned over and tenderly kissed the top of his head. As she did, Ben felt her tears drip into his hair.

"Ben!" Callie breathed out his name in a sound that combined joy and relief.

From a place of desperate need, like an irresistible thirst, he dropped his head deeper into the curve of her neck, the warmth of it sending a surge of new life through him. Somehow, though he couldn't understand it, Callie was returning to him what he'd given away, and the exchange was tightening the knot that bound them together. Callie released his shoulder and placed her hand along the side of his face, holding him tightly against her.

"Callie!" Ben whispered, his voice weak but content.

"Shh," she soothed, caressing his cheek with her fingers, then moving them up into his hair. "It's my turn to take away your pain this time."

She kissed him again before continuing in a shaky voice filled with wonder and gratitude. "I... I don't have the words to tell you what that meant to all of us, to me, to Lee, and I know to my dad. It was beautiful and I... I can't express how grateful we are that you gave everything you had to give us the chance to say goodbye."

As she kissed him again, fresh tears began flowing. "But, Ben"—she paused to take a steadying breath, her voice carrying her sorrow—"I understand now. I truly understand."

Ben turned his head, so he could look into her eyes. He wasn't sure what she understood, but he could see the genuineness of her conviction. As she returned his gaze, Ben's heart again filled with joy at knowing she could read the unspoken messages there.

"I could feel it. Well, at least a very small piece of it—the struggle, the fear, the happiness, but then the burden of having to let go, knowing it was almost time, and the feeling of desperation when you had nothing left to give. I understand what this does to you, how heavy a weight it is to carry. I'm so sorry."

A sob shook her, and Ben gathered up a morsel of his newly acquired strength to raise himself and shift toward her. He placed his hands along the sides of her face and used his thumbs to wipe her tears away. "It's not such a burden now," he said in a hoarse whisper. "The burden was in carrying it alone."

Callie closed her eyes and leaned forward, so her forehead rested against his. "You won't have to do that anymore."

Taking a deep breath, Ben allowed the relief and peace released by the truth in her statement to fill his entire being. "I'm sorry I couldn't give you more time with him." Ben's words expressed sadness for his own loss as well as hers. The brief but meaningful exchange with her father had carved a void that he wished he could fill with more memories.

"No! Please, please hear me." Callie leaned her head back, so she could look him in the eyes. "You gave us everything you had, and it was enough, much more than enough."

Pulling her to him, he gently wrapped his arms around her as they leaned against each other, exhausted and weak yet grateful and satisfied.

CHAPTER 21

THE WARNING

Ronald LeVray's funeral took place five days later. Callie was up and walking by then, aided by the effective assistance provided by Ben's touch. They held the service in their small family church, though the community wanted a much bigger affair. The police were still concerned about Lee's and Callie's safety, so they encouraged them to choose a location and crowd size that would be easier to secure and defend.

Ms. Essie sat with the LeVray family, and Louis came as well, Ms. Essie pushing him in his wheelchair. He offered Ben a warm and sympathetic smile, and Ben intentionally removed his gloves to shake his hand, passing along a moment of strength in the gesture. Ben and Ms. Essie had already agreed that when this crisis passed, he and Callie would spend some time at the Joneses' house learning more about the Succouri. Grace sat with them in the front row as well, though Lobster, ever uncomfortable in crowds, had opted to come alone earlier and pay his respects privately, which meant that Ben still had not had the chance to meet him.

The police officers on duty held their hats over their hearts as they guarded the LeVrays and their guests in honor of Callie's father and all he'd meant to them. Many others who had worked with him attended and spoke about Ronald with great regard.

When Lee got up to speak, offering beautiful memories of his dad and then listing the ways he hoped to be like him, Callie sat softly crying next to Ben. He held her close, but he was still puzzled by the fact that he couldn't seem to offer any help with her grief.

Though there were tears, there were many smiles as well. Sweet years of sharing and love had left a lasting covering of warmth over Ronald LeVray's family and friends, and that, Ben thought, was truly the best kind of legacy.

After the funeral, while Callie and Lee spoke to some of their relatives, Ben approached Louis and Ms. Essie.

"I've been holding her hand all day," he whispered to the older man, "but I can't stop her tears. I want to help ease her grief, but I can't."

Louis exhaled slowly, looking at Ben with eyes full of wisdom. "Sadness and grief ain't problems of the body, Mr. Sawyer. Those are problems of the heart. That kind a pain must be healed with a very different sort a touch. You'll help in her healin', but it will take more time and involve only that part a ya that's Ben, not Succouri."

Ben sat up straight, realizing that all these years he'd blamed everything that had happened to his mother on his "curse" and its limitations. That was why he had come to think of it in that way in the first place. He thought it had been the cause of easing her depression for the years he was with her and that it was the lack of it in her life that ultimately killed her. Now he wondered if his touch, as

Succouri, had ever helped her at all or if it had just been him, his love and presence as her son and companion, that had given her some comfort and peace.

Though this possibility didn't reduce the sorrow of losing her, it did dramatically shift the way he felt about the ability he possessed.

Being Succouri had saved Callie, and it had given Ronald LeVray a final moment with his son and daughter. Ben thought about the white car and that rainy night many years ago. It hadn't saved everyone, but he wasn't sure that any gift, no matter how powerful, could do that.

He needed time to think through everything, and he needed answers. Who had made him Succouri? Why had they chosen someone so young when that wasn't the way it was normally done? Why hadn't the giver stuck around to help Ben rather than leaving him lost and confused? To move forward, Ben needed to go back.

Before he rejoined Callie, he hugged Ms. Essie. "Thank you," he said with a grateful smile. "If it weren't for you, I'd still have no idea who I was. I would have run again, missed out on Callie, and been empty and desperate, maybe forever."

She beamed one of her contagious smiles at him. "Mr. Sawyer, are you knowin' that my full name is Esther Lilian Jones? Now one of the most famous verses in the book of Esther goes like this: 'And who knows if perhaps you have come to this kingdom for such a time as this." She laughed, and the sound of it resonated off the church walls like music.

AN HOUR LATER, Ben was holding Callie's hand as they made their way up the walk toward her front door. Family and friends were meeting together to have another one of Ms. Essie's amazing homemade meals after the funeral. The sight of the front porch would always inevitably stir strong emotions in them both after the events of that terrible night.

This time as they approached, the front door opened, and a short, stout young man in his early twenties, his unruly black hair reminiscent of Einstein's, stepped out. He walked toward them, limping slightly with his left leg. He stared wide-eyed at Ben's face.

Ben stopped and stared at him as well. Something was familiar about him. Then, recognition dawned, and shock and disbelief froze him in place.

"Roberto?" Ben inquired, not trusting his own eyes.

"You!" the young man stammered, looking just as stunned as Ben. "It's you!"

Callie looked back and forth between the astonished faces in front of her. "Ben, this is Lobster. Lobster, this is Ben."

They both stood speechless, staring in disbelief. Ben tried to make his heart accept what his eyes were seeing. "You're alive!" he exclaimed with such relief and joy that Callie laughed along with him despite her total confusion.

Lobster approached Ben, never breaking eye contact. When he was a foot away, he reached out and tackled Ben in an enthusiastic embrace. "Thank you! You saved my life. Thank you!" It was evident in his voice that he'd waited years to offer his rescuer this sincere expression of gratitude.

Ben returned his embrace while Callie looked on in stunned silence. Then, as quickly as he'd embraced Ben, Lobster let go and ran back into the house.

Callie moved to stand in front of Ben and gazed into his

tear-filled eyes. "Um, what in the world?" she asked. "I've literally never seen Lobster touch anyone, much less hug them."

"I thought he was dead. I was certain, absolutely certain that he died that night," Ben said with wonder, more to himself than to Callie.

Callie smiled at Ben's stunned delight until he felt composed enough to fill her in. He gave her the abridged version of the story—the white car, the rain, the deer, and his sorrow at not being able to get the driver out. He promised to fill in more details later.

"That's unbelievable! Our Lobster, this whole time!" she exclaimed, embracing Ben in a gesture of mutual celebration.

As they moved toward the porch and past the police officers standing guard there, Ben caught the eye of Sergeant Evans.

"I'll meet you inside in a minute," Ben whispered, kissing her cheek and releasing her hand. Smiling, she nodded in acknowledgment, moving inside to join the sounds of laughter.

Evans beckoned Ben toward the wicker chairs on the porch, and Ben chuckled, noticing that someone had returned the cushions.

"I'm so glad your girl's alright," he offered, his broad smile filling his face. "She's lovely! I don't think I've ever seen anyone so, well, so completely in love as what I saw in you that night. It's something, well, I'll just never forget." He shook his head as he recalled the memory.

Ben gave the officer a warm smile in response.

Evans closed his eyes, trying to figure out how to put his next thoughts into words. When he opened his eyes, he spoke to Ben, but his gaze focused down the road, as though watching for something he expected to come. "Mr. Sawyer, we've done everything we can to find that monster, but so far we've only managed to catch some of the minor players in this evil game. We've gotten some information from them, but to be honest, it ain't promising. We also got our experts hacking the dark web, tryin' to find and track these thugs. Mr. LeVray stepped into a hornets' nest here, and now all the hornets are active and eager to sting."

He paused to confirm that Ben understood the gravity of his words. Holding eye contact with the officer, Ben nodded, confirming that he was following him.

"Bottom line, Miss LeVray's in danger, serious danger," Evans said, his face solemn and his eyes intensely focused on Ben. "I wish I could tell you she wasn't, but she is. We're doin' our best, brother, but the guy who tried the first time and failed, he ain't givin' up. It's a pride thing now and a status thing. He's gotta get her, take her out, or he's nothin'. Do you understand what I'm tellin' you?"

Ben sucked in a slow breath. "Yes, I think so."

His heart contracted with the familiar fear of potentially losing Callie. With Callie by his side, Ben was confident that he could face anything, but now he knew he couldn't face a single day without her.

"My suggestion," Officer Evans continued, "is that you take her somewhere that no one would know or anticipate —just for a while mind you, until we catch these bastards. We don't mind protectin' her, but even with the extra security you're providin', we can't be everywhere, and we can't keep up the twenty-four seven thing forever. And right now they have the advantage 'cause they know where to find her."

"If I take her away, won't they go after Lee?"

Evans shook his head. "I doubt it. This isn't about

Ronald LeVray anymore. He's gone, so takin' revenge on him is gone with him. This is about finishin' somethin' Callie's shooter started. Like I said, it's now an honor thing. This guy must prove himself to the evil people he works for. If he can't take out..." Evans paused, looking regretful about the way he had to word his next phrase. "Well, frankly, if he can't take out a blind woman, he's as good as dead himself. You understand?"

Ben nodded even as he balled his hands into fists in anger at the thought of it.

"Ms. Essie Jones wants to have Lee stay with her and her husband for a while, just in case, and we'll continue to provide security for him, even though I'm convinced that won't be necessary. As for Callie, you and her need to go, Mr. Sawyer, and soon. Take her out of state, far from here, just for a while."

Seeing the intensity and sincerity of the request evident in Officer Evans's eyes, Ben's mind began to work on a plan.

Both men stood, and Ben held out his hand. Officer Evans grasped it firmly.

"Thank you," Ben said. "I know just the place to take her. I'll keep you in the loop."

Officer Evans reached up to pat Ben's shoulder, then turned to head back toward the other officers.

As Ben went inside to rejoin Callie, his mind continued to work through the details of his plan. It would be hard for Callie. She'd just lost her father, and she needed the comfort of friends and family around her, but it couldn't be helped. He'd talk to her tomorrow, give her the night to grieve and rest. Tomorrow they'd pack and prepare.

Their destination was far enough away to keep her well out of this monster's reach. He'd already decided he had to go there anyway. It was where he needed to go to find some answers and figure out what had happened to him all those years ago.

One thing was certain. He'd never let anything happen to her. He'd freely give up his own life for hers, protect her, no matter the cost.

AFTER ANOTHER OF Ms. Essie's unbelievable home-cooked meals, Callie and Ben worked in the kitchen as the others gathered around the piano to hear Lobster's latest classical masterpiece. The music drifted into the room, and they listened in enjoyable silence while they worked.

Ben was at the sink again. Callie's arm was no longer in a sling, thanks to the miraculous rapid healing that they both suspected had something to do with their unique bond, though when they asked Ms. Essie about it, she just smiled and reminded them about how much she was determined not to ruin their fun by giving them too much information.

Though Callie had gotten rid of the sling, Ben wanted her to be careful not to overuse her arm, as her shoulder was still healing, so he washed while she, mostly with one hand, dried and put dishes away.

It surprised Ben how much the LeVray house had come to feel like home, much more so than any house he'd ever lived in. The warmth, love, and laughter that saturated the space made it that way, but it was also because those within its walls knew him and accepted him fully. When he came to this town, he had no family and not a single person in his life who really knew him, but now he had family, friends, and love. He didn't want to leave, and he didn't want to take Callie away from her brother or the memories of her father that echoed through the rooms of this house.

But he had to, just for a while. He knew he'd look forward to returning just as much as she would. After all, this was the place where his heart had finally found a home.

"You've definitely got a lifelong fan in Lobster," Callie teased, breaking into Ben's reverie as she set a glass in the cabinet. "He's pretty much followed you around all night."

Ben chuckled. He had noticed, but he hadn't minded in the least.

"You might be the one person on the entire planet that he feels comfortable being around. Do you think he knows, like *really* knows about you?"

"He knows something, but how much or how he interprets everything that happened that night in his mind, I have no idea."

Setting the last of the dishes in the dishwasher, he grabbed a towel to dry his hands. "I really thought he died that night. I was convinced that I hadn't saved him, that I hadn't done enough, just like with my mother. This whole time since I've had this, well, this ability, I've always looked at it as a curse because It never seemed to actually rescue anyone. I focused on what it couldn't do, so I labeled it a curse."

Ben stepped behind Callie and placed his hands on her shoulders, then gently turned her around to face him. "Then I met you. You changed my whole world, changed my perspective on everything." He placed his hand on her cheek, and the warmth and pull began to build between them.

"I thought, when I touched you like this, I'd lose you, that you'd run from it all, just like I've always done. But..." Ben leaned forward and softly kissed her forehead, stoking the smoldering fire. "You didn't. You accepted something about me that I've never accepted about myself. And..." He brushed her lips with his, and she closed her eyes. "You've helped me to accept who I am, even begin to welcome it. I never thought I'd feel that way. I don't think of it as a curse anymore. It's a gift, and it's not mine alone. We share it. What I am is yours, Callie LeVray, completely yours."

Taking Callie's hand in his, he held it to his heart, both out of affection and as a precaution, creating a small barrier between them. Though his desire for her raged in him like wildfire, his love and respect for her wouldn't be overcome by it. So, he kept the space, for now, respecting the powerful pull of their bond while still leaning in to press his lips passionately to hers. She wrapped her free hand around his neck, pulling him to her and returning his kiss. She parted her lips, and her breath flowed into him, fusing fire through every part of his body and soul. For a moment, they both allowed their usually restrained desire to run freely as they expressed love and longing, like melody and harmony, in tender yet hungry kisses.

The sound of Lee clearing his throat and chuckling awkwardly pulled them out of the moment.

"Alright, Uncle Ben," Lee teased. "I know that *that* is supposed to charge your batteries and all, and doesn't every man I know wish he had that for an excuse? But we've got dessert to get to, and it may be a little awkward to work around you two if you're, well, doing that. Don't make me channel my inner protective father voice again." He cleared his throat as if he was getting ready to do just that, but Ben turned and held his hands up in surrender.

"Alright, no need, backing off." He laughed, still a little breathless.

Lee pointed at the chocolate cake on the island. "Dessert, plates, forks," he instructed as if trying to bring them back to the real world.

They all laughed, and Callie and Ben helped Lee serve up generous portions of cake and ice cream but before they moved to join the others, Ben stole one more moment, pulling Callie back into his arms and whispering in her ear.

"Thank you, sweetheart. You've changed my life, filled up my heart, and given me a home. I love you with all of me, with all that I am."

She smiled at him, her exotic green eyes sparkling as his touch focused her vision, and she stared lovingly into his eyes. "I love it when you call me sweetheart," she whispered in response.

Acknowledgments

A special word of thanks to those who helped with the editing and designing of this book.

In particular:

Melanie Underwood (editor)

and

Hannah Linder (cover design)

And my numerous beta readers who offered me valuable feedback during the book's development.

THANK YOU ALL!

ABOUT THE AUTHOR

As an Adjunct Professor of Communication for more than two decades, writing has always been a part of Meridith's life and career. Her novels combine her love for romance and storytelling with her communication and writing background. Legally blind since birth, Meridith's unique point of view and experiences bring intriguing and fresh perspectives to her storylines and characters. Beyond simple romance novels, Meridith writes unforgettable, epic love stories that sweep readers off their feet.

Meridith resides in Kansas with her husband, Jason, and her two sons.

www.ingramcontent.com/pod-product-compliance
Lightning Source LLC
Chambersburg PA
CBHW061232310726
48971CB00007B/2035